SHADES C
DARKNESS

By the same author:

Novels:
Elegy for a Revolutionary
Send War In Our Time, O Lord
Death of Fathers
A Messiah of the Last Days

Biography:
Patrick Duncan, South African and Pan-African

Poetry:
Occasional Light (with Jack Cope)
I Live Here Now
Hong Kong Portraits
In the Water-Margins
Holiday Haiku
Requiem

SHADES OF DARKNESS

A NOVEL

Jonty Driver

Jonathan Ball Publishers
JOHANNESBURG & CAPE TOWN

In memoriam: Marius Schoon, Jenny Curtis
and their daughter Katryn

Published in 2004 by
JONATHAN BALL PUBLISHERS (PTY) LTD
PO Box 33977
Jeppestown
2043

ISBN 1 86842 197 X

Although I have drawn, in some places extensively, on transcripts
of the hearings of the Truth & Reconciliation Commission,
all of the characters, most of the institutions and nearly all
of the incidents in this novel are imaginary although,
as always, one hopes that even the lies will have verisimilitude.

[CJ Driver, 2004]

Typesetting and reproduction of text by Alinea Studio, Cape Town
Cover design and reproduction by Flame Design, Cape Town
Printed and bound by CTP Book Printers, Duminy Street, Parow 7500

Acknowledgements

I am grateful to family and friends who read early drafts, who helped with detail, or who offered advice and suggestions, in particular Ann, Tamlyn and Dorothy Driver, John Adams, John Clare, John Coetzee, Mary Hoogewerf, Dan Jacobson, Kevin and Sally Kay, Jeff Opland, Frank Pike, Neville Rubin and Randolph Vigne. Valda Strauss, Francine Blum and Barry Streek have been careful and thoughtful editors. I am grateful to my literary agent, Andrew Hewson of Johnson & Alcock, Authors' Agents.

Acknowledgements

As for the way of the wicked, he turns it upside down.
Psalm 146

When I lie where shades of darkness
Shall no more assail mine eyes ...
Walter de la Mare, *Fare Well*

PROLOGUE

He left the jeep parked out of sight of the road behind the blue-gum trees, but then moved quite openly and quickly, working his way through the thorn bushes towards the river. Only when he had gone about a mile did he begin to move more cautiously, checking his direction against a rough map he had drawn the day before, and looking back to double-check that he had not been observed. Once, because he thought he heard a noise somewhere to the side, he stopped completely, sheltering behind a thorn bush, and watching carefully to make sure no one was following. Satisfied that he had heard nothing of significance, he shouldered the rifle again and moved on. Twice, he took a compass from the breast pocket of his hunting jacket and checked the direction in which he was moving, though the lie of the land seemed obvious. He dropped down to the bed of a stream that would serve as a tributary to the river if it ever rained, and for the first time hesitated there, looking at the sand; it was so dry that his boots left no detectable prints and, anyway, there were so many other prints – cattle, goats, sheep, buck perhaps, humans probably. Still, to be safe, he left the cover of the stream and climbed up the other side, to work his way carefully down through the thorn bush on the edge of the stream towards the dam across the river.

About two hundred yards before he got to the dam, he turned sharp left and, keeping well below the skyline, worked his way upwards to a point behind the brow of the hill. It was hot in the sun, particularly as he climbed the rocky outcrop near the top, but a slight breeze from the dam cooled the sweat on his face. A few yards short of the top of the hill, he took the rifle from his shoulder and, holding it carefully in the crook of his elbows, dropped to his hands and knees to crawl upwards to a gap between the rocks and a thorn bush, from which he could look down at the dam.

The bakkie was parked on the dried grass at the side of the dam wall; the man fishing in the dam hadn't even bothered to close the driver's door and stood now, fifty yards further up the dam, on the edge of the water, his khaki haversack nearby. For several minutes, the man with the rifle on the hillside watched to make sure that the fisherman was alone; then he felt in the pocket of his jacket, to take out a telescopic sight which he clipped to the rifle. Carefully he adjusted his elbows on the ground until he was balanced, then brought the rifle to his shoulder and the barrel up slowly, using the bakkie as target until he had the sights clearly adjusted: a bare hundred yards to the haversack, he reckoned, and some fifty yards further to the bakkie. He shifted his position slightly, then checked the sights again, switched the safety catch off, took a breath, held it, and squeezed the trigger once, then again.

The fisherman looked up suddenly as the shots reverberated from the rocks above him and swore, but made no effort to move away from where he was fishing; he seemed not to have noticed that a back tyre of the bakkie had collapsed. The man on the hillside fired again, the same pattern of shots, one after the other, and this time the fisherman realised his bakkie was the target. He dropped his fishing rod and began to run towards the bakkie, shouting furiously, first in Afrikaans and then in English. The next shot shattered the windscreen, and now the fisherman stopped, realising there was someone on the hillside above him. He stared upwards to where he thought the man with the rifle must be, and shouted again. This time he could be heard. 'For fuck's sake, are you fucking mad, man, shooting like that? What the fuck do you want?' Then he began to run again, this time towards his haversack. He probably has a weapon in there, thought the man on the hillside; he had guessed he might have a rifle or a shotgun in the bakkie; he might have a pistol or revolver in his haversack instead. He waited until the man was ten yards away from the haversack, then fired twice into it, making it jerk and leap in the dust. The fisherman stopped, then moved a pace nearer the haversack; he looked at a different point of the hillside, trying to see where the hidden rifleman was, and shouted again: 'What do you want, you fucking lunatic? When I catch you, I'll fucking kill you!'

Once again, the rifle on the hillside answered, and the haversack jerked as the bullets tore into it. The man turned sideways now, and began to run for some thorn bushes on the edge of the dam that might provide cover. The man on the hillside let him run for twenty yards, then carefully fired, just once, into the ground ahead of the running figure. The man stopped; he was clearly winded even by that short run. He faced the hillside again, panting and then shouting, now more or less incoherent in rage and terror, though he seemed to have at last spotted the vantage point from which the rifle fire came.

The man on the hillside waited for the cursing and shouting to subside into silence, then got to his feet slowly, with the rifle still against his shoulder. The man at the dam could see now who held the rifle, and swore just once more, then was silent again. There was nowhere to run now, nothing more to be said. The rifleman planted his feet wide for balance. Slowly the rifle came up until the cross hairs of the sight were on the man's sweating forehead. The old instruction came back to him: *breathe in; hold steady; then squeeze.*

PART ONE

Chapter 1

Jamie Cathcart checked yet again that his seatbelt was firmly tightened and then peered sideways out of the window. No, there weren't even lights visible, even though somewhere down there was one of the great sprawling cities of modern times; *Egoli*, blacks called it: the City of Gold. The City of something else, he thought to himself. *Descend only.*

He was stiff and a little sore from sitting so long, though he had stretched out as best he could and had walked up and down the aircraft whenever it seemed not too inconvenient for air hostesses and other passengers. He had managed to avoid almost all conversation with other passengers, though he had slept hardly at all. Thank God he wouldn't be in Johannesburg for long. He had tried to get a direct flight straight through from Heathrow to Cape Town, but there had been no seats available at such short notice, even in the business class. In three hours' time, he should be on a connecting flight to Cape Town.

He wondered again, wryly, if this descent counted as coming home or as something else. Once upon a time he had resolved (he reminded himself yet again) that he wouldn't come back here until ... how had he put it to himself then? How English he had become that he was afraid it might sound pompous or pretentious, even if he only thought it, didn't say it out loud. How ironic it was, therefore, that he was now almost back again, where there had still been no change, except for the considerably worse. It was even more ironic that the people he would most want to vote for in an election here – if such a thing were possible – were precisely those who had least chance of doing so: those in prison, those expelled beyond the boundaries, those consigned to pretend-states invented only to try to fool the world into keeping quiet for a while. Indeed, right now, it seemed to be only the children who were brave enough to risk everything to fight back.

And since it seemed to him – in the pessimism which he knew, deep down, was also a form of fear – that there was no chance at the moment that anything like that would happen, nor that the kind of state that he desired would ever exist here until many, many more children had died, and more soldiers had been slaughtered on the borders, and more old men and women had died despite the shelter of their shanty-huts, why then he had no desire to be here at all. He was merely weary with what he was going to have to do.

For a moment, he wished he could make this a dream. No such luck. He would have to go through with it. *Descend only.*

* * *

It took his eyes several moments to adjust from the early-morning glare of the runway and the reflections of the aircraft in the plate glass of the entry hall: 'South African Nationals' that way, 'Foreign Passport Holders' this. The South African queues seemed to be moving rather faster than the others, even though there wasn't much initial difference in the length of the queues: people coming home; people coming on holiday; people coming to do business; people coming to see family.

He dropped his bag at the back of what he hoped was the fastest moving of the foreign queues and settled to wait; he felt grubby, rumpled and possibly even rather smelly after the flight, and wondered whether there was somewhere he might be able to have a shower and a shave. Though the air hostess had hung his blazer up for him, it was – he realised now – probably a mistake to be wearing it, even though he had wanted to look respectable

14

when he came to the front of the queue. All the other men were in shirtsleeves or linen jackets, except for one over-heated man wearing a tweed sports coat.

There was a German couple in the queue ahead of him, and a pleasant-looking family, almost certainly English, on holiday, he guessed, given their carefully casual cloth-ing and veiled conversation. He smiled at the youngest member of the family, a small dark girl, but she had clearly been told to avoid smiling at even the most respectable-looking strangers, because she turned away and clutched at her mother's skirt.

There was some sort of a problem at the head of their queue. The official, a small white man in khaki uniform, gestured for help from someone bigger and bossier, prob-ably a more senior official with a roving commission over the various immigration kiosks; there was an earnest con-sultation, passports were looked at, and then clearly the matter was resolved. Papers were stamped, the couple at the head of the queue passed through, and he was a step closer.

He fell into desultory conversation with the young father of the family behind him in the queue. Were they stopping in Johannesburg? How long was their visit for? Had they been there before? Now that she realised he was safe to talk to, the little girl returned his smile, then announced that she was going to see elephants. 'We hope to see them, Jenny, darling,' said the mother. 'Sometimes you don't see them.'

He smiled down at the girl. 'You nearly always see ele-phants,' he said.

'Do you live here?' asked the father.

'Not any more,' he answered. He pushed his bag along the marbled floor. They were almost at the front now. His passport was in the zipped-up inner pocket of his blazer, next to his wallet. He took it out, consoled by the solidity of its dark-blue cover and the embossed lettering.

The immigration clerk opened the passport, turned the

pages of a ledger propped up on his desk, seemed satisfied, stamped the entry form, pasted it in the passport, and handed it back. 'Have a nice holiday, Mr Cathcart,' he said in heavily accented English.

Jamie Cathcart hesitated for a moment before picking up his hand luggage and crossing the passageway to where the heavier luggage could be collected. He wasn't sure whether to be disappointed or relieved. Oh well, he thought to himself, it was a long time ago, I guess. They must have forgotten. He had never expected to get through that quickly and without any kind of argument. He was Mr Jamie Cathcart, aged forty-two, clearly a respectable Englishman visiting South Africa for – as he had said on the immigration form – 'a holiday'. Occupational category? Well, 'Education' seemed both broad enough and harmless enough, as well as more or less true. Place of birth? 'Grahamstown', but that was during a war in which a good many thoroughly British people had taken refuge in South Africa. Nothing untoward there either. Details satisfactory; appearance respectable. He was back where he had started, back in the country of his birth and upbringing.

The luggage hadn't begun to appear on the conveyor belt when he felt the tap on his shoulder. For a moment he thought, oh, bloody hell, they've let me in only to arrest me. How typical. He turned, half-expecting to recognise one of the familiar faces from the old days, a bit older now, as he was himself, but still the same cold eyes and mouth pretending to smile; but it wasn't – it was the little immigration clerk in his khaki uniform and he was stuttering, Jamie realised, in a state of abject anxiety. 'He thinks he's lost his job,' Jamie thought to himself, almost amused. 'He's made a mistake; he's let me in – and now he's going to lose his job.' Perhaps I should make a scene, Jamie thought; there might be a reporter here, or someone might telephone a newspaper, and then this could become an international incident.

'Mr Cathcart, sir,' the clerk stuttered, 'There's been a misunderstanding; I must ask you to step back into the other room. I want you the other side of that line.'

Jamie shrugged: they hadn't forgotten. In some ways he felt almost smug that they hadn't. He still counted for something, all these years later. Getting in was going to be difficult after all. He shouldered his bag to allow the clerk to shepherd him back to where he had been standing a few moments beforehand. The English family was still there, looking concerned. 'I'm sorry,' he said to them. 'I think if I were you I'd join another queue.' He raised his voice a little to apologise to others behind them in the queue.

When he turned back to the kiosk, he was surprised to find that the mousy little clerk seemed to have grown several inches, or at least to have puffed himself out. 'What do you mean by sneaking through?' He raised his voice, Jamie realised, to make sure that the supervisor was aware that the fault was Jamie's own and not his.

'Oh, come on,' Jamie said. 'I'm too big to "sneak through" anything. Look at me. Anyway, you stamped my passport.' He held it out for the clerk to see.

The clerk jerked the passport open, tore out the immigration form, then crossed through the remainder of the stamped permit. 'Cancelled,' he said. 'You sneaked through,' he said again.

Jamie turned again to the queue behind him. A few people towards the back had already shifted themselves, but the English family was still there, uneasy about surrendering a place at the front when the other queues were so long. 'Really,' he said, as kindly as he could, 'I'm going to be here some time; you'll have a long wait.'

The supervisor was in the kiosk now, looking at the ledger and at Jamie's passport. He looked up, double-checking face against photograph, and then turning over the pages of the passport. 'Mr Cathcart,' he said, 'you don't have a visa for entry to this country.'

'British passport holders don't require visas.'

'A certain number of people have that exemption removed; and you are one of those people.' The venom in the man's voice alone is enough to paralyse, Jamie thought; thank God the bastard can't bite. This was Hell, after all, and he was at the entrance, asking for entry. Perhaps it would be better merely to turn around and to arrange a flight out of Johannesburg and back to London on the next one available. He had noticed a British Airways desk as he came in, presumably to help those flying direct to places like Maseru or Mbabane; but, even as he had that thought of immediate retreat, he knew he couldn't: he had made a promise. If he were refused permission to enter, at least it wouldn't be his fault.

The supervisor was still staring at him. He's probably never seen a real live prohibited immigrant before, Jamie thought, and certainly not one who looks so respectable, so perfectly like an Englishman. He probably thinks this is a deliberate disguise, part of the ploy for 'sneaking through'. There were bright patches of colour on the man's cheeks, unhealthy blotches under the sunburn. 'What happens now?' he asked.

'You may not enter the country without a visa, and you haven't got a visa.'

'I'm aware I haven't got a visa, but I didn't know I needed one.' That wasn't absolutely true, he knew. Although he had never been officially informed that he had been moved into the small category of exiles and opponents who, despite their British passports, nevertheless required visas, he had some years earlier heard a rumour from his brother that he had been made a prohibited immigrant. Therefore, acting on careful advice from within the country, he had then applied for a visa – for the purpose of a 'family holiday', he said – and, after a delay of many months, had been refused. He hadn't bothered to ask why.

'Mr Cathcart, you require a visa for entry; you haven't got one; you therefore may not enter.' And obduracy is a

18

celebrated national characteristic, Jamie thought, looking at the supervisor's tight-lipped but now triumphant smirk.

'But my visit is urgent,' Jamie said, tight-lipped himself now, hating the fact that he would soon be reduced to explanation and appeal. What right had this fat little Afrikaner to keep him out of his own country?

'You require a visa.'

'If I had waited for a visa, it would have been too late.'

'You still require a visa for entry.'

'May I know your name?' Jamie asked. Silently, the supervisor tilted up his security pass for Jamie to read. 'Van Breda, Klaas (Mnr)' the name read.

'Mr van Breda, I heard last week that my brother in Cape Town has cancer. It may be terminal. He asked me to come to see him.' He corrected himself. 'He asked me to come home to see him, before he dies. If I had asked for a visa, it might have taken months. He might have died while I was waiting for Pretoria to make up its mind. I'm not coming to make trouble for anyone; I merely want to see my brother. If you don't believe me, telephone his doctor.' There, he had said it; he was doing what he had always vowed he would not do: he was in effect apologising, or at least trying to make a private peace with what he had hated so much he had been prepared to give up everything to make disgust and anger plain. Futile and personal gestures, perhaps, rather than publicly effective, but still a sacrifice of privilege; and he was making his apology to this bag of guts, this discourteous and obdurate Aryan with his unhealthy tan and piggy eyes. How dare he expect an explanation.

The supervisor was unmoved. 'The regulation is clear, meneer. You require a visa to enter the country.'

'I suppose you expect me to fly back to London to apply for a visa.'

For the first time, there was doubt in the response. 'If you apply for a visa now, Mr Cathcart, you will have to

19

wait here while the application is processed. It would be better to return to London to apply.'

Jamie looked about him. Now that he was held here, he was beginning to suffer from claustrophobia again; he was trapped in this anteroom to Hell, and part of him wanted nothing more than to escape, to get on the next flight out of South Africa and back to the sure ways of England. He was, he realised, longing to be outside; even a moment or two back on the tarmac would seem a release. Yet he had no choice, really: he would have to see this through.

'Mr van Breda, I wish to apply for a visa.'

'You may have a long wait in that case.' The note of triumph was back in the man's voice.

* * *

In fact, it was nearly eight hours before Jamie achieved a temporary visa allowing him to enter the country ('for compassionate reasons') for twenty-four hours. When he protested that such a short time would scarcely allow him time to get to Cape Town, now that he had missed his connecting flight, he was told he would be able to apply from Cape Town for an extension.

The respite was not thanks to Klaas van Breda; at nine o'clock, he had gone off duty, along with all the other officials in the immigration kiosks, and a fresh set of men (there were apparently no women officials) came on duty. Jamie had already talked to the woman (not a South African, judging by her accent at least) who had come on duty at the British Airways desk in the transit lounge at eight, and had provisionally fixed a seat for himself on the evening flight out of Johannesburg and back to London. She seemed mystified that anyone should be refused entry to South Africa, yet sympathetic to his plight, and was very forthcoming about the fact that the flight was likely to be only half full. 'Not many people are wanting to visit Johannesburg at the moment,' she said. 'More go straight to Cape Town – but people are worried about the politics, especially up here. Such a pity,' she continued soothingly, 'because it's such a lovely country.' With her help, he telephoned his brother in Cape Town to warn him that he was being delayed and, on her advice, he arranged for his suitcase to be retrieved; it was now stored, rather inconveniently for her, behind her desk.

At ten, aware that Van Breda was quite capable of having gone off duty, merely abandoning his application in a pile of papers on a desk somewhere, he asked to see the supervisor again, to discover that he was now being dealt with by an English-speaking official apparently as sympathetic to his plight as Van Breda had been unpleasant.

'Have you had breakfast, Mr Cathcart?'

'Well, actually, I haven't. I wasn't aware I could.' He hadn't eaten much other than the fresh fruit provided on the breakfast tray handed him by the air hostess on the flight, and was now aware that he wanted coffee, and perhaps more than that.

'There's a dining room in the transit hotel.'

'Hotel?'

'Quite a few people stay there while waiting for flights to the territories.' Jamie realised the man meant what he was still inclined to think of as the High Commission territories, though they were now the independent countries of Lesotho, Botswana and Swaziland. 'If you have breakfast, I shall join you for coffee.' He was being careful, very correct, almost as if their conversation were being overheard.

Once they were in the cavernous dining hall in the transit hotel above the concourse, the man – whom Jamie saw from his security pass was called Nigel Smethurst – relaxed. 'Well, Mr Cathcart,' he said, 'we can talk now. I'm never quite sure who is listening in to conversations these days, but this ...' he gestured at the empty space above

21

and empty tables around '… this should be all right. We have a problem.'

Jamie nodded. 'Thank you,' he said.

'Don't thank me yet,' Smethurst said. 'Listen first. I telephoned as you suggested, and the doctor has confirmed that your brother is seriously ill. I'm very sorry for that.' Jamie nodded again, silently. One forgot the degree of distrust – as if he would lie about something like that. 'The trouble is that it's Saturday. You see, your file had a label on it saying that the Minister himself must be consulted. The Minister isn't available. He could say no, he could say yes. I have to say that, normally, I would want that yes in writing, just to protect my own back, if you see what I mean.'

'Thank you for helping.'

'I haven't helped yet.' Smethurst held his hands up to ward off thanks. 'I'm just finding out the difficulties.' He grinned suddenly, like a schoolboy caught in some innocent mischief. 'I must say, Mr Cathcart, you must have upset them properly. I mean, the Minister …' And he wagged his finger at Cathcart, cheekily. 'I suppose I'd better not ask what you did.'

'Actually, it was more a matter of saying than doing.'

'Well, some would have us believe there's not much difference. But I'm not going to talk politics with you, Mr Cathcart.'

'I call it morality as much as politics.'

'Be that as it may, Mr Cathcart. My job is to find out if I can issue you with a temporary visa and to do that I need to talk to a government Minister, who could be anywhere. I'll do what I can, but you must be patient.'

'I have booked a flight back to London this evening.' He looked at his watch. 'I missed my connecting flight to Cape Town hours ago.'

Smethurst shrugged. 'Who knows?' he said.

'Why you are bothering?'

Smethurst grinned his schoolboy grin again. 'Well, I

22

guess I'm remembering that nothing lasts for ever, and one day someone like you may need to do me a favour too. But it may not work, Mr Cathcart.'

'I'm grateful to you for even trying.'

* * *

As the day went on, Smethurst reported back periodically on his progress. By noon, he had tracked down one of the Minister's officials to explain the problem. By one o'clock, the Minister had promised a decision 'before too long'. At three o'clock, there was no decision. The last flight to Cape Town that day left at five, and the return flight to London left at eight; Jamie was not sure he could bear to spend a night, and possibly another day, trapped in transit. The weeks he had spent in solitary confinement before his last departure from South Africa, nearly twenty years before, were coming back like a bad dream. Not being able to get into the open air, even onto a balcony, even by stepping back on to the airport runway, became a matter of near panic. Even the business of there being one nasty and one nice immigration official began to concern him. It was one of the oldest tricks of the security police, he remembered: they would use one loathsome policeman to bring you closer towards fear and despair, and then substitute a pleasant and friendly one to trap you into being trusting. Were the personae of Van Breda and Smethurst merely ploys to make him trust the latter? When, at four o'clock, Smethurst reappeared, Jamie had almost persuaded himself that this must be the case, to the extent he failed to notice that Smethurst was carrying his passport. In the passport was a temporary visa.

'I know it's only for twenty-four hours, Mr Cathcart,' Smethurst explained.

'Does the Minister really expect me to catch a flight out of Cape Town back to London tomorrow night?'

'If I were you, Mr Cathcart, I'd risk staying on, and

going to the Immigration Department in Cape Town on Monday to get an extension.' The man seems genuine enough, Jamie thought. Is it paranoid of me to wonder if he is merely trying to get me to put a foot wrong, to give the security police a legitimate reason for chucking me out again, or for locking me up again? He had left careful instructions for his secretary about what to do if he were held in South Africa; he knew one junior minister in the British government well enough to call him by his first name, and his secretary was to telephone him in the first place. Would that become a necessary recourse? The problem with a police state was that you could so seldom guess which way the bastards would jump. Then he reminded himself of why he was there at all: he had come to see Peter.

'Thank you,' he said to Smethurst. 'You have been very helpful. I am most grateful.'

And so, Jamie thought, he had paid his penny to the boatman, and now he was to be ferried across the marble floor and into the kingdom of the dead – well, the nearly dead. The dog had barked, but not bitten; and the waters were warm, not cold. Charon had turned out to be friendly and helpful, even if his other half was nasty. And waiting for him was his beloved brother. Not the person he would want it to be if this were really Hades; no, his brother was merely dying, and she was dead. Dead, gone, broken up and buried. Not dust yet but – after twenty years – not much left. No chance – worse luck – of finding her here again waiting for him, as his brother was waiting. The only miracle he could hope for was that his brother might survive what seemed on first hearing uncommonly like a death sentence – and Jamie didn't believe in miracles, nor in an afterlife, even in Hades.

Chapter 2

Although he had telephoned Peter to give him the news, Jamie had not been expecting his brother to meet him; indeed, Peter looked as if he shouldn't be anywhere but in a hospital bed. Thinking he would need to take an airport bus into central Cape Town and then a taxi out to the suburbs, Jamie had not hurried off the plane, nor to collect his luggage, but had allowed himself to drift, now rather wearily, at the back of the crowd coming off the aeroplane and across the tarmac into the local arrivals hall to wait at the luggage belt. Having taken hold of his suitcase, he wandered into the main hall to find a taxi rank or the bus stop and there Peter was, white-faced and still so shaky on his crutches that he had positioned himself next to a pillar for support, his blonde hair too long and his thinness emphasising that he was even taller than most of the other men, all white, gathered to greet friends or family.

'You shouldn't be here,' Jamie said almost accusingly as, awkwardly, he avoided the crutches so that he could hug Peter. He tried not to look at the pinned-up left leg of Peter's corduroy trousers.

'I'm afraid I had to come in a taxi. My car's in the garage, being adapted so I can drive it.'

'Did the doctor say you could come?'

'I didn't ask.'

'You should be in bed still.'

'They get you up quickly, these days. They say more people die from lying down too long than die of what they are brought in for. I shall have to go back in to have the wound dressed in a day or two. I'm glad to be out of hospital.' He tried to joke. 'Too many sick people in hospital for me ...'

25

'Painkillers?'

'Oh, lots of those – I probably rattle as I walk. I have to slosh pills down every four hours, even at night. Sorry I can't help with the bags. Do you want a porter?'

'No, they aren't heavy. Where's the taxi rank?' Most people got quickly out of Peter's way as they noticed the crutches, and some stared quite openly. One small boy nudged his mother and pointed.

'Don't stare, darling. It's rude,' she said, but stared herself.

Peter raised his eyebrows. 'I'm getting used to being an exhibit,' he said. '*Look, Mummy, that man's got only one leg.* I've been thinking of stories: shark attack – trodden on by an elephant – a thief cut it off one night when I was asleep … There must be something more original.'

'How about being a fighter pilot? You could wear a white scarf round your neck. You'd look dashing and romantic.' Jamie tried to match his mood to Peter's attempt at cheerfulness.

'No longer, I fear, brother. People would think I'd been shooting up infiltrators on the borders. Anyway, wasn't it the Japanese who wore white scarves? The suicide-bombers?'

'I thought the Battle of Britain pilots did too – to keep the draughts out. I think the taxi rank's the other way.'

'No, I made the driver wait. He's parked just over there. I thought there might be a queue. Do you mind if I sit in the front? It's a bit easier, I find.'

When the bags and crutches were stowed in the boot, there was a rapid discussion in Afrikaans between Peter and the taxi driver. Jamie tried to follow, but they spoke too fast. 'My Afrikaans is very rusty,' he said when the conversation seemed to be over. 'Is there a problem?'

'I was wondering if we might take a short cut back to Wynberg, but the driver says he thinks it's better to go the way we came, though it's a bit longer.'

'Is the short cut through townships? Is that what they are called now? Not "locations"?'

26

'No, we haven't said "locations" for years. "Townships", nowadays.'

'Dangerous?'

'Yes – sometimes, at any rate. Sometimes they are very quiet, but there are terrible things happening there, Jamie. You don't read it in our newspapers, but you hear.'

'We sometimes hear overseas, too.'

'Yes, there's probably more in English newspapers than we get to read here. Anyway, we tend to avoid driving through townships unless one has a guide. Even then ...' Peter shook his head. 'I risk it sometimes when I'm in a hurry – but never after dark.'

'It's best for *witmense* to keep out, especially when it's getting dark,' the driver volunteered, not taking his eyes off the road; Jamie had gradually become aware that the driver was keeping as close an eye on pedestrians as on other cars, particularly when the main road passed under bridges.

'There's been quite a bit of stone-throwing at cars on this road,' Peter explained. 'It's not a good place to break down.'

And this, thought Jamie, is the safest way into town. What an extraordinary contrast it was between the mountains in the evening light rising so beautifully and so suddenly from the sea to make the 'fairest Cape in all the circumnavigation of the globe' and the dark and dangerous townships with their stone-throwing protesters and gun-mad policemen. It was a blissful evening too: clear, warm, but not too hot, with a small breeze blowing off the Atlantic Ocean. How extraordinary it is to be home, he thought, where it is no longer home, to be back where he had once belonged, but now no longer.

As if he had read Jamie's mind, Peter said suddenly from the front seat of the taxi, 'I'm glad the bastards let you in. I got a bit nervous. I thought they might keep you out.'

'I'll have to get an extension to my pass tomorrow – there's an office down on the foreshore.'

'They'll give it to you, won't they, now they've let you in?'

'You never know with these people, do you? But you're right: why let me in at all, unless they really want trouble?'

* * *

The original idea had been that Peter would, as soon as possible after he left school, come from the Eastern Cape to join Jamie and, together, they would take a cheap house somewhere. Jamie's leaving the country had forestalled that plan, though Peter had still come to Cape Town to take his diploma in commercial art and had found a house a little larger than needed because he had been sure that, sooner rather than later, Jamie would be coming back for good. At first, Peter had rented the house, but when the owner – a man classified as Cape Coloured and thus caught in the trammels of the Group Areas Act – had put it on the market several years after Jamie had left for London, he had (with Jamie's help from London) taken out a bond to buy it.

Even then, Peter had still thought it would be only a year or two more before Jamie returned to Cape Town permanently and so he had hung on to the place rather than moving somewhere else. Relative to the cost of property in England, the house had been very cheap. However, fashion had shifted and Wynberg was now an affluent part of Cape Town whereas once much of it had been on the edge of being a slum.

Peter's pride in what he had done with the house was obvious. Even before Jamie had unpacked his suitcase, Peter took him on a guided tour of the property, so meticulously it included his opening virtually every cupboard and wardrobe to show Jamie the contents. The house itself was a low-slung, white-painted place, fronting directly on to a quiet street; one walked up several steps from the pavement and onto a verandah that stretched round the side of the house. Behind the house was a small courtyard and only slightly larger garden, shaded by a pergola of vines and an old lemon tree. The courtyard was, for much of the warmer part of the year – though Peter clearly didn't count today as properly warm – in effect Peter's sitting room, and indeed his kitchen, because against the wall of the neighbour's house he had built what Jamie had learned overseas to call a barbecue but Peter still called a *braaivleis*, shaped to mimic an old bread oven, and (he explained) he actually did most of his cooking out there. Over the years he had gradually stripped out the interior of the house, making the original dining room, sitting room and kitchen into a single, long, open-plan room, with a kitchen at one end, a dining table in the middle, and comfortable armchairs and a sofa at the other end. A spare bedroom had been converted into two bathrooms, one for each of the remaining bedrooms. One of the bedrooms Peter named firmly as 'Jamie's room' and Jamie noted, with amusement as well as affection, that for all his proprietorial pride Peter made a real effort to refer always to 'our house', even though Jamie had never before set foot in it. Floorboards had been sanded and sealed, and doors, windows and lintels returned to the original wood. Peter had spent the money he had saved by not moving elsewhere on carpets, curtains, expensive lighting and a few really good pieces of old Cape-Dutch furniture: yellowwood (like the floors with their twelve-inch-wide boards) and stinkwood – not a stick of pine anywhere.

'Where did you get the paintings from?' Jamie asked.

'Most of them our grandmother left to me when she died. Don't you remember? I wrote to you to ask if you wanted some of them, and you said you didn't.'

'Of course,' Jamie replied; he had genuinely forgotten the complexities of their grandmother's will with its careful instructions about who was to get what – the 'what' including no money and many objects, most of sentimental value only. 'Some of the paintings are your own, aren't they?' Peter nodded; he had moved quickly from his own painting to commercial art to business but, once upon a time, he had had ambitions to be a proper artist and still, in his occasional spare time, he would paint a South African landscape in water-colour, though he never sold his work nor exhibited it, except on his own walls.

'It's a lovely house – and, little brother, remembering how uncommonly mucky you used to be as a boy – extraordinarily clean and tidy.' For most of their younger years, they had shared a room, and the contrast between Jamie's obsessive tidiness and Peter's habitual untidiness – he never put anything away that he could keep on a chair or the floor – had been one of the few conflicts between them. Jamie had given up trying to reform his brother, in the end, and each had kept his half of the room exactly as he wished, Peter's a circulating chaos, Jamie's an uncluttered minimalism.

'Do you have a maid?' Jamie asked suddenly. When he was growing up, most white South Africa households had had at least one maid, often living in one room out at the back somewhere; but the room that might once have been a maid's room Peter had converted to a workroom.

Peter looked uncomfortable suddenly. 'Oh, yes, I do, but Grace walked out earlier this week, soon after I came back from hospital, and I haven't got round to finding a new one. She used to come a couple of mornings a week. It's something I've got to sort out.'

'I hope her leaving isn't to do with my visit,' Jamie said, though in his heart he was glad there wouldn't be a servant constantly there; he had got used to a life without servants – he managed in England with only the occasional visit from a cleaning lady.

'No, it's nothing to do with you,' Peter said. The conversation is closed, Jamie noted; one always knew when that happened with Peter. A door was shut, the portcullis came down, the drawbridge went up. No further inroads into privacy were permitted.

Jamie was never very sure exactly how wealthy Peter's company was, nor how much money Peter had, only that he seemed able to travel abroad whenever he wanted to, though he almost always stopped in London to see Jamie. That – and knowing the Wynberg house was always there for him if he needed it and if he were allowed back – had made up a little for the years during which Jamie had not been able to come back to South Africa himself.

Because, thought Jamie, even after all these years, he and his not-so-little brother were actually still so close to each other that they hardly needed to talk. Jamie had only to look at Peter to know what he was thinking, and Jamie knew Peter knew what he thought too, so he didn't need to say anything either. They could sit in the same room for two hours having a conversation, and not speak a single word. They could go to a drinks party together, and then come home in silence. Over supper, Peter would say to Jamie, 'Ghastly woman,' and he would agree without needing to attach a name, though anyone else might have thought Peter had been responding to her flirtation. Or Jamie would say, 'I didn't think much of that,' and Peter would know that he was talking about the opening of an exhibition they had gone to the evening before; and Jamie wouldn't put it like that if he thought Peter had approved of it. He would say, 'I know you quite like that, but I'm not sure I do,' and Peter would have answered, 'Yes, I realise. Those distortions are hard to take at first, aren't they?' How did he know precisely what Jamie had found disturbing? Neither had any idea. Telepathy? Possibly, though Jamie wouldn't have thought so. It was just that they knew each other so well that they could tell, from the slightest movement of the head, or from a twitch of the shoulders, or from a space between words, or an apparently irrelevant reference, what was happening in the mind of the other. Even though they had been mainly apart for the past twenty years. When Jamie read about twins, they seemed to communicate in the same way:

31

Peter and he weren't twins and for all their physical similarities – the same blonde hair, the same tall skinniness – they were by no means identical to look at, and differed in habits and manner, not just in attitudes to tidiness either. However, they thought and felt in the same way. And for the twenty years before they had been separated they had been inseparable.

Yet they had so many secrets from each other. For the past fifteen years, for instance, Jamie had known that Peter had a mistress, the wife of one of his business partners, not especially beautiful or sensual but, as far as one could tell, an ordinary, well-kempt and pleasantly dressed housewife with sun-bleached hair and a figure she kept in shape by visiting a gym three times a week, who spent most of her time looking after her house, her husband and her children. Jamie had never met the husband, though he had no doubt he would have done if he had been living in Cape Town. He knew his name and that was all. Peter and he seemed to get on very well together; the business flourished, without any suggestion that it might be floated on the stock market or anything expansive or grandiose like that. Jamie had no idea what ages the children were, nor what sex; he thought there were two of them, and for all he knew one or the other or even both might actually have been his niece or his nephew, by blood if not by name. Was the husband complaisant? Did he know that, one or two or even three nights a week, his calm and sensible Jessica left their smart house in Bishopscourt and came to his brother's house in Wynberg to sleep with him? He must surely have known that much, Jamie surmised – or at least that, when his brother travelled, Jessica as often as not travelled with him.

That's how Jamie knew about her in the first place: Peter had brought her to dinner at his flat in Battersea. 'This is Jessica Barnard, the wife of one of my partners, Anton; she is in London at the moment,' he had said. Neither of them had made any pretence that their friendship was anything other than sexual. She had stayed that night in Peter's room in the flat, and there had been … well, there had been some noise. If it hadn't been Peter, Jamie knew he might have been upset, but Jessica was there for breakfast the next morning, wearing one of the old dressing gowns that Jamie kept for the occasional guest in his spare room. After she had gone Peter had said to him, 'I hope you aren't too upset that she stayed for breakfast. We almost never get the chance back in Cape Town – she has to leave very early for the children.'

'How many nights a week can she come to you?'

'It varies: one or two, usually. Does that shock you?'

Jamie had shaken his head. Thereafter, when Peter wrote or telephoned to say he was coming to London, Jamie knew without asking that Jessica would probably be with him, and would come to stay in the flat, though she was sensible about not intruding too much into his existence.

Peter's letter about his cancer had been typical, too – both what he wrote, and that he wrote at all, rather than telephoned, even though the question was urgent. This was news better put in a letter than in a conversation; better by far to read – 'to read, mark, learn and inwardly digest' was the phrase from childhood – than to hear.

'You will remember,' Peter had written, 'that I thought I must have a deep varicose vein in my thigh. In the end, it began to ache rather too much and too often, and Disprin didn't help. So I took it to the doctor. The x-ray shows I have a tumour on the bone, not very small either. By the time you get this, the surgeon will have had a look. He thinks that, rather than just getting at the tumour, he will have to take the leg off at the hip. That way, there will be a chance that the cancer won't have gone further up. I was offered the choice between a relatively quick and apparently painless exit in a few months' time and this op. The op may not work, and the exit will then be certain; but I thought I should try to fight. By the time you get this

33

letter, the surgeon's decision will have been made. He may have sewn me up to die very quickly, or he may have cut my leg off, in which case I could die quickly or merely in the usual course of events.'

And then: 'I know you don't want to come back here, and I understand why. I know too that you may not be able to. But I think they'd let you in, now, if only for my sake. I would very much like it if you would come home.'

And that was it. Jamie knew. There was no choice. This was something that had to be done.

* * *

These were what Jamie had taken to calling – whenever anyone he met in England remembered he had been, or was still, a South African and thought to ask his opinion – the dark days, when it seemed that nothing would ever change in South Africa, except for the worse. Whatever happened to be the long- or short-term merits of what they were trying to do inside their own countries, as far as Jamie was concerned, Ronald Reagan in the USA and Margaret Thatcher in Britain seemed intent on making the wrong choices in the rest of the world. If there was a dictator who needed admonishment, they provided admiration; if there was a system that needed amendment, they provided support; if the rest of the world seemed to be moving towards consensus, they provided dissent.

In South Africa in particular, it was clear enough that the white Nationalist government was prepared to do almost anything to stay in power: commando units would strike across international borders to destroy opponents; death squads got rid of awkward activists; one could actually pretend to dispense with some of the more draconian laws because the police or army did what they wanted to, anyway. Though the black townships – which apartheid had so ruthlessly segregated from the white towns and suburbs – had become largely ungovernable, and black schoolchildren in particular were in an almost constant state of revolt, which dogs, sjamboks and even machine-guns seemed unable to quell, the black population was apparently very divided, and the government and the press – both national and international – played up the divisions as vigorously as they could.

Yet Jamie (despite his suspicion of any kind of collective or even communal politics, and though it was difficult for him to say this even to beloved Peter) was sure that things were going to have to get even worse before they got better. In one sense, he could greet every new horror, if not with approbation (for who could approve of prisoners 'being shot while trying to escape', when everyone knew they had been taken out of their cells to be murdered in the bush? Who could approve of the communal punishment of 'necklacing' – pushing a car tyre down over a victim's arms to trap him, then pouring petrol into the tyre and setting it alight?) at least as bringing the inevitable final conflagration a little closer. These were the many circles of Hell into which one would have to walk deeper and deeper before one (not, in Jamie's view, 'the people', but 'one') found a way out – and the way out is up through the Devil's anus.

Though even Hades has its pleasant corners, Jamie thought, as he and Peter sat having breakfast in the courtyard on the day after he had been given a week's extension to his visa.

'What happens if I want to stay longer?' he had asked the clerk in the office down near the Cape Town docks.

'You come back,' the man said. 'Just like everybody does.'

'Silly of me not to realise,' said Jamie when he had walked back to the car where Peter sat waiting for him. 'In a major port like this, they'll be used to dealing with all sorts of odd characters wanting visa extensions.'

'Less and less major,' said Peter. 'Sanctions are really

biting, whatever the government pretends. You see it here most of all.'

'It looks very prosperous to me,' Jamie replied. Peter was steering his car carefully out of the harbour complex. They had retrieved the car from the garage earlier that day, and Peter had taken him for a drive round the peninsula, partly – Peter said – so he could learn to use the new accelerator fixed to the steering wheel like an old-style throttle, though Jamie guessed it was as much for the pleasure of being free to move again. 'I must say, all the same, I'm glad I'm legitimately here, not an illegal immigrant,' he said.

'Anyone can tell, just by looking at you, what a shady chap you are, Jamie.' Peter smiled at him. He had already teased Jamie for looking 'just like a bloody Englishman, needing to wear a tie so your shirt won't fall off'.

While Peter had struggled to shave, shower and dress – 'you forget, when you have two legs, how often you stand on one to do something like putting soap on, or pulling on your trousers. What the hell am I going to do with eight right-footed shoes?' – Jamie had put breakfast on the wrought-iron table in the courtyard: orange juice, coffee, rolls, butter, some cold sausage left over from the night before. The sun was pleasantly warm and he was wearing a T-shirt he had borrowed from his brother, and shorts and sandals which he had added to his luggage at the last moment – relics of a summer in Tuscany a couple of years earlier. He was, he realised, almost happy. Perhaps I am back where I really belong, he thought to himself. If one pushed politics to the back of one's consciousness; if one ignored the pinned-up leg of Peter's jeans; if one wrote off the years of exile; why then this was where he might still have been. The sun poured into the courtyard; the doves called throatily to each other; the leaves on the lemon tree stirred in the slightest possible breeze.

'What are you going to do today?' he asked his brother, though he thought he already knew the answer.

'Well, if you wouldn't mind too much, I thought I'd drive myself into town just to see that all is well at the office. Unless you've got other plans, that is.'

'I thought you said you were dispensable.'

'Disposable, more like. No, they don't really need me; I'd just like to keep a semblance of normality. I can't go tomorrow – I have an appointment with the doctor, the cancer lady, at Groote Schuur.'

'Do you want me to come with you – tomorrow, I mean?'

'Could you bear that? I'd like you to meet the doctor. I'm not seeing the surgeon again until next week, though the dressing will need changing sooner, I think.'

'Not today?'

'I hope not; anyway, I do want to go into work for a few hours. I'll feel better if I make an appearance.'

'Of course.' Work mattered; work was what kept you going when things got difficult. It wasn't need, or duty, or loyalty; it was order and sanity. 'I thought I might drive in with you and then catch a train out to Simon's Town. Are the trains all right still?' He meant: are the trains still safe?

'You should be all right. There've been a couple of nasty incidents, but it was single women, generally.' He hesitated, then said, 'Will you be all right, yourself?'

Jamie knew that Peter was referring not to any danger that might lurk on the suburban trains, but to something else. Once upon a time, that journey – or, rather, that part of the journey that lay between Muizenberg and Simon's Town, so close to the sea that on wild winter days it was quite common for the sea-spray to splash upwards to the train windows – had been Jamie's very favourite outing. Once, when Peter had come from school to visit him in Cape Town, it was that which Jamie had insisted on taking him to experience – before an ascent of Table Mountain, before a visit to the docks, before a journey in a car borrowed from a university friend on the precipitous road around Chapman's Peak, before a night visit to the fleshpots of central Cape Town and Sea Point.

'I'll be all right,' Jamie said, unsmiling. 'By the way, while we're on that subject, what about Jessica Barnard? Do you see her still?'

'We've not seen much of each other since I went into hospital. I think she may be worried about having someone else to look after. I think she may feel she has enough people to look after already.' He spoke wryly but then added, 'Anyway, I'm not that concerned.'

So, when they had cleared away breakfast, Peter drove them both into Cape Town, where he dropped Jamie outside the central railway station before taking himself off to work. 'No,' Peter said firmly. 'I'll manage. One of the office boys is waiting for me outside; I'll get myself to the lift while he parks the car for me. I'll be fine; it's all arranged already. I'll see you at home for a drink at about six.'

* * *

There is nothing particularly special about the train journey on the suburban line from central Cape Town to Muizenberg. If one sits on the right-hand side of the train, one gets the occasional glimpse of Table Mountain and its attendant peaks and ranges as they rise so surprisingly and abruptly into rocky precipices from the closer suburbs. On the other side, one sees the squalor of the industries of Salt River and Woodstock, and thereafter the train runs through suburban houses, schools, playing fields, sports clubs, more houses, the backs of shops, until one is past Claremont. Then, on the left, if it's a clear day, one can see across False Bay to the Hottentots Holland range and, on the right, the vineyards of Constantia, with mountains behind, almost like a Renaissance landscape, with the ordered vineyards directing one's eyes to the wild mountains above.

It is only after Muizenberg that the journey becomes altogether spectacular, when the railway line runs between the road and the Indian ocean, the whole way to Simon's Town and the main naval docks. Compared with the Atlantic coast, the other side of the peninsula, this is much calmer, and all three bays – Kalk Bay, Fish Hoek and Simon's Town – provide shelter for fishing boats. The sea here is generally warmer too than on the other side, though it can't be particularly warm today, Jamie thought, as he watched from the train window; there was hardly anyone swimming, except some hardy youngsters in wet suits surfing out in the bay.

Perhaps, Jamie thought to himself, it is only possible to be really happy when one is still innocent enough to think that happiness continues. As soon as one has learned how transient it is, there is such grief in any moment of happiness that it is hard to distinguish grief from happiness. Or is it the other way round? Is grief so powerful that one cannot be more than momentarily happy? It hadn't always seemed liked that – but then he hadn't really known grief in any major sense until later. He had learned all right.

What had she said that day? The train had been almost empty, and they had been so cold that they had run most of the way up the hill from Simon's Town to Seaforth. 'Ballet dancers don't like running very much,' she had said when they stopped, scarcely panting herself, though he was almost winded. 'We always stand with our feet at right angles – look, like this. It makes running very difficult,' and she demonstrated. 'You run too fast.'

'I shamble,' he said, laughingly. 'I'm too tall to be fast.'

'You're quite fast, my Jamie,' and they had both laughed before she took his hand and walked him onwards towards Seaforth.

Was that the first time she took possession of him by calling him 'my Jamie'? It had become a joke with his friends and, when they wanted to tease him, they would call him 'my Jamie' too. 'My Jamie' – and then, when he had caught the mannerism from her, 'My Jenny'. The first time he had taken her to a café down the hill from the university; and then he had wanted to be with her so much he used to wait for her outside the women's residence and would walk down the hill with her to the ballet school almost every afternoon. Sometimes he took a book and sat reading outside, waiting for her dance class to end; more often he went to the music school himself. Was it her idea to take the train to Simon's Town or his? No, it had been his, because he had remembered the journey from a holiday with his father when he was much younger.

There was an old man in a patched and tatty tweed overcoat on the seat opposite him. He must have got in at Kalk Bay, Jamie thought. I didn't notice him. The old man stared at him, then said, 'Are you all right, kêrel?'

'Yes,' said Jamie. Have I been crying? he wondered. How embarrassing to be middle-aged, English and in tears on a train. 'Yes, I'm fine. It's just the sea-salt in my eyes.' He had, it was true, opened the window a little when the train arrived in Muizenberg, so he could smell the breakers.

'It's too cold today. You should close that window.'

Jamie didn't reply, but the old man was determined to make conversation. He leaned forward and said, 'You here on holiday? From England?' Jamie nodded. 'I was in England once – right after the war.' He didn't look or sound like a man who had travelled much.

'Why?' Jamie asked.

'I was in the war – taken at Tobruk – and then we were in Italy and Germany. Prisoners of war, you know. I was only a boy then.'

'Have you been back to England?'

'No way – too cold for me. Cape Town winter is bad enough. You know they call the south-easter the "Cape Doctor"? Doctors always make me ill.' He chortled at his little joke, then coughed noisily, and Jamie caught the smell of his sour breath.

'Have you always lived in the Cape?'

'No, I was in the Transvaal mostly – in timber, near Tzaneen. Do you know it?' Jamie shook his head. 'No, I came back here to the seaside when my wife died. My daughter was here, but she's gone to PE now. She wanted me to go too, but you can't keep shifting about, can you? No, they'll bury me here.'

'You look good for a few years yet,' Jamie said.

The old man grinned craftily. 'You couldn't spare a couple of rand for an old man, could you, kêrel? The pension doesn't go very far these days.' Jamie took his wallet out and handed the man a ten-rand note – more than he needed to, he realised, but it was little enough, translated back into pounds.

The old man pocketed the note without any sign of embarrassment and moved off down the carriage. When they got to Fish Hoek station, Jamie saw him leave the train. In the old days, he remembered, Fish Hoek had been a 'dry' town – no off-licences, no *drankwinkels*. Had that changed? he wondered. Probably, if the old man hadn't waited to get to Simon's Town, which certainly wasn't 'dry'.

Was it so wrong to give money to drunks? His father had always refused beggars, not out of any particular meanness, but because he said it merely encouraged them to continue begging, and so made life uncomfortable for others from whom they begged. In reaction, Jamie had always found it almost impossible to pass by a beggar without giving him something. Jenny had teased him about it: 'You'd give away your bus fare to a beggar, wouldn't you, my Jamie, even if you had to walk eight miles as a consequence? And it isn't as if you are rich.'

My goodness, he had been poor in those days – well, relatively poor, Jamie corrected himself, not poor-poor, not Indian-poor, not township-poor – just poor for a middle-class white South African. That day at Seaforth, for instance: after their laughing run up the hill, they had walked down to the little sheltered beach and had sat on a bench looking out across the bay back to Muizenberg, before Jenny had said, 'I'm so hungry. Shall we get something from that restaurant?' There was an Italian restaurant on the water's edge; Jamie had noted it, but had assumed it would be too expensive by far for students. He fished in his pocket and produced a handful of coins.

'That's all I've got,' he said. 'I bought return tickets. Perhaps we can get a hot dog at the station on the way back.'

'I've got money,' Jenny answered. 'I keep some for emergencies.' She opened her purse and produced two notes folded small. 'I think this counts as an emergency, don't you think?'

'Are you sure?' He felt diffident. Few girls paid their own way – it was the boy's job to produce funds.

'Let's see what we can get. Give me your change too.' She marched determinedly across the verandah with its wooden benches and tables, and umbrellas folded – it was too cold to sit outside for long. Jamie stood nervously at the door of the restaurant while she engaged the man at the counter in conversation. Fortunately, the restaurant was almost empty. After several minutes, Jenny came back to him. 'Come and sit down,' she said. 'I've ordered for both of us. He says we can have a bowl of spaghetti each – I hope you like spaghetti – and then coffee afterwards.'

Jenny had clearly exercised her charm well, because in the event the proprietor served them not only what she had negotiated – and very good and filling it had been too, Jamie remembered – but as well as their coffee gave them gratis a pudding which they shared, something warm, rich and tangy that he had never had before, though he guessed there must be a quantity of cream and brandy in whatever it was. He could still remember the taste of it all these years later.

The train was in Simon's Town now. There would be several minutes' wait before the return journey. Shall I walk up the hill to Seaforth? he wondered. Is the restaurant still there? No, I don't think I can bear it. I'm not even going to leave the train. I'll stay on the train until it gets back to Kalk Bay, and then I'll walk along the pavement and the seaside walkway to Muizenberg; I did that once or twice with her and it was lovely, though it wasn't the same as that day in the restaurant. Jamie turned his face away from the rest of the carriage and rested his forehead on the cool glass of the window. Could one be said to enjoy grief? Was this merely self-pity, then? Forget Jenny, forget himself, remember Peter – poor Peter, maimed in the hope that his life might be saved, maimed even though it might not save his life. Think of an old man reduced to begging on a train. Think of real poverty. Think of all the misery of this benighted country, of those locked up, of those shipped away from their homes to some arid location in a so-called homeland. How pathetic to grieve for his own loss when he had so much.

* * *

It was a Thursday, in the afternoon. Because of the trouble in the township, the boy was sitting in the house with his father's new woman and her children. He didn't know where his mother was that day; the last time he had seen her she had been very angry with his father and said she would tell the township about him. Now he heard, outside the house, the sound of a crowd toyi-toyiing; he peeped out of the curtains to see a big crowd of men, some women and a few children – including some of those from his school. They were all shouting and some were waving sticks; one man had an axe. After a while, when no one came out of the house, the crowd went away and he ran to find his father to warn him.

That night, the cars outside the house were set on fire and the crowd came back, still toyi-toyiing; so his father dropped the boy and the other children out of a back window and they ran away to the boy's mother's house to be safe that night.

Next evening, the boy heard the crowd again and ran to his father as he was coming from work to beg him not to enter the township; but his father said, 'No, they won't do anything to me, because there is nothing I have done.' So he went on. Although his father had a gun, he had never before shot at any person. When he met the crowd, he fired the gun in the air. Then he faced the crowd, but they kept coming towards him and he moved back, still facing them. A man got behind him suddenly to trip him, and another man tackled him to take the gun. The boy's father was on the ground now, and this other man swung the axe at his neck; then they put a tyre round his neck and his body, and they poured petrol in the tyre, and they burned him. Then someone saw the boy and shouted, 'Look, there's his son, his offspring' and some of the crowd began to chase the boy, but he ran away to friends in another township.

Later, he heard his father was dead.

Chapter 3

'I'd better warn you,' Peter said over his shoulder to Jamie, 'this so-called oncologist – it sounds like some sort of musical instrument, doesn't it? – looks about fourteen.' Once they had got from the car park to the entrance of the hospital, Peter had accepted – with evident relief to be off his crutches – that he could now allow himself the luxury of a hospital wheelchair, not that it was very luxurious, being as battered and difficult to steer as a farm bakkie. A porter had offered to wheel Peter, but Jamie shook his head and took over.

'Show me the way,' Jamie said, as they weaved their way from side to side of the long corridors, into crowded lifts and out again, avoiding trolleys with tea-urns, patients being wheeled to or from operating theatres, white-coated professors with gaggles of medical students following noisily, clergymen walking slowly with sad-eyed families, patients walking very carefully in dressing gowns and pyjamas. Food or bedpan, scalpel or painkiller? wondered Jamie, as he twisted the wheelchair to avoid a large black nurse carrying a covered tray; the one thing that seemed sure was that there wasn't much apartheid in practice in this hospital, at least as far as he could tell.

The waiting room outside Dr Immerman's office was crowded. After he had found a place to park Peter's wheelchair, Jamie went to the receptionist's desk to report Peter's arrival. 'I'm afraid your brother may have a wait,' the nurse said. 'There are some double-bookings and the doctor had to do a ward round before she started this morning.'

'Are all these people just for her?' Jamie asked.

'No, not even Dr Immerman can see that many,' said the

nurse. She did not smile – there clearly wasn't time for smiling.

'That's all right, then,' Jamie answered. It's odd, he thought: he was usually the most impatient of men, who would in England walk out of a restaurant if he thought the service too slow, but he seemed now to be taking on some of Peter's own peacefulness – or was it a wise passivity? Jamie looked across the room at his brother, sitting there, apparently unworried, not talking to other patients, not looking at the newspaper they had bought from a salesman when they stopped at a traffic light – a 'robot', Jamie reminded himself (he was having to relearn South African names for things) – en route to the hospital, and which Jamie had tucked down the side of the wheelchair for Peter. It was almost as if Peter had begun to move away already, as if he had accepted something Jamie didn't and couldn't know about – and Jamie suddenly found himself hoping that his brother was going to go on fighting his disease and would not merely drift away into dying.

'The nurse says we'll have a long wait,' he said when he rejoined Peter.

'I'm afraid it's always slow. It's amazing how many people get cancer, isn't it? All sorts of people, all sorts of ages. Look at them.'

'Lots of them are just supporters, surely. Sometimes it's a whole family with only one person ill. I mean, look at that lot,' and he gestured with his head to a family group on their right. An old woman with a headscarf hiding most of her dark face, a tartan blanket over her knees, and a shawl around her shoulders was huddled in a wheelchair, and around her four more – one presumed – members of her family: an old man in a blue serge suit, silent, solicitous of the old lady, presumably her husband; a younger man, wearing a blazer with a sports-club badge on the pocket who had assumed control of the wheelchair – the old lady's son, perhaps, or son-in-law, because that was probably his wife next to him, wearing a black dress down to the ground, with a shawl covering her head; and then another woman, younger, very smartly dressed in a dark coat and short skirt, with a white blouse and high heels, and nothing to cover her shining black hair. Where the other members of her family were still and patient, she was restless, jumping up to fetch a magazine or a glass of water, looking at her watch, going over to talk to the nurses at the reception desk. 'That's the one who's got a good job somewhere and she thinks she needs to get back to it,' Jamie said *sotto voce* to Peter and, sure enough, after another glance at her watch and another consultation with the nurses, she hurried off, leaving the rest of the family to wait with the old lady.

'Lots of Coloured girls are holding down quite big jobs now,' Peter said. 'There's a real shortage of manpower here, and those girls are very ambitious and very efficient. They work, where the white girls only want to play. We've taken on three or four in the office and they are bloody marvellous.'

'Very good-looking too,' said Jamie, then laughed. 'In England, now, you can get arrested for saying that kind of thing. It's sexist.'

'Sexist to be pretty? At least we've got rid of the Immorality Act here.'

'Yes, I read that. I was surprised. I always thought it would be one of the last bastions of apartheid. Why did it happen? Too many Dutch Reformed ministers caught having it off with black maids in the garage?'

'Maybe,' Peter shrugged. 'Maybe it just began to seem unimportant. There are lots of things that used to seem important but which we are forgetting about now. We don't say "maids" now.' His voice was gentle.

'Sorry. One forgets. It's a pity we don't seem able to forget about apartheid entirely,' Jamie said, and then felt embarrassed that he had sounded censorious when he did not mean to. He noticed something across the room that

47

helped him change tack abruptly. 'Peter, look at that man over there. You don't know who he is, do you?' It was obvious who Jamie meant: a tall, grizzle-haired man had come into the waiting room accompanied by a white policeman in uniform and another white man in plain clothes whom Jamie was fairly sure he could remember from the old days as a security policeman. 'Good Lord, he's actually handcuffed to the policeman,' Jamie said to Peter.

'It's not Mandela, is it?'

'No, I don't think so; probably not old enough – and not at all like the photos one sees, though they're more than twenty years out of date. But he's a fine-looking man, isn't he? He has "chief" written all over him. I wonder who he is. He makes the policeman look cheap and silly, as if the handcuffs were the wrong way round.'

Other people had clearly noticed, too, because several people were staring at the oddly-assorted party. The security policeman had gone over to talk to the nurses at the reception desk and, while he waited at the desk for an answer to whatever he had asked, he turned to stare about the room. He seemed to look long and hard at Peter and Jamie and, for a moment, Jamie thought there might have been some recognition of his presence; but then he looked away, and Jamie realised he was checking almost everyone in the room. The black man sat bolt upright on the hard hospital chair, paying no attention to anyone, least of all the person he was handcuffed to. A moment or two later, the receptionist spoke to the security policeman, nodded to the guard, and the prisoner was led through to the doctors' offices. 'I wonder what's wrong with him,' Jamie wondered aloud.

'Well, it's going to be cancer of some kind, isn't it? I hope they save him. He's jumped the queue, hasn't he?' Peter sounded suddenly weary.

It was nearly forty minutes before they were summoned to see Dr Immerman. She stood up from behind her desk to shake hands with her patient's brother from England, a small, serious-faced young doctor in horn-rimmed glasses, worn (Jamie realised) mainly to counteract her very youthful appearance because she often forgot to use them, either for reading or for looking at people. Still, when she spoke, she seemed as authoritative as anyone their own age.

Carefully, she took both of them through the notes: the operation had been a complete success in itself, she said, and it had been necessary. The tumour had been even bigger than they realised, and of a very malignant kind; it must have grown very quickly. When had Peter first noticed the pain? He really couldn't remember; it was just something which had nagged away for a while and which he hadn't bothered about. It wasn't like toothache or a pulled muscle, just an ache – at first – until it got really bad.

Jamie wanted to know whether it would have made a difference if the surgeon had operated earlier.

'Who knows?' Dr Immerman replied. 'Early on, we might not even have picked up the tumour on an x-ray if it was very small and very deep.'

'When will we know if we've caught it in time?' Jamie asked. 'If it's spread beyond the leg?'

'I wish I could tell you that,' Dr Immerman answered, 'but no one knows: sometimes very soon, sometimes not for months. You can never know for certain; in a way, don't know is the best to hope for.'

The brothers looked at each other and then at the young doctor sitting seriously behind her desk, taking her heavy glasses on and off, as she tried to answer their impossible questions as plainly as she could. 'There's one other thing,' Jamie said. 'Peter asked me to ask you this: if you haven't caught it in time, is there …' – he hesitated, then rushed at the terrible question, as if by asking it quickly the obstacle would be better cleared – '… is there going to be a lot of pain? Peter asked me to ask you.'

'That's one thing I can promise both of you. These days, with the drugs we have, there'll be no pain. I promise you.'

'When our mother died, she had been screaming for a fortnight,' Peter said. Jamie looked at him, shocked; he hadn't been told that. That had been the first time he had applied for a visa, when Peter had warned him their mother was dying, but the answer had not come through until after her death – and had been a refusal, anyway.

Dr Immerman looked at the papers in the file. 'Yes,' she said. 'You told me: it was in her spine, wasn't it? Well, all I can tell you is that the drugs are better now and we use them more specifically.'

'Are you going to put me on chemotherapy now?' Peter asked. 'You said that you might do so.'

'We could, if you want. We could wait to see. A lot of medicine is not an exact science. If we start you on a drug treatment now, we could be preventing something else developing. On the other hand, it will make you feel very ill sometimes – for a few days after each treatment.'

'Would I have to come into hospital for the treatment?' asked Peter.

'Oh, yes, of course.' She looked astonished at the question. 'We put a drip up overnight, and we give you other things: anti-emetics and so on. It would have to be very broad-spectrum. You'd have to be in each time for three or four days.'

Peter was already shaking his head. 'No,' he said. 'No. I don't want to be back here. I'm feeling perfectly well just now; I mean, it's bloody awful, but it's not the same pain as it was before. It's only now it's gone that I realise how bad it had got.'

'It was a big tumour right in the bone.'

'Well, now I want to think that I'm going to be all right. I want the wound to heal; I want to get used to having one leg only; I want to get a false leg, even if I have to clank along like a tin man.'

50

And what you want you shall have, thought Jamie. I've no idea about the medical side, but if this is the way you need to go, then I'll be with you. He looked at the young doctor on the other side of the desk; she had her heavy glasses in her hands and was staring down at the papers rather than looking at Peter or Jamie. If this were me, thought Jamie, I'd probably ask a question now about the statistical chances. It's always been a difference between Peter and me: he would always bet on the most absurd outsiders, and only when the odds were very high; I, on the other hand, would always start by assuming that the favourite was favourite for very good reasons. However, if he has a reason he doesn't want to go back into hospital, he'll tell me when he's ready; I guess he has a reason.

In the car going back to the house in Wynberg Peter said suddenly, 'Jamie, brother, would you mind very much if someone else moved into the house with us?'

'Of course not. Do you want me to move out? I can go into a hotel or a boarding house or something.'

'Don't be silly,' Peter answered. 'It's as much your house as mine.'

'So she'll share your room, will she?'

'Well, she's certainly not going to share yours, brother mine.'

'Who is she, anyway? Not Jessica Barnard?'

'Good heavens, no – though Jessica does know about it. I told her when it started.'

'Who, Peter, who?'

'It's one of the girls in the office, Jamie. I know it won't matter to you, but she's a Coloured girl. She's called Sharon, I'm afraid. It's the only bad thing about her. Oh, and she's very young: twenty-six – too young for me,' and he grinned suddenly, like a schoolboy. 'She's why I didn't want to go into hospital.' He pulled the car over to the side of the road, abruptly, so that he could turn to look at his brother. 'It's the most extraordinary thing, Jamie. I mean, I've known her for a few months now, in the office: she's

51

very pretty, sexy, and I flirted with her a bit, you know, like any boss with a pretty new girl in the accounts office would, just very gentle and teasing. Then a gang from the office came round when I was in hospital, after the operation, with flowers and chocolates and so on, and she was there, and she stayed on a bit, afterwards, talking, until I went to sleep. And then another crowd came to the house, when I first came back here, and they had stocked up the fridge and brought in flowers, and then I must have been looking weary and they left, but Sharon stayed – and we went to bed together. She sort of invited herself. You know, I'd thought that with my leg like that, either I wouldn't be able to, or that a girl wouldn't much fancy it with me, but even with the dressings on it wasn't like that.' He laughed and started the car again. 'Sorry. I've been wanting to tell you. Actually, I thought for a while we might have pulled the stitches out.'

Jamie didn't think he had ever heard his brother make such a long speech, and certainly not one which touched on that particular subject. No doubt some brothers did, but they didn't. So now all he said was, 'Well, it sounds to me as if she'd better come to stay as soon as possible. I'll make myself scarce.'

'No, you don't have to. She's actually quite shy. She's been staying in the house already but she moved out when you said you'd try to come out. I think she's the reason the maid – you know, Grace, my old cleaning lady from Nyanga – stopped coming.'

'Do the blacks feel like that – about the Coloureds, I mean?'

'No, I think Sharon thought Grace was helping herself from the pantry cupboard and said something. I knew we seemed to get through a lot of groceries, but I sort of counted that as part of Grace's wages. Sharon wouldn't tell me what happened, but Grace didn't come back.'

'How awkward,' Jamie said.

'Well, not really. Grace shouldn't have been helping herself like that, or maybe I should have been paying her more. I thought I was being reasonable.'

'Was Sharon upset? At having to move out? She didn't have to.'

'No, I told her that. When I saw her in the office yesterday, she pretended at first that nothing had happened between us. I wanted her so much that I would have done it on my desk if I could have done. She said that if I didn't have to go back into hospital she'd come back to the house after work today, and that she'd stay. You can meet her then. And hands off, brother.' He was, Jamie realised, only half-joking; there was a real warning in his jealousy. 'I'll tell you something else, Jamie. You know how white people always think that blacks and Coloureds have fantastic prowess at sex. Well, Coloured girls think that white men are the best lovers – and that's for sexual reasons, not for money.'

Jamie didn't answer. It's also just possible, he thought to himself, that inhibition, or a lack of inhibition, might come into consideration in these matters, but he was not going to start a conversation along those lines even with his own brother. For Jamie, it was sufficient that Peter had fallen head over heels into sexual love, in his early forties, with someone called Sharon, who might or might not be a suitable person, but what would it matter, since Jamie had a feeling that Dr Immerman knew that Peter should probably be starting on a course of chemotherapy right now if he was to have any chance at all of survival. For reasons he did not wish to examine, Jamie suspected that the doctor knew perfectly well that the chances were remote – and he was not at all sure that Peter didn't know that himself. So let him have what he wants, Jamie thought, and let him have as much of it as quickly as he can get it, with Sharon or whoever; there is only a short way to the precipice.

* * *

53

Sharon Danialls moved back into the house that evening, arriving with two suitcases. Looking at the cases, Jamie thought that either she must have packed very quickly and efficiently or this must have been actually decided, not merely planned, even before Peter had seen Dr Immerman. No wonder he was so unkeen even to consider going back to hospital when he had this to look forward to. However, despite what Peter had said about her, she was not – in his view – a raging beauty, merely a pretty, slim, dark-eyed girl, with an Indian abundance of hair, so dark that it was almost lustrous, though she herself was the colour of creamy coffee. Clearly, she wasn't a stranger to the house, nor was there any evidence of what Peter had called her 'shyness'; the word Jamie would have attached to her after a couple of days was 'watchful'. She watched over Peter like a hen over a chick, and she watched Jamie too, for instance at meals, to make sure (Jamie decided) that she was behaving as an Englishman thought she should.

However, from the very moment she arrived, it was obvious that Peter was besotted with her and could hardly keep his hands off her, despite Jamie's presence. She in her turn seemed to accept Peter's adulation very easily, almost as if it were her due, though she was more formal with Jamie than he would have expected, shaking hands with him rather than letting him kiss her cheek as he had rather diffidently set out to do when they were introduced.

She had hardly arrived before Peter said that he was going to help her unpack, but immediately shut the bedroom door firmly behind them. Jamie stood still in the middle of the big room for a moment or two, wondering what was the best thing to do. It seemed sensible that he should clear out of the house for a couple of hours; perhaps a long walk in the early evening might be appropriate. Anyway, there was a particular place he wanted to find again, and he thought he might do so more easily if he walked, as they nearly always had to do in the old days. Quickly, he grabbed a jumper and let himself out of the house into the cool evening air.

Even when, half an hour later, he thought he had found the house, he wasn't sure. It had to be hereabouts, he thought, but the combination of dusk and twenty years' growth of trees made it difficult to see. What confused him most of all were the high walls and fences around nearly all the houses, often topped with razor wire or random spikes or electric wiring which must be, Jamie thought, electronic warning systems. Almost every wall had a sign promising instant and armed response, and at the entrances to gates there were automatic lights.

As the evening grew darker, he could have measured his own progress by the growling and barking of dogs behind the walls and fences. In the old days, he remembered, garden boundaries were marked with boulders painted white or with small rockeries or beds of flowers or, at most, fences so low one could have stepped over most of them. Provided their dogs knew one, one could simply walk not just up to the house but into it, calling as one did so, 'Anyone at home?' Even if the family were out, there would be servants there to greet one and offer tea or coffee. If I tried that now, Jamie thought, I'd probably be shot if the dogs hadn't mauled me to death.

Eventually, despite the dark trees obscuring the short drive, he decided he must have the right house. God knows who lived there now, but the garden still fell away down the hillside towards Bishopscourt, offering a spectacular view over towards Kirstenbosch. Well, they may be strangers here now, Jamie thought, but Simon and Adrienne would be pleased that the garden was still cared for. The Du Plessis family had moved to Australia fifteen years earlier, five years after he himself had left. He had tried to persuade them to join him by settling in England, but Simon du Plessis said he didn't think he could cope with a National Health Service. 'I've tried government service, Jamie, and it doesn't like me any more than I like it; I think I shall be entirely independent now,' Simon wrote – and there he stuck, no matter how Jamie tried to explain that, really, the National Health Service wasn't like that.

Remembering now, Jamie smiled wryly to himself. Dear old matter-of-fact Simon had probably been quite right all along because he would have hated what the NHS had become and was probably much better off in Australia anyway. Certainly, their Christmas cards and their family form letters at Christmas – all the communication that remained between them now – made them seem very settled and happy. They kept on wanting Jamie to visit them and he kept on inviting them to England, or to join him on holiday in Italy, but somehow other plans, other commitments, took priority, for them and for Jamie himself.

It had been an odd friendship, anyway: Simon had been seven or eight years older than him, and already a houseman in the hospital at Groote Schuur and married to Adrienne when Jamie had arrived at the university; both were the children of farmers in one of the most prosperous areas of the Western Cape. Simon had apparently been named after one of the Dutch Governors of the Cape, Simon van der Stel, even though his family had originally been French Huguenot, and Simon's elder brother still ran one of the more celebrated of the Cape wine estates out at Franschhoek. Adrienne's father had been a Member of Parliament for many years, a pleasant and wealthy farmer-cum-businessman who had loathed the narrow-mindedness and bigotry of the Afrikaner Nationalists even before they came to power in 1948, but who couldn't quite bring himself to disown his own Afrikaner roots. He therefore hovered uneasily on the fringes of the mainly English-speaking United Party until, thankfully, he found an issue over which he could resign, not just from his party but from all politics.

The wealth of both families had meant that Simon and Adrienne could marry while they were still at the univer-

56

sity. As a wedding present, their families had bought them a double plot of land up near Bishopscourt on which they had built a pleasant, low-slung house with a green roof and white gables, designed by a family friend, one of the better-known young architects in the Cape, who taught part-time at the School of Architecture as he built up a practice in domestic architecture – modern but clearly in the Cape Dutch mode. Jamie had sat next to Simon and Adrienne in a political lecture at the university; they had exchanged pleasantries then and, the next day, entirely by chance, had met again, this time at an opening of an exhibition of paintings in a gallery in Rondebosch. Finding that not only were their politics very similar – Simon and Adrienne were as instinctively liberal as Jamie was – but that they liked the same kind of paintings, and recognising his loneliness, they had invited Jamie to come to supper to meet some of their other friends.

Soon, he had become a regular visitor to their house and, when he met Jenny, it seemed natural that he should take her with him to make sure that they approved. Although he was never certain he wanted to be like them, he recognised in them qualities of warmth, security and even of solidity that he had never experienced at home himself, except in Peter – and, really, the love that existed between him and Peter was in part a defensive response.

What was it Jenny had said to him in their garden? There had never been any talk between them of marriage or engagement; they hadn't even been to bed together. Some of their friends did, and some talked about it, but he and Jenny seemed to agree that, when they did, they were going to do it properly, in a big bed, not furtively, not leaning against a wall or squiggling about in the back seat of someone else's car. A few times, they had almost made love completely, but then either one or the other had said 'No', or 'Wait', or had merely turned away. It wasn't as if they could have gone to a hotel together or taken a cottage somewhere; Jamie lived at a men's residence at the university and Jenny at a women's residence, and each was out of bounds to the opposite sex. Jamie didn't have the sort of money one needed for what their more sophisticated friends called 'dirty weekends'.

Then, one evening, walking through Simon's and Adrienne's garden – then still only half-made, though Adrienne was giving more and more time to it and less and less time to finishing her Fine Art degree – Jenny had said to him, 'Of course, when we are married, my Jamie ...' He hadn't heard the rest of what she said.

'Did you say "when", or was it "if"?' he asked, smiling.

'Did I say "when"?'

'You did. I thought it was men who asked that question.'

'You can ask it if you want.'

'And if I don't want?'

'Well, then, I'll ask it.'

'Do you want me to ask you?' Jamie said, suddenly doubtful.

'On no account,' she smiled up at him. 'Think how awful it would be if I said no.'

'I still don't understand.'

'Well, if you don't ask, I can't say no, can I? A kiss might be better.'

So he kissed her and, when they had separated, she said, 'Well, if you kiss me like that, my Jamie, perhaps we should get married, sooner rather than later.'

It wasn't that night, but a week or two later, when they had again been visiting Simon and Adrienne, that they had, perhaps deliberately, stayed so late that, suddenly, it was too late for them to get back into their university halls of residence. 'You'd better stay the night, hadn't you?' Adrienne had said. 'You can have the spare room if you don't mind a double bed.' Neither he nor Jenny had managed to say either yes or no, but soon afterwards they found themselves together in a bedroom with the door shut, and an enormous bed. Although he had not gone into any detail, Jamie had told Jenny soon after they had met that he wasn't a virgin. She had told him she wasn't actually sure whether she was or wasn't, because she had got very drunk at a party before she came to university, and she was uncertain whether or not the boy she had been with that night had managed to do it – '... though,' she said, 'I think I wanted him to, which is really the same, isn't it?'

Jamie had offered to turn out the light. 'No,' she said. 'I want you to see me, and I want to see you.' So they had, rather solemnly and awkwardly, undressed each other, and had then climbed naked into the bed where, to his astonishment but also relief, she had fallen suddenly sound asleep. So he had slept too until, some time during the night, she had woken him. Both still half-asleep, they had made love very rapidly and then, in the early morning, had taken their time. By the time they woke again, both Simon and Adrienne had left the house. There was a note from Adrienne propped on the kitchen table to say that the maid didn't come on Wednesdays, that they were welcome to use the pool if they wanted a swim, and that there was plenty of food in the fridge.

So now, twenty years later, Jamie Cathcart stood in the shadows of the road as he tried to peer though the automatic gates and into the garden, and said to himself, 'Well, God bless Simon and Adrienne, and their sons and daughters, and their hospitality, and I hope they are as happy in New South Wales as I once was in their house' – indeed, not just the once, but constantly, because he and Jenny had treated the place almost as if it were their own home. We must have spent almost every weekend there that year, Jamie remembered – and long weekends we made of them too. We ended up keeping some of our clothes in the wardrobe of their spare room because Adrienne said she was tired of having to run us back to the university in her little car to get a change of clothes on Saturday evening, and all we ever did in return was to buy the odd crate of beer or bottle of wine – and Adrienne's father anyway kept their cellar stocked with bottles Jamie couldn't have afforded in a month of Sundays.

As he wandered slowly back towards Wynberg, Jamie went on thinking about Simon and Adrienne, wondering, for instance, whether they could still afford to live so comfortably, but then reckoning that, even if they no longer had the money they had seemed to have in South Africa, their hospitality was more a matter of style and manners than of material things. He must go to see them in Australia, he said to himself. It was senseless that he avoided them now, though he acknowledged that he did avoid things now, probably too often for his own good. For instance: would it be safe to go back home now? he wondered – and he was aware how ambiguous that term 'home' still was for him. He was home, and he was not at home.

Back at the house in Wynberg, he found Peter sitting in an armchair in the big room, looking tired but pleased with himself. Sharon was down the other end, working efficiently at the stove, wearing an apron of his brother's over her well-cut slacks and smartly embroidered navy-blue blouse. 'Can I help you?' he asked.

'No,' she said. 'I'm just getting something to eat. You must be hungry. You've been a long time.' She didn't sound at all embarrassed.

'Thank you,' he said. 'I am. I walked a long way. Shall I open a bottle of wine?'

'Not for me,' she said, 'but I think your brother will probably join you.' There was still no evidence of any shyness; she was working as quickly and competently in the kitchen as if it had been her own place for years, Jamie noted, with wistful admiration.

'You've clearly found yourself a treasure, Peter,' he said after he had chosen a bottle of red wine from Peter's wine rack near the kitchen end of the room and had taken it and two glasses down to the other end of the room.

'It's lovely to be looked after sometimes, isn't it? She won't let me anywhere near her when she's cooking. She's as efficient there as she is in the office. I think she probably bosses her family around like mad. I can't say I mind.' He looked hard at his brother. 'We've both waited too long, haven't we?'

'I didn't know that I had waited,' Jamie said, for once a little abruptly.

Peter took the hint. 'Where did you walk?' he asked.

'I wandered up to Bishopscourt to see if I could find the house Adrienne and Simon du Plessis used to live in. I took you there, didn't I?'

Peter nodded.

'They went off to Australia.'

'Yes,' said Peter. 'I was here, remember. I used to go to see them after you left. I drove them to the airport when they went to Sydney.'

'Of course,' said Jamie. 'I knew that – silly of me. You became quite good friends, didn't you?'

'Not like you were, Jamie, but they were very kind people, always. It's tragic people like that left here. We could do with more of them.'

'It's likely to go on happening. I'm never sure whether to be pleased or not, though I understand why you don't like it.'

* * *

My name is Nombi. I am baptised also with the English name 'Grace', but when later I went to work for an English family they said I must be not Grace and they gave me another name, which I shall not tell you because it is now not my name. I am Nombi or I am Grace. No, do not call me 'Mrs Gweni', even if you mean it out of respect. Do as our people do: call me 'Mama' because I am old enough to be your mother, even if I am not your mother. Then you will be showing me the respect you show your mother.

61

*I am baptised 'Grace', and my sisters are 'Mercy' and 'Hope'
because my mother and my father were Christians in the St
Cuthbert's Mission at Tsolo in the Transkei. My sister Hope is
still with me; Mercy died when she was still young – only six-
teen years of age. She had the TB; many in the Transkei died of
the TB. Some days I must think Mercy is the lucky one of the
three of us sisters. She died when she was beautiful, and she
was still happy because she did not know she would die. When
she walked through the town, men's heads would turn and
they would smile, and she would smile too, though she had had
no man when she got that illness which made her cough till she
had no blood left to cough. Then when I remember her I am
angered with myself for thinking she was the lucky sister of the
three.*

*I have had, in total, five children: three sons, two daughters.
Of the daughters, one is dead and one is with me – or I am with
her because I live in her house with her children, my grandchildren. Because my daughter must work in town, I am often
the mother to her children as I was to my own, but I too work
in town, five days of each week. I am a domestic servant
because that is all I know how to do, but I work in four houses,
and I will not stay where I am insulted. Even though he is a
sick man, I will not call him 'my master'; I will say only 'my
employer', and if the woman who is now his girlfriend but who
is no better than a whore tells me an insult I will work there no
longer. I will do without his money and the groceries he lets me
take for my sister's children in the township if I must also be
insulted.*

*Of the sons I bore, one is deceased of natural causes, one is
still alive though I do not know where he is now, and one is
murdered. It is this last I shall speak of so you may write down
carefully the words I say. This is the truth I speak, as best I
know it, although there is much I do not know. There is truth,
and there is ignorance; but the ignorance is not lies. I cannot
tell you what I do not know, only what I know with my own
eyes and ears.*

When my first husband went to work in Egoli, I waited for

him in the Transkei, because there were already three children. He did not wish to go, but there was insufficient grazing for the cattle, and the children's mouths were always crying for food. At first, the money came every month, but then there was no more money. So I left the children with my mother and I too went to Egoli, but to find my husband, not to find money. He was a good man and I was still well shaped in those days. There were many men who said to me, 'Well, if your husband is gone, I will be your husband,' but I had made my promise to him in the church before God.

I could not find my husband in Egoli, though I asked many people. There were others of our clan there. Then some other woman told me that my husband had been taken by the Boers because he had no dompas *when he was coming from the church on Sunday afternoon, and the Boers had put him to work on a farm that was also a prison.*

Then I went to the magistrates' place to find where they had sent him, but no one could tell me. When I grew angry with the jokes and the deceits, the Boers said they would put me in a prison too if I was not silent; but one Boer said he would help me and take me in his car to find my husband. But then he put his hand where no man who is not a husband should, and I fought with him and made his face bleed with my fingers, so he left me in the veld. After that I went back to my children in the Transkei.

After my first daughter died – there was no money for the doctor, and no one could say what it was that made her die, but she was very small and her stomach was swollen – I took the other children and went to my sister Hope in Port Elizabeth, and my sister found me a domestic post with an English family. It was that family who gave me the other name.

After three years that family left Port Elizabeth because they said they had seen enough of South Africa and were going back to England now. Though they gave me the wrong name, the mother and the father were kind, and their children cried when they left, and gave me clothes and toys for my children.

Then I went to work in the house of an Afrikaans family; but though they called me by my baptismal name they did not like it when my children came to see me in my room in the back yard on a Sunday and they said it was against the law for my children to come there, and they should be again in the Transkei. So I took the money they owed me, and my children and I went to Cape Town, though I had no permit to be there.

I will not tell you what it was to be in Cape Town when the wind and the rain were there too, and the Boers constant in their searching in the townships for those who have no permits. If Cape Town has beauty I did not see it. The beauty did not stretch as far as Nyanga. The wind blew, the rain reached through our skin to the bones, the Boers were on every street and street corner, and there was no work except for so little money that the taxi drivers took it all.

It was there I found my second husband, though I was too cold to find a church before I went into his bed; may God forgive me, if He has time to consider such small things. My new husband had good work, being a mechanic of motorcars and lorries, white people's or our own people's, it mattered nothing to him as long as it was an engine – and from Monday to Friday we were content. But on Saturdays he would go with the other men to the beer hall and when he came back to the house he would be angry, and he would beat me – or, if I hid myself from him, he would beat the children, and worse than that for my daughter – so I did not hide myself for long. Later, he would weep and ask for forgiveness, especially when I showed him the hurts he had given me. I had nowhere to go except into his forgiveness. If you have no dompas you are not a person.

What I did not know was all the cause of his anger. This is not his story; it is the story of my son. But the last son I bore was his son, though he would deny it when he beat me, saying it was the son of a wizard, the son of a tokolosh, or of a policeman, or of his friend. I did not know then that people said his money came not just from the engines he fixed.

In the end the comrades caught him when he came back from his work and they killed him with an axe and then they burned

64

him for an informer. Myself, I think he was a good mechanic and a bad drinker, and when he was drinking he said many things and made many enemies. I do not think he took money from the police. I was his enemy too, if he took another woman or if he took money from the police to tell them things about his own people, but I think it was merely his talk and I would not have taken an axe to him, even in my anger, and I would not have burned him.

But it is my son, also his son, whose story I will tell you now.

He was never an easy boy, not like my other sons or my second daughter. Even before the comrades slaughtered his father, my second husband, he was a trouble in his school and the township, to his teachers and to our neighbours, and to me too, though because he was my last child perhaps I looked on him with too much kindness when he was troublesome. But now he is dead it is different. I say he is dead because that is what I have been told, but where he is buried I do not know. For all I know he is not buried. He may be in the veld still somewhere, with no name and no memory. Perhaps when I go to my own grave I will find him. I do not know.

Sebenzile – that was his given name, Sebenzile Africa, as his father desired – was a constant trouble at his high school; all the time he was organising, never was he doing his books or his homework. *Why should I study when there is no freedom to be found at the end of the studies?* he would say when I tried to make him change his ways. *Eh, mama, when you tell me the answer to that I will tell you why I do no bookwork.* And when I raised my hand to him he would laugh and run away to his friends.

In the end the police took him and two of the other students from a meeting in the school playground, and they held them in confinement in some gaol. Myself and the other parents could not find the three of our children in any gaol anywhere, and the police told us, no, we have no students here, we have no students anywhere; we have agitators and communists only, no students. We have never heard your son's name. What

65

did you say his name was? How do you say that? What kind of name is that? Is that a baboon's name? That is no student's name.

In the end, the Boers let him go, but only after one of his friends arrested with him was dead: the Boers said first he killed himself out of a window, and then they said he hanged himself in his cell. Sebenzile himself was silent. I think myself there was so much anger in his heart that if he had spoken he would have been like a bomb, but at home he showed me the burns where they put the electricity into him to make him tell them other names. I think he learned the silence then, and found more anger than he already had after the slaughter of his father.

Very quickly after that he went away, I knew not where. There was no news of him anywhere, just more silence. When I spoke to his friends, they would tell me nothing, or perhaps they knew nothing to tell me.

Then there was more trouble in the township, and the Boers came for him, and I told them, I do not know where my son is, though he is my son. I have not seen him, except in those days after he left your gaol. And then I thought, in my heart, that perhaps they had taken him silently and killed him too, had thrown him from a window too or had buried him in the veld, and came to me only in pretence that they were seeking him.

And then there came a letter to me from Lusaka, a very short letter with no name, but I knew it was him, and I was over-joyed because I knew he was safe and no longer silent. He said he was not permitted to tell me anything, but he wanted me to know he was now a soldier against apartheid.

Then the Boers returned to my house, and they searched and they searched, but they could not find the letter because I had hidden it away very privately. And when they asked me, I said, What letter? I know of no letter. I have had no letter.

So they took me too and held me in a gaol for two months. I knew it was the letter from my son that was the cause because they called me among all the other names which I shall not tell you a terrorist's mother, but they made a pretence that it was

66

because I lacked permission to be in Cape Town. But I told them that this was my country, not their country, and it was they who should ask permission to be here, not me. And then they stripped me in the courtyard, for all to see my nakedness, and they threw water over me, and left me in the cold, naked. But the other prisoners would not look at me naked, and they began to sing for me, and later the Boers gave me a blanket and put me in the cell again.

When they had let me out of the gaol, one of my son's friends came to me to say that he too had heard my son was in Zambia, training with uMkhonto weSizwe to be a freedom fighter against apartheid, and he was learning how to put a hand grenade in a police station and a gun to his shoulder, and I was pleased for him and pleased for us. And it was from then I gave my name as 'Nombi', never more 'Grace'. The comrades had burned my second husband for an informer, but our son was a soldier who would soon return to drive the Boers back into the sea they came from.

And then – almost half a year later – I heard a message from another person in the township, who says to me, Nombi, mama, I have very hard news for you to bear: your son has been killed on the borders, fighting for our freedom; he was a brave boy, for all the difficulty he gave you. You should be proud of him; he is an example to all of us – and when our liberation comes he will be remembered. Then he put his fist in the air and said, only not so loud so others outside the building would hear, 'Amandla!' But though I too put my fist in the air and tried to say Amandla – izwe lethu, my heart was too full of grief for my last child, and I choked. And I did not know where they had buried him after he was dead.

Sometimes I wonder if it was God who made me choke then, so that I should not say words except from my heart. Because next I heard from another person, also in the ANC but not so important, that maybe my son Sebenzile was not dead but only wounded. She said she had heard another story, that my son and five or ten others had gone on a patrol across the borders into Angola, for my son and the other young men to learn how to fight in the veld. They had made my son walk in front, and he had walked on to a land mine that had taken off his feet, and more than his feet, but he was not dead, not then. Then the others had feared this was an ambush, perhaps by the Boers, perhaps by the enemy in that country, whoever they are. (I do not know of an enemy in Angola; for me it is only the Boers who are an enemy.) So they had run away, leaving my son there wounded.

Now I was so heartsore because I knew neither if he was dead nor if he was only wounded, nor where he was buried nor if he was buried at all, but lay a heap of dry bones somewhere on the borders of Angola.

So I took the money I had saved and I skipped the country; it is not so difficult when you are a woman no longer young. You put your bundle on your head, you catch a train to this place, you walk a long way, someone will give you a lift in his lorry, you talk to your own people to tell them you are going to find your son and – when they have finished telling you you should not go – they show you the way past even the most wakeful of the Boers because this has been our country long before the white people made borders.

Yes, it is dangerous, but there are so many dangers now for our people that if you do not walk where you wish you will be nothing, nothing at all.

Then I was in Lusaka, and I went to the offices of the ANC, and at first I thought: this is my home among strangers. So I said in the office, 'I am Nombi, and I have come to find my son, Sebenzile Africa, who was killed on the borders.'

And then the lady in the ANC office shakes her head at me and says, 'There is no one of that name who has been with us here, and no one of that name killed. You are mistaken, mama.'

And I said to her, 'I have come too far on too hard a journey to be mistaken. My son was here, and here is the letter he sent me,' and I took it from deep in my bundle where I had hidden it, sewn into some article of my own clothing.

That lady now tries to take the letter from me, but I will not let her, even when she says it is not permitted for the soldiers

68

to send letters. Nevertheless, I say, he was here, and here is proof. Why are you telling me he was not here? And then she will not talk with me for any longer, though I went back to the office each day to wait for an answer from her or from anyone.

Then one of the big men – I must not tell you his name, for the Boers desire to kill him by any means – came to me where I waited in the offices and he sat next to me to hold my hands and he says to me, 'Mama, it is true your son is dead. He died as a hero fighting on the borders, and his name will be remembered when we have our liberation.'

But I remembered the story I had heard, that he had been wounded and that his comrades had left him there, and I asked this big man for the truth. Then he told me that I did not understand war and what he called 'the necessities of warfare', and I told him I was not a child, but I did not think that to leave a comrade wounded in the veld, after he had led them through the land mines, was a necessity for soldiers, but was a necessity for cowards.

And then he grew so angry I wondered if perhaps he had been among the cowards on that patrol himself, for he demanded to know how I knew that story and who had told me that story; but I would not tell him any name. And when he threatened me I laughed at him because the Boers too had tried to frighten me, so he said he would see to it I was deported from Zambia back to South Africa, and I asked him what kind of freedom fighter he was who could threaten a member of the ANC Women's League with deportation. So he went away.

Then I waited more time, visiting the ANC offices every day, and waiting in the vestibule. And when anyone entered I would try to find out the response to what had happened to my son – and the lady in the office, who was now my enemy, told them I was a mad old woman, out of her right mind.

At last, one day, someone in the leadership cadre, not so important as the other man but still in the cadre, came to tell me he had found out the circumstance of my son's death; and he said those who had left him there in the veld, wounded badly but not yet dead, had been disciplined as soldiers, for they should not have run away, leaving a comrade wounded. He said he thought my son must be dead, given the injury the land mine had given him, but he did not know for sure, and no man knew where he was buried, or if he was buried at all, but just left there where he lay. And when I said, perhaps he still lives, he answered me, no, the wounds were terrible, his feet were blown away, and more than his feet. He was dead for sure.

When I said I should go myself to find my son's body, if they would send a soldier to guide me to the place, he showed me on a map how far away it was, so many miles from any town, and across rivers and across the border in a strange land, and even then no one could now be sure the place was here, or here, or here, all the while his finger pointing at different places on the map. And then I knew for sure I should never find my son, and I wept for him and for all other mothers whose sons die where they are never found.

So that is my story, except that, when I left Lusaka and tried to come home to my own country, the Boers caught me and put me back in gaol. And when they asked me my name I told them, I am Nombi, and I am also Grace, and my son is Sebenzile Africa, and he is a soldier against you.

But I never told them he was dead on the borders; and though I did not lie to them I was contented that they thought he had come over the border back into his own country with me, but they had not taken him a prisoner when they had taken me. And they kept me while they sent many men to look for him, many men for many days. So I think he is still a soldier against them – as I am myself too, am I not, even if I am a domestic worker?

Chapter 4

It had never been Jamie's intention to leave South Africa permanently. He was – he had always maintained – through and through a South African, even though he was to discover, once he had moved to England, that his Englishness was more deeply rooted than he had supposed.

On their mother's side, he and Peter were descended from one of the British settlers sent to the Eastern Cape in 1820. On their father's side, his great-grandfather had come to South Africa as a young officer in the later stages of the war against the Boer republics, but had fallen in love with a South African woman from the Cape, and indeed with the country itself, and had, when a peace treaty was eventually signed at Vereeniging, surrendered his commission and set up as a farmer in the Wellington area of the Cape. When it became apparent that the First World War wasn't after all going to be over in a matter of weeks or even months, duty called him back to his regiment and armed service in Europe. Invalided out of the trenches in 1917, he had died of pneumonia in a Sussex hospital, leaving his wife and two children to survive on his pension in South Africa.

There had been some talk among the English Cathcart cousins that Jeremy's young wife and sons should come to live closer to the English family, but Emma Cathcart had no desire to move to an England she had read about but had never visited. Eventually, even the sending of occasional cards between the cousins lapsed. Her total attention was devoted to her boys and their education; her first-born – named Hamish after a grandfather – went to what was regarded as the best school in Cape Town,

71

where he did exceptionally well, eventually winning a scholarship to Cambridge and, in due course, settling permanently in the home country and becoming a successful city solicitor. Although he at first tried hard to persuade his mother to come to live with him in England, she said she would stay where she belonged, particularly as the second son needed her. He had been christened William, but was Will to everyone but his mother. Less noticeably clever than his big brother, he had been manoeuvred by his mother into the school in Grahamstown to which her own brothers had gone, on a bursary which took account of a father who had died – if not actually in the trenches – at least as a result of the trenches. Very happy at a boarding school which paid more attention to prowess on the games field than to academic ability, he had decided to stay on in Grahamstown for his university education too, partly because he could keep a close link with the school. It was no surprise to anyone that, even before he had left school, he had settled on schoolmastering as his career. As soon as he had taken his degree and a teaching certificate from Rhodes University, he went back to work full-time at his old school. Even if he wasn't as academic as his elder brother, he had in fact a bright and lively mind, though he often pretended otherwise, partly because his games-playing friends affected to despise intelligence and partly because Karoo farmers – and the school always depended on them as basic clientele – didn't want their sons contaminated by intellectuals.

This was Jamie's and Peter's father. 'It is a tradition in our family,' Will Cathcart had joked, 'to have two sons, one very bright, one just ordinary; the ordinary one is however good at games, where the clever one is a duffer at pretty well everything except books – and, in your case, Jamie, music too. It's God's way of evening things up in this strange country.'

Though he was in almost everything what he himself called 'an ordinary English-speaking white South African', in one thing he was – in that country – extraordinary: he was apparently entirely without racial feelings. He attributed this to the application of his simple-minded and devout Christianity. 'It seems to me quite idiotic to go to church on a Sunday to worship someone who was undoubtedly a Jew and on Monday to be anti-semitic,' he would say not only to his wife and sons but to anyone else – even Karoo farmers who claimed to know their black workers more intimately than any 'silly liberal with missionary ideas' – if they spouted any kind of racism in his company. 'And that being so,' he would add, 'it's surely just as crazy to be anti-black or anti-Afrikaner or anti-anyone just because they are pink or yellow or green; you are you – nice, nasty, clever, stupid, pompous, unpretentious, kind, cruel – and you like or dislike individuals, not whole sets of people.'

Long before the war, and while most men and women of his class and age were arguing that Hitler was doing considerable good in Germany in particular and Europe in general, he had been passionately anti-Nazi. When the Afrikaner Nationalist Government came to power in 1948, he had talked seriously of taking his wife and their two small boys away from South Africa to settle in Rhodesia. Only a visit there to spy out the land had made him realise that most white Rhodesians were at least as racist as most white South Africans, even if they did pretend to be British. What he would make quite certain of, he said therefore, was that his boys didn't grow up believing all that nonsense.

Like his father, he had joined up soon after war was declared and had served with the South African forces in North Africa, narrowly avoiding capture at Tobruk, and had then fought with them through Italy; demobilised in 1946, he had returned to the same post at the same school, quite content, he said, to be an ordinary schoolmaster for the rest of his days.

Which he would have been, except that, when Jamie

had just turned ten and Peter was eight, Will Cathcart collapsed one day as he was leaving his classroom. A stay in hospital revealed that he was seriously diabetic; he had, the doctors said, probably been diabetic for years, but his physical fitness must have concealed the worst of the symptoms. Despite treatment, his condition deteriorated hopelessly over the next few years and he was dead before he was forty, leaving Alice – his young, pretty and rather helpless wife – a tiny pension and the two boys.

The school allowed her to keep their school housing until she managed to find something of her own to rent, which eventually she did – a small semidetached cottage in an older part of town. She had been a piano teacher when she married Will, and now she went back to it, taking pupils at home and occasionally at her husband's old school. Although she had no choice about working, by the way she did it she showed she was not born to that sort of work. If life had been kinder, she would have been a concert pianist, or perhaps a headmaster's wife (if she could ever have persuaded poor Will to be properly ambitious), not a teacher of six-year-olds who came to lessons with grubby hands and chewed fingernails. Feeling that life had treated her like dirt herself, she treated those who worked for her ('beneath her' was what she said) as dirt too, and, when her sons reminded her what their father used to say, she would answer, 'Well, he would, wouldn't he?' making a gesture which included them in her sad dissatisfaction.

Though the boys recognised the sadness, they found it hard to cope with the dissatisfaction, and took refuge in their own company. Their grandmother gave them bicycles for Christmas, though she could hardly afford them, and they took to cycling for miles into the countryside around Grahamstown. Unusually for white South Africans, the family had no car, which gave another cause for complaint to their mother, especially when Jamie said, 'But we like cycling, Ma, really we do – and if ever anyone invites us to the seaside we can always go by train, can't we?'

Port Alfred was about forty miles away, on the Kowie River, and one could get there by train. Actually, even if one didn't have an invitation but had saved up for a couple of months, it was possible to get there by train and back again in a single day, and still spend most of the daylight hours swimming in the lagoon or picnicking at Shelly Beach. Better still – though one couldn't get there by train – was the wilder and more isolated Bushman's River Mouth, though their mother didn't like it as much, because it was (in her words) 'really very Afrikaans now'. Kenton, the other side of the river, was better and more English, but the houses there were more expensive and the sort of people who owned them were less likely to have known Will and now feel sorry for the boys. Alice Cathcart was not wise enough to realise that a main reason for there being fewer invitations was that even old friends were not sure they could cope with a whole week of Alice's 'moaning and snobbery', and so she moaned even more, and regarded fewer and fewer people as fit to be friends.

Particularly during holiday time, the boys spent more and more time in each other's company. Often, they would cut themselves jam sandwiches, take a banana and an orange from the larder, fill their father's old army water-bottle with water, or orange squash if there was any left in the pantry, and choose two books from the four they had each taken from the library the day before. They would then pile everything in an old military haversack that had belonged to their father and ride miles out of Grahamstown, either up the Cradock Road towards and then past the military airport, or towards Table Farm, or the other way, up on to Mountain Drive, or towards Port Alfred or, if they were feeling especially energetic, down the steep hill towards Southwell – marvellous, if a little scary, going down but, in the evening, coming back on bicycles which had no gears, they would end up having to push all the way uphill – or, rather, Jamie would find himself having to slow down for Peter's sake and then having to dismount to wait for him.

Once they took the risk of hiding the bicycles under bushes so they could leave the road and explore a little further on foot, but they felt very unsafe doing that; suppose some passer-by had spotted one of their bikes and had taken it while they were exploring?

However, as holidays passed, and they explored further and further afield, they found some idyllic hideaways – what they always called 'secret places'. Out to the north of Grahamstown near Table Farm there was what looked like a massive and solid clump of thorn bush which turned out to be in fact a circle of thorn bushes with a grassy centre which was, even on the windy days so common in the Eastern Cape, completely a suntrap. The boys speculated that once this might have been a kraal made out of cut thorn-bush branches which had somehow taken root and survived as a secret stockade.

In the other direction, over the top of Mountain Drive, there was a rough track which led down towards Featherstone Kloof, and down there was a stream, a waterfall and a pool … Well, there was water there for only a part of the year, and there was also at least one and probably several of the spitting kind of cobra, the *rinkhals*, which was reputed to lie in wait and then to spit venom which could blind someone at a dozen paces, so the boys had to throw a lot of stones into and around the pool before they ventured there themselves; but it was still another secret place.

Best of all, on the road down towards Port Alfred, at what was the limit of their cycling range, just where the tar ended and the dirt road began, there was a pool that seemed never to be quite empty, even in the driest season and, above the pool, in the cliff face, a cave that one reached by shuffling carefully along a ledge. On the back wall of the cave Peter (who was inclined to explore a little more bravely than his big brother) discovered a painting in ochre and yellow and brown of little men hunting eland and what the boys thought must be a kudu bull because it was so huge in relation to everything else, though there were strange lines sticking into most of the animals which didn't seem to be spears and, anyway, the little men carried bows and arrows, not spears.

They had seen rock paintings like these in the Albany museum, quarried from their original sites and then put on display; and Peter wondered if it might be proper for them to go to the museum to tell a curator what they had found, but then both boys decided, without much discussion, that they wouldn't mention their discovery to anyone. 'After all,' Jamie said, 'whoever put it there wanted it there, and not in a museum somewhere; so I think we should just keep quiet ourselves, and come to see it when we cycle out here. That's what I would want if I had painted it, anyway.' Peter – allowed to do Art at school because he was meant to be less clever than his big brother, who had to be in the top Science set which did Latin and Additional Maths rather than Art – nodded; he had already brought a sketchbook out there to copy the mass of small figures and animals of the mysterious hunt. When his teacher asked him where he had got the drawing from, he had answered that he had made it up out of his head after seeing the rock paintings in the Albany museum. Secret places were secret places, after all.

The boys talked often of cycling all the way to Port Alfred; it would be tough going, they realised, especially since the second half of the road was dirt, not tarmac, but they reckoned they could do it if they started early. What was less certain was whether they would be able to get back the same day. They talked about cycling down and then catching the evening train back and then they wondered if they knew anyone who might put them up overnight at the Kowie, or if they could borrow from someone a tent small enough to carry on the back of a bike. Jamie found an advertisement in an old compendium of the *Boys' Own Paper* of exactly the kind of tent they would need, but the advert was several years out of date, and anyway required one to send a postal order all the way to England. He took the risk of showing the picture of the tent to his mother, but she pooh-poohed the very notion of camping anywhere, and then wondered where on earth he and Peter thought she was going to get that kind of money from anyway. So he and Peter made an A-framed structure of bamboo in the garden and threw over it a groundsheet that must have belonged to their father in his soldiering days. But even though they pegged out the four corners and weighted the sides down with stones, the wind lifted the groundsheet off the frame before the night was out, and both boys abandoned the makeshift tent to climb through the window of their bedroom and back into their own beds.

The groundsheet was useful, all the same, because it rolled up small enough to be tied to the parcel rack on the back of Peter's bicycle (Jamie always carried the haversack on his back) and it gave them something to lie on when they rested after a long ride and read their books, and once or twice they used it as a shelter when they were caught in a sudden rainstorm (the weather of that part of the Eastern Cape being crazily unpredictable). It also gave them an opportunity to talk to each other about what they remembered about their father when he was alive; they couldn't really talk about him in front of their mother because it seemed to make her so miserable, and they had stopped asking her questions about him because she seemed almost angry with him for having died. 'I suppose,' Jamie said to Peter once, 'I suppose she's sort of punishing him.'

'Punishing us, more like,' said Peter, but not too loudly.

* * *

Their greatest adventure of all wasn't an exploration, but something much closer to home, indeed, right in the centre of Grahamstown itself.

They had known Mr Gadla all their lives; most white people called him merely John, and knew him in his capacity as the swimming-pool attendant at the school. He was a tall, straight man, taller even than their father, though much skinnier; he seemed to talk to very few people, black or white, and even the cheeky white boys from the town who used the pool during the summer holidays were afraid of him. He had a fierce temper, and had been known to threaten the young with the long pole with a net at the end which he used for catching frogs and hurling them high into the air over the swimming-pool fence and into the road, where – if the hurling didn't kill them – a car would. If a child misbehaved in the pool – say by jumping off a diving board when the sign said plainly that diving boards were for diving, not jumping – Mr Gadla would not merely remonstrate but actually turf the offender out of the pool enclosure, using his killing pole to emphasise his instruction. Most small boys were convinced that Mr Gadla was quite capable of catching one of them with his net and flicking them over the fence to be squashed flat, just like a frog. Yet they still called him 'John', just as they called the women servants 'Elizabeth' or 'Mary', even if they were quite old and were known to be married women with children of their own. Jamie and Peter, however, had been told by their father that they must call him 'Mr Gadla' and not 'John': 'You see,' their father explained, 'he is in fact a chief among his own people up in the township; I have heard them calling him by the Xhosa name for "chief", and I found out that he used to be a chief until the government sacked him because he did what he thought was right, not what they thought he should do. That's why he is so fierce, you see. So you boys will not call him "John", as if he were a garden boy, but you will call him "Mister".'

'Honestly, Will,' their mother remonstrated. 'He may be a chief in the township, but here at school he's just a swimming-pool attendant, just another boy.'

'Darling, you can call him "John" if you want; but the boys and I will call him "Mister". If I were in his shoes …' And he didn't bother to finish his sentence, though in fact Jamie and Peter knew that their father often called Mr Gadla not just that but, sometimes, quietly, 'Chief Gadla' in English. Actually, they got to like calling him that themselves because they knew that, although in public he treated them just as fiercely as he treated the other white boys who used his swimming pool, in private he called them by a Xhosa name which their father explained to them meant that they too were the sons of a chief: *Nkosana*.

A year or so after their father's death, when Jamie was just eleven and Peter still nine, there was trouble up in what white people called the 'location'. Black people had apparently decided – according to their mother's view – that they were going to ignore the laws of the country and do what they liked. There was to be a big demonstration in the centre of Grahamstown, in the High Street outside the magistrates' court – a high street that had in the old days been made wide enough for an ox-wagon to be turned round in, though now there was a row of jacaranda trees down the middle of the road, as well as at the sides of the road on the pavements, so that cars parked there had shade.

'You will stay indoors today,' said their mother firmly. 'The police are predicting big trouble, riots even, and we are going to lock our doors and close our windows. I've told the maid' – because even a family as constantly hard-up as Mrs Cathcart said they were had a daily maid – 'she is to have the day off. We don't want Elizabeth getting into trouble because she is working when everyone else is on strike, even though she assures me that the people calling for the strike are troublemakers who have no respect in the location.'

The boys, long since used to agreeing that they would do as their mother said, and then quietly doing the opposite, said they would be in their bedrooms reading if she needed them to help with any chores. ('Oh, no,' their mother answered, 'Elizabeth will do them tomorrow, as usual, but you are good boys to offer.') Soon afterwards, having taken off their good shoes and put on tackies, they opened the latch of their window, pushed the bottom halfway up so they could squeeze out, then from the outside pushed it down again. After a moment or two of waiting to make sure they hadn't been heard, they took their bicycles quietly from the verandah where they were stored, wheeled them past the dining-room windows and not past their mother's bedroom, and set off downtown.

Though it was mid-morning, the town was even quieter than it usually was in the early morning; most cars had been parked in garages, not on the streets, and there were no black people on their way to work. All shops were shut, too, and some were boarded up. The boys cycled down Bathurst Street, then past the Cathedral of St Michael and St George, and then into the High Street; there, outside the magistrates' court, was a huge crowd of black people, almost all of them very peaceful except for two or three men who seemed to be drunk and were cavorting in the road; only they were dressed like tramps – the rest of the people seemed to be in their Sunday best. Nearly everyone in the crowd was listening attentively to a speaker who stood with a small group of others facing the crowd who spilled off the pavement and into the road. Seeing no sign of any danger, and noticing that there were policemen parked in three police vans on the other side of the road, in front of the High Court, Jamie signalled to Peter that they should ride their bikes a little further down the street. They stopped, about thirty yards away from the crowd. 'Jamie,' said Peter suddenly, 'that man talking to them – that's Chief Gadla, isn't it? I'm sure it is.'

Jamie looked at the tall, thin man in his black suit and

white shirt, with a smart homburg on his head and a knobkerrie in his right hand, which he used to emphasise whatever he was saying to the crowd. Peter was right; it was Chief Gadla, all right, and one could see now that his father had been right all along: this really was a chief – you could tell that by the way the people listened to him. He was speaking in Xhosa – long, slow sentences which neither Jamie nor Peter could follow though they could recognise a few words.

Just then, the police must have decided they had to do something about the two wildest drunks who were dancing and shouting in the middle of the road. About six black policemen, led by two white officers, the blacks carrying sjamboks and truncheons, the whites with pistols drawn, rushed forward to grab the drunks. At least one resisted, and the boys saw him struck so savagely with a truncheon that blood spurted as the police pinioned his arms to drag him and the other man to a police van.

Immediately, some of the young men in the crowd began to shout. A group seemed about to gather together to march across the High Street to where the police were, but then the older men in their hats and dark suits who were acting as marshals intervened, and the group dispersed. Instinctively, as this had begun to happen, Jamie had shepherded Peter – both boys still on their bicycles, not dismounted, but each balancing with one foot on the ground – closer to an alleyway on the other side of the road which he knew led through to a garage and a path down towards Beaufort Street; but when he saw that there was to be no retaliation he allowed Peter to come closer again.

The speeches went on and on; there were occasional shouts and cheers from the crowd, and often laughter at something a speaker had said. The police lounged against their trucks and cars on the other side of the street, and once a junior policeman wandered over to them and told them to '*voetsak*'. When neither Jamie nor Peter showed any sign of budging, he repeated himself in English: 'You two, it's dangerous here; now bugger off.' However, he didn't sound very convinced himself of any danger and, although the boys pretended to get on their bikes to leave, they in fact merely went a little closer to where the blacks were gathered.

'I wonder if Elizabeth is here,' Peter said; she had been his nanny and, when he and Jamie had disagreed about something, he was still rather more inclined to seek her out for a cup of sweet tea and one of the rusks she made from old loaves of bread than he was to go to their mother.

'I don't expect so,' Jamie answered. 'I don't think Elizabeth will be much interested in politics.' In fact, he did recognise some of the men and women in the crowd as people he had seen working in the school; but now there were so many people – so many more people than he had realised could possibly live together in the location – that somehow one didn't need to recognise them. He wished, suddenly, that his father were there; there was so much he would want to ask: why, for instance, were there no white people in the crowd? In the newspapers, there were a few white people who were joining in with the blacks, though most white people called them 'idiots', 'renegades', even 'traitors'.

'I wonder if Dad would have been here,' he said suddenly to Peter. 'I bet he would have been.'

'I don't think Mum would have been very pleased; I don't think she would have let him come, do you?'

'No, probably not.' The boys looked at each other and, without saying anything, both mounted their bikes and rode around behind the policemen, down the High Street towards the Drostdy Arch and the university, and then back home. Here they managed to get their bikes onto the verandah and themselves through their bedroom window and on to their beds with books in their hands so that when their mother called them a little later she was able to say, 'My, but you have been good, quiet boys this morning. You must have got a lot of reading done.'

It was a day or two before Jamie said to his brother, 'Peter, whose side were you on?'

Peter put his book down. 'I've been thinking about that too,' he answered.

'But which side?'

'Well, it certainly wasn't the police.'

'I'm on the side of the black people,' Jamie said, suddenly. 'It was their country before any of us came here, and we should at least let them share.'

'The Afrikaans teacher at school said the blacks came at the same time as the whites.'

Jamie looked at his brother; the Afrikaans teacher had also given Peter three cuts with the cane he kept on his desk because Peter had said that he didn't see why he had to learn Afrikaans as well as Latin, when neither was any use in Grahamstown. 'I tell you something, Peter; it wasn't your Afrikaans teacher – or your Art teacher – who painted that rock painting on the wall of the secret cave. I think there have been people here for a long time.'

Both boys also made sure, over the next few days, that they saw John, the swimming-pool attendant, and both called him, as their father used to do, 'Chief Gadla'. '*Nkosana*,' he called them, but he also said to Jamie, 'I saw you, young Master Cathcart, and your little brother on your bicycles at our meeting.'

'I hope you didn't mind, Chief Gadla.'

'No, Nkosana, we were very glad to have you there. Your father was a good man.'

A few weeks later, Chief Gadla was no longer at the swimming pool, and there was a new man there, a Coloured man, who killed the frogs by dropping them in a bucket of poison rather than by throwing them high over the fence and on to the road. At Jamie's suggestion, Peter asked Elizabeth about this, but all he got was a shaken head and repeated remarks of 'Shame'. Jamie then asked a couple of the other black men up at the school where Chief Gadla had gone, but all he got was apparently blank incomprehension; when he substituted 'John, the swim-ming-pool attendant', they seemed more forthcoming, and he gathered that John had gone away, one said to the Transkei, one said to Johannesburg.

Eventually, Jamie was reduced to asking Mr Karel, the khaki-clad Estates Manager who drove everywhere in his bakkie, even from one side of a field to another, which was one of the reasons he had a beer-belly, a *bier-boep*, the size of a pillow, and who was an enemy because he had once chased Peter and Jamie out of the cricket nets. Mr Karel, who had still not forgotten what Will Cathcart had said to him after the boys had complained about the episode in the nets, told Jamie to mind his own bloody business, but then muttered something about 'troublemakers and the sons of troublemakers', which Jamie wasn't sure meant him, his father, or Chief Gadla. He couldn't ask his mother to find out what had happened without giving her a reason for asking, and that would mean letting her know that they had been to the demonstration, and he couldn't think of anyone else to ask.

He also had the oddest feeling that his father might still be somewhere close by him, saying 'Well done, my son' or, as he did when he was really very pleased with some-thing he or Peter had done or said, 'Well done, thou good and faithful servant.' That didn't remove the concern he felt for Chief Gadla, but there didn't seem much to be done. Perhaps that was a part of being grown up, too.

* * *

In later years, when Jamie tried to work out why he felt as he did about South African politics – which meant think-ing about all sorts of things that in other countries seemed to have very little to do with politics – he acknowledged always that what his father had taught him and Peter was crucial; he explained to Jenny in due course that, really, he was doing nothing else but apply what his father had

85

taught him: everyone had value and therefore everyone must be treated as deserving respect.

It took him longer to learn that, actually, in some ways equality was even more necessary because it seemed so obvious to him that people weren't equal; for instance, giving everybody and not just the qualified and the deserving the vote meant that those who didn't have much power or position or privilege at least had some say in what was done to them. He remembered explaining to Jenny, when they had got themselves involved in a political discussion, that there was a real sense in which he, Jamie, and she, Jenny, didn't themselves really need the vote; they had so much else instead to give them power. They were born into privilege. That they were clever too confirmed that birthright. Even if they didn't have the vote, they would have power.

What created Jamie's frame of mind was more than that, of course. Though many of the people who lived there liked to think of Grahamstown as a city of schools, universities and churches (Grahamstown people always insist that it must be called a city, even though it is only the size of a town, because it has its own cathedral and it is run not by a town council, but by a city council), really, however, it was still in some ways a frontier town. That was the purpose of its foundation: to be a barrier between a black tribe and a white tribe. One could almost draw a line down the middle of the city, at any rate in the middle of the night, and say that this was the white city, and that the black. Oh, there were a good many blacks who slept in the white part of the city, but they slept in the maids' quarters out at the back, not in the houses (unless they were baby-sitting because the parents were out, in which case they usually curled up on a blanket on the kitchen floor until the white people returned). It would have taken a brave or foolhardy white to risk sleeping in the black town, though no doubt whites went there in search of dagga or women.

86

In the 1960s, during a time of strikes, boycotts, trials and tension following the massacre of black protesters by policemen at Sharpeville, Jamie had found visible evidence of this division into two: at the lowest point of the town, where once there had been a small river (usually dry), the other side of which lived the other side, there was now a road – and this was where the police and army parked their armoured cars, ready for any intrusion into the white city by armed blacks. This is really purely symbolic, Jamie had thought when he had come across the armoured cars waiting silently on what might anywhere else have been a border. If he had been a black revolutionary who wanted to raid white houses to cause the most panic and mayhem possible, he would have taken his armed men out of the township the other way, round behind the hills, and then he would have come swooping down in the darkness, not from the obvious place, but from nowhere. Perhaps the police and army were lying in wait here because they planned to make what the textbooks called a 'pre-emptive strike' – which Jamie had never been able to distinguish from 'the first blow'.

Or perhaps it was something to do with Makana's Kop, the coppice of pine trees to the east of the township, which was meant to mark the point over which once upon a time Makana Nxele – Makana the Left-handed – of the amaXhosa had brought his warriors in their crazily brave direct assault on the cannons of the army garrison and the rifles of all the settlers who had hurried back here from the surrounding districts in anticipation of the attack. The veld which ran away to the east behind Makana's Kop was the part of the countryside around Grahamstown that Jamie and Peter had barely explored because to get there they would have had to cycle either through or right round the location. They had only ever done that once, on their way back into Grahamstown after they had got lost and had to follow a farm track which led them back not to where they had been expecting but to the East London road – and because it was getting late and they wanted their supper, they had come back that way into Grahamstown – and perfectly safe it had been, too, though they had attracted some stares and a comment or two in Xhosa from black children of their own age.

Neither Jamie nor Peter had any black friends; there were no blacks at their school and they didn't get to meet black children in the township; indeed, they were rather friendless boys generally, though never unfriendly. They were so close to each other that somehow it didn't seem necessary to have another 'best friend'. Because their mother felt she was too poor to do any formal entertaining except occasionally when, between lessons, she would invite a friend to morning tea, the boys felt that they shouldn't invite their friends home either. It would be hard to explain to friends why they had to keep quiet when their mother was teaching or practising.

Occasionally, one of their father's old friends would invite the boys to stay for a weekend. Ted Impey, who farmed out near Bedford, would pick them up in Grahamstown himself and then drive them out to the farm for a few days before delivering them home again. However, his children were much younger than they and, though they enjoyed the farm, the horses, the food, the evening drives up into the green and yellow mountains, and the apparent luxury of a spacious farmhouse with servants for everything from early-morning tea to picking up towels from the bathroom floor, they were still quite relieved to get home again.

There had, once, been a problem on the farm about shooting. Their father had taught them to shoot, first with a pellet gun, then with a .22 rifle; when their mother had remonstrated, Will Cathcart had said, 'Listen, darling, I know more about guns than you ever will, and I hate them more than you will ever know. I've taken dead bodies out of tanks that have stood for days in the desert, remember. But I want our boys to know what guns are for and what they do, because – God knows – they're bound to see and maybe even to use guns in this benighted country.'

So he taught them, first using an air-rifle to knock tin cans off a post at the bottom of their garden at school, then with his old .22 in the school range, and then up near the stony outcrop known locally as Hill 60. There, one day, because Jamie had wanted to, his father had allowed him to use the .22 to shoot a bird; when he and Peter had retrieved the mousebird with its head blown clean off and a few drops of blood spilling down onto the dust and gravel, they had looked at each other, said nothing, and buried the bird under a bush nearby. Their father had said nothing either, except later, when he came in to kiss the boys goodnight, and said to Jamie, quietly, 'Don't worry about that bird, darling. It wouldn't have known anything at all, no pain or anything.'

Jamie did not reply, so his father said, 'If it's any consolation, when I was your age, I used to cross the road rather than walk past a butcher's shop.'

From the other bed, Peter said, 'Did you really, Dad?'

'Yes, though it's a bit hypocritical, really, because I still eat meat.'

'Only cats eat mousebirds,' said Peter thoughtfully.

'And hawks,' Jamie added, but later, when their father had gone, he said to Peter, 'I don't think I want to shoot any more.'

So, when they were staying on the Impeys' farm outside Bedford and were offered the use of a .22, both boys hesitated. Seeing this, Mr Impey thought they might not know about rifles and cheerfully offered to teach them to shoot. Since to do anything else would have seemed disloyal to what their father had taught them, Jamie answered, 'No, we know how,' and took the rifle and the box of rounds from the farmer. Having collected ten empty beer bottles from behind the kitchen, Jamie and Peter lined them up on the old stone wall at the bottom of the garden. With Peter well to one side of him, Jamie paced out fifty careful yards back across the lawn and, reciting under his breath his father's instructions ('feet well apart; barrel up slowly; breathe in and hold; steady up; then squeeze'), and reloading as rapidly as he could, Jamie smashed the first five bottles with five shots, then handed the rifle to his brother who, with a quick grin at Jamie, repeated the trick.

Mr Impey was clearly delighted, guffawing and applauding. 'Well, boys, I see you inherited your father's eye, all right. He was a bloody marvellous shot, too. And I can see he taught you properly' – this because, when Peter handed the rifle back to Jamie, he had automatically cleared the bolt and checked that there was no round in the barrel. 'If you like, boys, I'll drive you up to the mountain in the bakkie and you can shoot some dassies.'

Peter started to say, quietly, 'Jamie, will it be rude if we say no?'

But Jamie had already begun his answer: 'We don't like shooting except for the pot, if you don't mind, Uncle Ted.' So they were excused, though they could see that Ted Impey was puzzled: if one had the skill, why should one not get the pleasure too?

'Well,' he said, 'we do get some springbuck up there, and the occasional kudu, but we're not hunting them at the moment, and there are sometimes guinea fowl, and I got some ducks on the dam last year – but they tasted of mud, I have to say. So perhaps we'll leave the shooting till next year, eh, boys?' And that, fortunately, was that.

* * *

When Peter got back from his office with Sharon next evening, he said, 'Oh Jamie, before I forget: there's a bloke from the university trying to get hold of you. He says he knows you.'

'What's his name?'

'I think he said Euston Stillman, but I might have got that wrong.'

90

In fact, when Jamie got the man on the telephone, his name was Huston Stillman. In due course, when Jamie knew him well enough, he was able to ask the origin of the name, and it turned out to be nothing more or less than a mother who had 'liked the sound of it'; there was no reference either to an American town or to any film director, and – as Jamie told Peter – he might just as well have been named after an English railway station. Moreover, it turned out that Huston Stillman hadn't said he knew Jamie; what he had said was that he remembered him from university days: he had been a junior member of the university when Jamie was a senior figure among the students. 'You were very much a hero in those days,' he told Jamie, who was not sure whether he liked having heroic status attributed to him; it was pleasant to be called a hero, but if one was no longer in that mode what was one now? There were very few post-heroic heroes he could think of; most heroes ended up dead very young. So he deflected Stillman by keeping silent, and then asking what it was he could do for him.

'We'd like you to give a lecture in the Department,' Stillman said. Jamie had already established that Stillman was senior lecturer in a new Department of Inter-Cultural Studies, which seemed to be an odd mixture of the study of literature, some dollops of History, Geography and Anthropology, a spoonful of Economics, and a slice of Education.

'I'm not much of a lecturer,' Jamie said, untruthfully; he spoke regularly to academic and other audiences about the work of the Foundation, but he thought of himself as being free of those duties at the moment, as he had – with the permission of the chairman of the trustees – taken an accumulation of leave that was owing to him. 'Look, Jamie,' his chairman had said, 'you've been working like a Trojan for fifteen years; you never take the leave your contract allows you; it's a quiet time of the year for us; and, as you said yourself in your last report, the office

91

runs so smoothly now that your secretary can quite easily manage it in your absence. So for goodness' sake disappear from the scene as long as you want or need. Why not call it long leave and be away for three months? I'll square it with the trustees.'

In fact, Jamie had no desire to be away that long, but Sir Ronald was quite right: he could easily afford to take three months off; the Foundation would continue to run along its usual pathways, even in his absence. Actually, it might be good to demonstrate that he wasn't indispensable, so that, if he did ever want a change, the trustees wouldn't regard his departure as a crisis.

'I've done my homework, Mr Cathcart,' Stillman said to him. 'You're said to be an excellent lecturer, and the work of your Foundation could be very interesting to those of us who think that, one day, apartheid will be bound to come to an end – and then we are going to need to reform education in a hurry.'

'I have to warn you, Mr Stillman,' said Jamie, 'I am by no means an optimist about the end of apartheid. I abhor it, but it seems to me deeply entrenched – though I'm not going to start saying, in public or in private in this country, what I think will dig the country out of the massive ditch it has got into.'

'How long are you here for, Jamie? May I call you "Jamie"?'

'Of course.' Most South Africans went on to first-name terms the moment they were introduced, sometimes even before. 'I've no idea: weeks perhaps, if I can get another extension of my visa.' He did not say: and once I've given a lecture I may find it much harder to get a visa. He had already compromised himself by coming back at all; to give a lecture which resulted in his being thrown out again might negate that compromise – and, though that might hurt Peter, it wouldn't hurt himself that much.

'Tell me, Jamie, is your reluctance to do with this so-called "cultural and academic boycott"?'

92

'Not at all. I've never approved of it.'

Although Jamie had never been pressed to say so in public, it was indeed his view that the cultural boycott then being advocated was utterly self-defeating. He was a convinced proponent of the probable efficacy of economic sanctions. He had also supported (though a little less enthusiastically) the sanctions against all-white South African touring teams, even though he felt that they were sometimes a diversion of attention from more important things, simply because they got so much public attention. However, when sporting boycotts were extended first to films and plays and then to books, and then ever onwards until the academic boycott – whereby university people refused to visit South Africa to teach or to lecture – it seemed to Jamie a version of self-immolation: the only cultural artefacts that would be withdrawn were precisely those that either the South African authorities would ban themselves as likely to correct their narrow vision or those which might encourage change. Those who wanted no change, or as little change as possible, would rush in enthusiastically to fill the gap. Anyway, Jamie was persuaded that in some way he stood outside the normal political framework; it would be hard for anyone to argue that he had not given his full commitment already even though – since Jenny's death and because of it – he had opted out of any personal and immediate commitment.

So it was agreed he would lecture the following week, provided the authorities granted him another extension of his visa, and that any publicity for the event would be muted. His subject would be 'Public and Private: the future funding of education'. There would be no explicit reference to South Africa in the title, but Stillman hoped that he would concentrate on that side of things, rather than merely explain the work done by the Sturrock Foundation in the UK. Jamie would talk for perhaps forty minutes, leaving twenty for questions and answers; and the Department of Inter-Cultural Studies would almost certainly want to publish the lecture in its occasional journal, so would Jamie please provide a text, and not merely speak from notes? It was also, Stillman said, a bit of a protective mechanism these days to have an actual text; the lecturer might deviate from his written words but, when there were problems with the authorities, it helped to have the words written down which might have actually been spoken. Perhaps, Stillman suggested, he and Jamie might meet later that week to talk over the details – over lunch, perhaps.

Thus it was, having got a second extension to the visa, and having had a very pleasant lunch with Huston Stillman at the restaurant in the old Company's Garden in central Cape Town, that Jamie found himself a week later facing an audience of some two hundred in a lecture theatre at the university. Because he knew that some of what he proposed to say would shock those in the audience who regarded themselves as Marxist or even socialist, Jamie had decided to begin his talk by referring to the last time he had spoken in this place, shortly before his arrest and detention, more than twenty years earlier. The occasion had been a protest against the banning of one of their lecturers and Jamie had been the main speaker. 'If the man has done something wrong,' he had declaimed, 'then charge him with an offence and bring him to trial. We suspect however that he has done nothing but hold opinions the authorities find offensive – odd that they should be opinions the rest of the world finds right, proper, sensible, democratic ... Ah, now "democratic", that's dangerous, isn't it? That's just about the same as "communist", and we can't have that in sunny South Africa, can we?'

It made a good starting place for what he now had to say, Jamie said, because the Foundation he worked for in the United Kingdom, the Sturrock Foundation, was doing something which had initially seemed subversive to conventional thinking about mainstream education. It was, wherever possible, providing private funding – either from its own resources (and Jamie desisted from saying how considerable they were) or by encouraging others to join in the provision of private funding – not just for private education but also for worthwhile activities in government-funded schools. Most of the world had learned (he said) that the state wasn't much good at running things like railways, farms, factories or schools. The Sturrock Foundation didn't think it was much good at running things either; but it did like to give money to people who were good at running things, rather than giving it out evenhandedly to anyone who claimed it. So, for instance, if a school could demonstrate that it taught music well, it could get grants from the Foundation to do it even better: not just capital grants for buildings or instruments, but grants to buy in good musicians for substantial periods of time. Of course, that led to claims that the Foundation gave money to those who already had it, and to accusations of elitism; there was an element of truth in that, he accepted, and the Foundation therefore tried wherever it could to give money to good people who wanted to start something that seemed likely to succeed. However, it had learned by experience that money given to reinforce success was better spent than money given to repair failure.

Knowing the reaction that could be provoked even in liberal England by the policies of the Foundation – policies which he had himself passionately advocated, after his own experiences of visiting too many third-rate schools in England, and which had, in the early days of his time in the Foundation, been regarded as dangerously radical, though now they were beginning to be quite widely accepted, even by some who liked to see themselves as left-wing – Jamie wasn't surprised that part of his audience became quite quickly restive. The mode of mind of most of the world was still collectivist. Individualist answers – and individualist solutions – were regarded as reactionary, not as a step forward into personal responsibility, which was how Jamie saw them.

When he was talking about what the Foundation did, everyone listened with apparent interest. Actually, Jamie thought to himself, so everyone should, because the range and the depth of involvement are very impressive: music, dance, art ... those were obvious enough, given the interests of the Sturrock family which had set up the Foundation in the first place ... but then there was all the rest: training schemes that tried to bring back some of the old advantages of apprenticeship; adventurous training; community education; and so on. It was the theory behind what he said that seemed to cause an abreaction: one would suppose, he thought to himself as the questions began, that these people had seen enough of how corrupt, cruel and inefficient a centralised state can be to make them realise that the substitution of one kind of state for another wasn't going to solve any problems. One would have assumed that people even here knew enough by now about the nonsense – and the misery – which the imposition of Marxist thought on the real world had created not to need persuading that there had to be something flawed, not just in the way the system had been applied, but in its very nature. But, no, one of the strident voices – no longer even pretending to ask a question – asserted that only the rigorous imposition of democratic socialism by a people's government would ever produce an equitable education. Jamie resisted the impulse to ask if the young man making the statement had ever thought of visiting Cambodia, but patiently again explained some of the evidence for thinking that education might be better provided by agencies other than central government.

Just as he was beginning to feel a little dispirited by the dogmatism and mindlessness of the questions, Jamie found a source of support. An old man with a magnificent head of white hair – which a beret had concealed until he was actually seated in the front row of the lecture theatre – got to his feet to ask a question. This was clearly someone even the strident students in the back rows wanted to hear, and Stillman pushed a note over towards Jamie: 'Dr Liebermann', the note said. Good God, Jamie thought, looking at the old man and remembering now who he was; so he's still around. I wonder if his brain is still as formidable as it once was; in the old days, when he had been Professor of Comparative Law, he had been thought of as a communist. He had been gaoled for five years under the Suppression of Communism Act, and then banned for another ten years on his release from actual imprisonment. Now, he gestured to the back rows, and then faced Jamie.

'Well, Jamie Cathcart,' he said, the Middle European accent unaffected by nearly fifty years of living in South Africa, 'it's good to hear you again after all these years, and to know that you are still someone with your own ideas, not the easily received opinions. You have perhaps forgotten that, once, you spoke up for me when I was saying things people here didn't like to acknowledge,' and he gestured at the back rows again. 'Ironically enough, the best example I can think of to contradict your idea that state education doesn't work is close to home: by that I mean the hideous policy of Bantu Education here in South Africa. It has worked brilliantly, in that it has almost killed black education – and most of us think that is what it set out to do. And so I would agree with you that, when democracy comes to South Africa – as it will do, I think sooner myself than most people here think, because they are waiting too lazily for the days of reckoning, not doing enough reckoning themselves – when the revolution comes, it had better come with some new ideas about education, or we will just get the same again, only in a different direction.' He smiled; the back rows were silent at what seemed like treachery from their own side. 'Now, Jamie, that was a statement, not a question. Here is my question: when are you coming back to live here? We need you back here, not running some Foundation in England.'

To Jamie's relief, Huston Stillman decided to treat Dr

Liebermann's question as a vote of thanks rather than as a question that needed an answer, and – ignoring some of the hands still being raised – he added his own thanks to those of Professor Liebermann and invited those who wanted to continue the discussion to have tea or coffee in the lobby.

At the prospect of actually arguing face to face, most of those who had wanted to ask what they thought were difficult questions drifted away, and Jamie was left with Dr Liebermann and a handful of others, a few of whom he recognised from the old days, though he wasn't sure he could put names to any faces. Huston Stillman brought Jamie a cup of instant black coffee, which he sipped without much pleasure while he answered Dr Liebermann's questions, trying to fit his own in too. 'No, I'm an old man now, Jamie, and my views aren't of any great relevance. I just wish sometimes that those who talk loudest had read a few more books – or even if they haven't read the books, had done some more real politics. In the old days, if a man got up and talked about trade unionism, at least you knew he had organised one himself. Nowadays he's just picked up one or two slogans. Now, tell me, Jamie, do you ever see the people in London ...?' and he named with great rapidity and some conspiratorial lowering of his voice three or four of the better-known South African exiled politicians.

'I'm really out of those things now, Prof,' said Jamie, using the old nickname without thinking. 'I'm really more or less English now.'

'Yes, yes,' said Liebermann; Jamie decided he couldn't really have been listening because he immediately asked after two or three more of the exiles. Jamie shook his head. Even if he saw these people, he thought, they weren't going to be as responsive to his views as they had once seemed to be. He was too pessimistic and too disillusioned to be of any great use to anyone in exile politics where a sanguine optimism was the main requirement.

And London was London, not Cape Town nor even Johannesburg; the circles there didn't intertwine, as they seemed still to do here.

Dr Liebermann clearly thought Jamie was being merely discreet, however. He smiled happily and tapped the side of his nose. 'Ah, well, young man,' he said. 'Better to keep silent, eh? Did you see there was a Special Branch policeman at your lecture? He was writing names down.' He cackled loudly. 'I'm glad to say that they still don't have to ask who I am. Some things don't change.' He started to move away, saying that he must find his transport home, when he suddenly turned back to Jamie. 'Whatever happened to that beautiful girlfriend you used to have? Did you marry her? Such a lovely girl; she was a dancer, wasn't she? I can still see her.'

Isn't it extraordinary, Jamie thought, even as the wound which he thought long since healed tore open again as if it had only just been made, isn't it extraordinary that someone who knew me and knew her shouldn't know what happened? He couldn't turn his back and walk away from this kind and clever old man. He breathed in, took another sip of his disgusting coffee, then said, as quietly as he could to avoid anyone else overhearing, 'Jenny was killed in an accident in England, a year or so after she got there.'

'I'm terribly sorry for that,' said Dr Liebermann. 'I'd no idea.' He looked suddenly devastated. 'I see that I have distressed you in asking what I should have known. Forgive me.' Before Jamie could say anything he had turned and gone.

'There's no reason you should have known,' Jamie said to Liebermann's back as he disappeared across the room. It's a long time ago, he thought; really, I should be able to talk about it now – but I can't. Even with my beloved Peter I can't. No, I could, but I won't. This is my grief, no one else's.

* * *

The car they had been told to target was parked, not in a driveway as they had been told it would be, but just outside the house, with two wheels on the pavement so that it was more out of the roadway. Using a shaded torch, he checked the number of the car against the number he had printed on the base of his thumb, under the glove – they had been told to carry no papers. The number was right. All the lights in the house were out and there was no perceptible movement inside. Nonetheless, he stayed in the shadows, waiting for the others to take up position. Though he had stripped down to underpants before he put on the black overalls, the gloves and balaclava made him very sweaty. He hated working in gloves.

First one, then another dark figure came down the road. They had parked the vehicle in the next street. There was still another person to come. He checked his watch with the shaded torch: still two minutes to go. There was a whistle from the road ahead, and he motioned the other two into the dark driveway. A car came slowly down the road but didn't stop. After another minute, the man who had whistled joined them; he swore in a whisper about stupid bastards who drove around the streets looking for kaffer whores at this time of night – why didn't he just go home and fuck his hand like any normal man? His three companions separated: one up the driveway, one down the road, one back up. Carefully he took the small bag off his shoulder and laid it on the ground next to the car, then lowered himself down on to the road and slid, head first and on his back, under the car, pulling the bag with him very carefully.

When he was right under the car, and his nose up against the underside of the engine, he peeled off the gloves. He knew what the colonel had said – 'Gloves on at all times' – but even the colonel couldn't do this job wearing gloves. He pushed the gloves into his pocket, pulled the bag closer, and laid the torch next to his head so that it shone upwards into the engine. He was glad two of the wheels were on the pavement; it gave him a few inches more within which to work. It was not a big car and usually there was very little clearance.

Carefully he took the thing from the bag and pushed it up into the engine. He had built it that afternoon in the workshop, using stuff anyone could buy in most ordinary hardware shops. It's got to look like a homegrown job, the colonel had said: we don't want one of these clever bastards saying this is professional. Use an ice-cream container – leave the paper on – and tape it on with ordinary tape. You want the fuel to do the work for you; it's not the thing that burns the car; the thing fires the petrol, the petrol fires the car. That's the point: the best option is for the papers to say, 'It is thought that a faulty fuel pipe may have been the cause.' I know you've got to put a switch in, but with any luck no one will find any part of that switch, will they? The second option is: this was homemade, probably the comrades quarrelling among themselves.

He was sweating so much he couldn't see properly; he tugged the balaclava off and used it to wipe his forehead and eyes. He used some more tape, then gave the thing a careful push. It seemed rock-solid. He shook it harder, and then as hard as he could. The car rocked a little, but the thing stayed firm. Now all he had to do was to put the switch in.

There was an urgent whisper from the pavement: 'For fuck's sake, pull your fucking finger out. There's a light come on in the house.'

'Fuck you,' he whispered back. With your face six inches from that thing, and most of a petrol tank not two metres away, this was not a moment you rushed, light on, light off, whatever. Carefully he shifted the switch into the active position and held his breath.

Very carefully, he pushed himself back down the road, making sure he didn't touch the car. When he was clear of the chassis, he wiped his face again with the balaclava and then put it on. It was cold and damp with his sweat. He found the gloves too, and pulled them on, then sat on the edge of the pavement for a moment before standing up. If there had been a light on in the house, he couldn't see it now.

He whistled quietly. Two men joined him and, after a

moment or two, a third. 'What took you so fucking long?' said one. 'Fuck you too,' he answered; only a fucking lunatic messes with these things.

* * *

He was off-duty the next day because of the late night, so was at home with the family when he caught the news bulletin. Mother and child killed by a car bomb. Second child badly injured. He moved closer to the radio so he could hear the details. A few minutes later, he rang the special number. 'Shit, Colonel,' he said, 'we got the wrong ones.'

'You can't make an omelette without breaking eggs,' the colonel told him. 'I'm recommending you for promotion, Sergeant. You did a fucking marvellous job, I tell you. It wasn't your fault the wrong people got in the car. We thought it was the husband who would take the car. We didn't think the wife drove.'

Chapter 5

Having been more than a little bored by the work in his last year at school – except by a serious and punctilious teacher of Latin and a brilliant teacher of English, an elderly widow, who interspersed rigorous lessons of old-fashioned grammar (including spelling lists and exercises in punctuation) with passionate readings of the English love-poets, and who was quite capable of silencing the largest rugby-playing oaf even while tears ran down her cheeks as she read John Donne aloud – Jamie found the academic side of the university immediately exciting. Always inclined to be systematic, indeed, almost obsessive in his orderliness, except only that – mainly because his mother nagged him so about it – he never practised his violin enough to be as good a player as she and his various teachers said he could be, he took to getting up in time for breakfast in the men's residence and making sure that he got not just to the prescribed lectures but to the library early enough to be able to find the books he needed before others started to hog them. Most of his fellows stayed in bed for as long as they could, got others to sign them into lectures, and then had to rush madly to get the reading done in time before they went off to play games in the afternoon. Jamie had never had much interest in games; most of them bored him and, while he was physically competent, he tended to become bored at exactly the moment others became competitive, so they would say that he wasn't really trying. Well, he would mutter to himself, I'm not; and if I hurry up and lose I can then go off to do something a bit more interesting. He certainly had no intention of spending his afternoons either rushing about in games kit himself or, worse still, watching others rushing about.

Instead, he preferred to explore Cape Town, walking down into Rondebosch to catch a bus along Main Road into the centre of town, or hitchhiking from outside the university campus. He had visited Cape Town with his father once, when he was very young, and his first free afternoon was spent re-creating that visit as best he could. He remembered in particular the Gardens in the middle of central Cape Town; his father had bought a packet of peanuts from an old woman at the entrance to the Gardens and had then shown Jamie how to feed them to a squirrel. Now, he watched other parents doing exactly the same with their children, and then he wandered through the leisurely crowds up the main thoroughfare of oaks, agapanthus and hydrangeas to the national gallery where he remembered his father had shown him pictures of the Karoo landscape, then back into the open air and through the rose garden, down to the restaurant in the Company's Garden and through the old trees to the library and the cathedral, past the statue of Queen Victoria standing with sceptre and orb rather forlornly in front of the Houses of Parliament, and back to the place from where university students used to hitch lifts back to the campus.

On another afternoon, he found by chance a cinema that combined showing films – sometimes newsreels, some-times feature films of a kind one didn't get in ordinary cinemas – with serving tea. Going in first because it seemed cheaper than most restaurants, he guessed it might be used mainly by Cape Coloured people prohibited from entering other cinemas in the centre of town, though – given the dimness of the lighting – one couldn't be sure of anyone's race. To his astonished delight, the film showing was *Carmen Jones*, an all-black American production. He had heard some of the music of the show at school – he had been secretary of the tiny Music Society, and ordered most of the records entirely on the basis of his own taste – but now was able to see the film for himself. It seemed extraordinary that the censors had let the film into the country uncut – *South Pacific,* shown briefly in a Grahams-town cinema, had been so censored that it had been almost entirely meaningless – but he guessed that, because the whole cast of *Carmen Jones* was black, it didn't offend the doctrine of apartheid, whereas *South Pacific* could be read as a praise-poem to what white South Africa called 'immorality'. A week later he was back to see the even more extraordinary *Black Orpheus.*

One afternoon, a few days later, walking down St George's Street, he heard a pianist playing some of the tunes his mother sometimes used to play after supper when she was sad. He followed the sound and found himself in a palm-court, where a young man sat at a grand piano playing very gently and dreamily to a scattering of mainly middle-aged couples. After a moment, he realised that the young man was one of his fellow students in the men's residence at the university, though he wasn't sure of his name; Frank Someone, he thought and, while this was hardly jazz, it was quite fun: the tunes flowed seamlessly one into another, there was a scattering of musical jokes, he shifted key from major to minor and back again, very skilfully, and most of the middle-aged couples were hold-ing hands; two couples were even dancing, very sedately. The pianist had noticed him, for he now gestured with his head that Jamie should sit down. He did, then found him-self presented with a menu by one of the waitresses. He had discovered that the cheapest thing on any menu was Russian tea, so he ordered a glass of it.

Before he had finished, the pianist took a break and walked over to the table. 'Hi,' he said. 'You're in the men's res, too, aren't you? I thought I recognised you. You're Cathcart, aren't you?'

'Jamie Cathcart.'

'All right if I sit down? I'm Frank – Frank Harris – not unfortunately the great pornographer. I'm the other Frank Harris.'

'I don't know the other one.'

'You've not missed much. He wrote a very dirty auto-biography – probably all lies.'

'I really enjoyed your playing. Do you play here a lot? Are you paid to play?'

'Of course I'm paid – you don't think I'd play that kind of crap if I wasn't.'

'You play well.'

As if in answer, Frank Harris went back to the piano. Picking his hands up dramatically high, he crashed out the first few bars of one of the noisiest concertos Jamie had ever heard, then, without a pause, shifted to a Chopin prelude – one note at a time, as limpid as a forest pool – and then began to play Mozart at a very brisk pace. Someone, probably a manager because he was wearing a bow tie and a black jacket, appeared, frowning; without turning a hair nor missing a beat, Frank let Mozart turn into *Stormy Weather*. The couples resumed their hand-holding, the manager went back to this office, and Frank grinned happily at Jamie. Jamie finished his tea and walked over to the piano.

'I see what you mean,' he said.

'Do you play yourself?'

'The violin – but not as well as you play the piano.'

'Have you done grades?'

'I scraped through Grade 8 last year. My mother's a music teacher – pianist.'

'Grade 8 violin is good – bloody hard instrument.'

'It was a real scrape,' Jamie confessed. 'The examiner knows my mother, if you see what I mean. I played in the school orchestra – it was not very good.'

'You should audition for the university orchestra.'

'Are you in it?'

'When they need a piano, which isn't often, though I bash away at the timpani; it helps to be able to count. Not all the string players can count.' He smiled to make it plain he was teasing. 'We practise on Wednesday evenings; it's not that demanding – just the occasional concert –

and we play for the university ballet company and so on. Come next Wednesday. I'll introduce you to the conductor.'

So, five days later, Jamie Cathcart found himself, after a cursory audition with Philip Whitehead, one of the lecturers in the music school who doubled as conductor of the orchestra, firmly positioned in the back row of the second violins. He had hardly touched his violin since he arrived at the university – indeed, he had tried to leave it behind when he packed up his belongings, but his mother had made such a fuss that he had capitulated, though it soon became apparent to Jamie that someone who played the violin in his bedroom in the men's residence was liable to be dumped, along with the instrument, in a bath of cold water – but Frank Harris was right: though there were a couple of outstanding players in the orchestra, most were of much the same standard as Jamie was himself, no more than competent amateurs. Some of the players were studying music, but more were not; there were a few university lecturers, and even a professor in the woodwind section – with whom Philip Whitehead had to be particularly patient – but most were students of subjects other than music.

The outstanding musician in the orchestra was in fact a young Cape Coloured man, Willem Bearer, a 'cellist. He was full-time in the music school, and clearly heading for a professional career – given his race, probably overseas. Despite the increasing imposition of apartheid on and within even the university, the orchestra was in those days able to remain multiracial, mainly because it was multiracial without being political in any sense. Jamie was still relatively innocent; at the third rehearsal, he found himself talking yet again to a dark-haired, dark-eyed girl who sat in front of him among the second violins. He hadn't yet taken a girl out – although he had met quite a few already, not only was he shy but he knew he hadn't any spare cash to squander on expensive entertaining. Now, to his slight surprise, he found himself asking her if she'd like to go to the cinema with him one afternoon.

Carole looked at him quizzically. 'You do know, don't you, Jamie, that I live in Grassy Park?'

He didn't understand. Willem Bearer, who had been eavesdropping, laughed at him. 'Come on, Jamie. She says she lives in Grassy Park. That means she's a *kleurling*, a *Kapie*, a Coloured, just like me. If you take her anywhere, you'll both get arrested and done for immorality.'

Jamie was so embarrassed he could hardly speak. 'I'm sorry, Carole. I simply didn't think.'

She was smiling at him, clearly unoffended, and Willem crowed with laughter. 'I tell you what, whitey, I think she fancies a bit of immorality with you, eh Carole?'

'Don't be dirty, Willem Bearer,' she snapped. 'You're just a moffie.'

Willem shrugged. 'A moffie could be useful to you, Carole. I tell you what: let's you, me and Jamie all go out somewhere; then if we get caught by the cops, I can be with you and he can be our chauffeur.'

Jamie was still not sure how much of a game this was. He thought he knew now that a 'moffie' must be a homosexual, and Willem's frank admission had explained several things which had puzzled him, in particular the oddly close friendship that seemed to exist between Philip Whitehead, Frank Harris, Willem himself, and a couple of other men in the orchestra. 'I'm afraid I don't have a car,' he said, seriously.

Carole moved off, Willem saying to her back as she did so, cattily, 'Well, as you see, Jamie old son, girls from Grassy Park can't go out with whiteys if they don't have transport. You could come out with me, though,' he said, suddenly hopeful.

'I don't think so, Willem. I really do prefer going out with girls. I hope I didn't upset Carole.'

Willem was serious for once. 'Never,' he said. 'A whitey asks a girl out because he really fancies her, not having noticed what every other South African would – that she's Coloured? Carole will love you forever. I'm the one she's cross with.'

Willem claimed to have no interest in politics whatever. When others talked politics – which happened to be most of the time – he would sigh ostentatiously and turn away, or try to divert the conversation, or simply go away to find someone else to talk to. 'All I want,' he told Jamie once, 'is to get away from this place to somewhere one doesn't ever again have to give a damn about politics; I want to live in London or New York or Paris, where it might actually be an advantage to be a black moffie.'

'Come off it,' Jamie would tease him. 'You're a very white coffee, not black at all. It's the English boys you're after.'

'But no, old son.' Willem was serious. 'I'm not keen on boys, you know, and I'm certainly not keen on little boys. Actually, I think, if I had no choice, I'd prefer women to little boys. No, what I like are middle-aged men with nice flats, big motorcars and fat chequebooks.' He giggled suddenly. 'Though I'd better be honest and say I prefer it when they don't have *beer-boeps*. I like nice flat tummies, like yours; it's a pity you're not middle-aged, Jamie.'

'I don't have a flat, nor a car, nor even a chequebook; I still keep my very little bit of money in the post office,' said Jamie. He liked Willem and admired his musical skills, but did find the flirting a bit off-putting, especially when there were others around. Suppose someone thought that he … No, perhaps they wouldn't.

Despite Willem's denial of politics, it was through him that Jamie began to become acquainted with some of those who seemed to be more actively involved. White students who tried to attach themselves to black groups were viewed with suspicion. There had been some well-publicised exposures of students in the pay of the security police and, given the number of black students who had been either taken into short-term custody for questioning or actually banned, they were learning to keep their views to themselves if they weren't sure of the company. There were, of course, white students who could probably be trusted, but generally they were those who had already got themselves into so much trouble with the university authorities or the police that one knew whose side they had to be on. (These were still the days of innocence, before one learned that the best – and cheapest – way of 'turning' someone was to terrorise him or her in custody, so that on release the leash could always be re-tightened.) Willem's talents as a musician were such that everyone made something of an exception of him; he was allowed to be scathing about the futility of politics because it was clear that he was going to end up elsewhere than in South Africa. His homosexuality was accepted because he was so open about it that no one thought it peculiar. He could be found talking to students so right-wing in their views that, if they had been asked, they would have denied his theoretical existence; but he was Willem the 'cellist and even the most khaki-clad, lager-slurping, catcalling thug from Driekoppen men's residence would admit that talent, saying things like: 'Have you heard him play, man? I mean, I don't go for classics, but he can make that thing sing to you.'

If Willem was an oddity, the outstanding leader – both intellectually and practically – among the black students was Barney Jacobse. Although technically classified as Coloured, he was in fact as dark as any black South African, and used to make a joke of his ancestry, claiming that, of all South Africans, he was the most typical, and therefore the most pure: ' My great great great grandfather was Khoikhoin; my great great grandmother was a San; my great grandfather was an Afrikaner – man, was he in trouble with his family when they found out what he had been up to; and the rest were Xhosa, except for the time the Zulu impi came to visit. The one thing I haven't got is any English blood at all – not one drop.' Physically unprepossessing – he was small and thin, with a wispy beard and bent back – he was however a brilliant orator. 'My voice makes up for my looks,' he told Jamie once, and he claimed to have been trained to preach by a crazily aberrant sect of Evangelical Christians who believed – like the Zionists – that Heaven would be made upon Earth, and it was all there in the Bible. Even now his favourite gesture – left hand held to his heart, as if holding a Bible, right hand making (and emphasising) each sally, each point, each joke, each demolition of an opponent's argument – derived from the days of his youth when he had preached on the Grand Parade each Sunday morning.

Das Kapital had supplanted the Gospels, and then Trotsky had purified Marx; but, Barney maintained, he was racially predisposed to abhor slavery of any kind, intellectual or otherwise, and he took his ideas where he found them, to make a surprisingly liberal creed, though he affected to despise liberals of the South African variety, saying that they were neither fish nor fowl, and one never knew how to take them.

On the other hand, he worshipped Gandhi, though he had to jump through several hoops to get there, claiming for instance that *satyagraha* – the doctrine of 'soul-force' by which one overwhelmed one's opponents by the righteous force of one's moral probity – need not be applied only to pacifism. When attacked for contradictions in his views or in his arguments, he would invariably cite Gandhi: 'Why do you taunt me with the hobgoblin of consistency?' Loathing Afrikaner nationalism, he was in fact a considerable student of Afrikaans literature and, despite his racial classification, was allowed to be a registered student – postgraduate – of the university. He was, he said, working very slowly on a doctorate about the early Afrikaner poets and, in the meantime, working much faster to overthrow the Afrikaner state. He had recently begun to be deeply influenced by the Africanists in – and out of – the proscribed ANC, and had made speeches at the university which had caused him to be called, variously, an 'inverted racist', a 'traitor to the working class', and a 'renegade'.

Though Jamie was, by any standard, in those days merely a rather unformed liberal politically – indeed, as little an ideologue as it was possible to be in such a deeply politicised community – he found himself immensely attracted to Barney Jacobse's hotch-potch of ideas and attitudes. Habitually systematic himself, he enjoyed Barney's constant ranging over ideas, picking up this titbit there, rejecting this crumb, nibbling this morsel, spitting out that mouthful. Most of his white contemporaries at the university who became involved in politics found room for themselves in the broad church of a students' union which was affiliated to – and influential in – a small but vociferous national union of students. When the leaders of that national union were detained, banned, expelled from the country, Jamie joined in the protests – then went back to Barney and his 'fellow workers' to be criticised for having joined in 'too little, too late', like all liberals.

Exactly what Barney and his comrades were up to was never very clear to Jamie, partly because of an inevitable residual suspicion of even the most apparently sympathetic white man; they were, they said, 'organising', but who or what they were organising was never clear. There was much discussion of workers' movements, and a couple of Barney's older friends were apparently minor officials in trade unions in other parts of the Western Cape who would turn up at the meetings he organised – though they were always known as 'discussion groups' because that made them less attractive to the security police. Periodically, Barney would drop out of view for a few days and then reappear at the university, but he was as secretive about his own activities as he was vociferous about ideas.

At first, it was clear that Barney and his comrades regarded Jamie as a potential source of funds; after all, he was white, and most whites had money. When it became apparent that Jamie wasn't in a position to make handouts of any kind, either personal or as a contribution to whatever it was they were organising, what might have been disappointment was in fact quickly subsumed in a kind of relief that here was a white boy really as short of funds as most of them were used to being. One evening, after a discussion group in Salt River, Jamie had set off to walk back to the university; he nearly always walked if he could. It was a small but easy economy, but on this occasion he had to; it was late in the month and he was broke. Some of those who had left the discussion group a little after he had, had caught a bus going towards the terminus in Claremont; seeing Jamie walking as the bus went past, one of the young men dropped off at the next stop to wait for him. 'Why are you walking, Jamie, man?' he asked when Jamie came to the bus stop.

'I do my thinking on my feet,' Jamie replied. He wasn't absolutely sure of the young man's name; as the only white in the group, everyone knew him, but Jamie didn't like to keep on asking people to repeat their names so he could learn who they were, particularly as several of them seemed to have interchangeable nicknames.

'No wonder you're so skinny,' the young man answered.

'I'm also broke,' said Jamie. 'It's the end of the month, and I've spent my allowance.'

The young man stopped. 'You mean, no money even for bus fare? Christ, man, it's only peanuts.'

'I've not got even peanuts,' Jamie said; in a way, it was pleasant to be able to confound expectation with an admission of poverty.

'What do you do for food?'

'Oh, I'm not starving. I get my meals in the men's res. I just don't have much for extras.'

'Well, neither do I; but I can always find bus fare. Eh, man, can I lend you a couple of rand? I mean, my family's in building – not big, but ...'

113

Jamie stopped. 'I try not to borrow,' he said, seriously, and then grinned. 'And walking is good for you, especially when buses are segregated.'

'Not upstairs, man, not upstairs,' the young man laughed, and they walked together until another bus came along.

This was Fred Carelse and, in due time, he became Jamie's closest companion in the group, though he wasn't at the University of Cape Town, but at the new University College of the Western Cape, out in Bellville. This was one of the creations of the Extension of University Education Act which had closed the older liberal universities to all but a handful of blacks, and had opened others, known at first in the liberal universities as 'tribal colleges', though the term fell out of favour when it became apparent that, in modern times, even the older universities were just as much 'tribal colleges' since they, too, were limited mainly to people of a single 'population group'. Fred was reading for a degree in Commerce at Bellville, in the expectation that he would, in due course, take over the business side of the family firm – a small building company, prosperous enough but without the capital resources to permit expansion. One brother had emigrated to Canada; two more brothers, already married with families, worked for the father, as Fred would have been doing if his mother, who had been a teacher, hadn't insisted that one of the boys should get a degree; there were three sisters too, one married, two still at school – a large and cheerful Catholic family living in relative comfort in Athlone.

'I was telling my mother about you,' Fred Carelse said to him when they next met. 'She asked whether you would like to come to Sunday dinner next week – with the family.' It was obvious from Fred's whole demeanour that this invitation was unusual.

'I'd love to,' Jamie replied.

Fred let out his breath explosively, relieved to have got

the invitation out, and now to have it accepted. 'Sunday dinner is a bit special for us,' he said. 'You know that we are a Catholic family.'

'You told me,' Jamie replied gravely.

'You're not Catholic, are you?'

'No, but I still like eating.' Despite the teasing, he was actually very flattered to have been invited at all, quite rightly suspecting that the Carelse family was so close knit that outsiders were seldom included – and a white boy was an even odder inclusion.

Sunday dinner at the Carelses' house was a formal affair. The men of the family – all in suits as for church – gathered in the front room for a small glass of sweet sherry beforehand while the women finished cooking in the kitchen. Then all were summoned to the dining room to listen to Mr Carelse – a short man, so powerfully built that he was almost square, and in whose huge hands even the family Bible looked minute – reading a psalm and saying grace before the family consumed a meal more substantial than Jamie could remember since his last visit to a Karoo farm: pickled fish, *bobotie* and yellow rice, various vegetables, stewed fruit, and then sweet, milky coffee. Conversation was in English at first, for Jamie's sake. He understood classroom Afrikaans well enough, but when the family relaxed into the more colloquial and vividly punning *argot* of the Cape Coloured community he would have been totally lost without Fred's occasional translations and Mrs Carelse's strictures on what was appropriate in front of a guest and for a Sunday dinner. There was no mistaking where the central authority of the family lay, despite Mr Carelse's formidable presence: Mrs Carelse, very formally dressed in a floral coat and skirt, was half the size of her husband and quiet in voice and manner, but when she spoke the family listened and did not interrupt.

'That was a wonderful meal,' Jamie said to her as the dishes were being cleared by the unmarried daughters.

'I thought I would give you a proper Cape meal,' she smiled at him. 'Fred said you were too thin.'

'The whole of my family is very skinny,' Jamie said. 'No matter how much we eat, we stay thin.'

'Not true here,' said Mr Carelse, patting his midriff.

'I'm not fat,' Fred joked.

'You wait, my boy,' his father answered. 'By the time you're forty you'll be as fat as butter.'

'I shall take after Ma,' Fred answered. There was an edge in his voice that Jamie recognised – even wholesome families had their tensions, he knew. Fred had already confessed to him that his father wanted him in the business, not messing about in a university, costing good money and making none.

'People change,' Mrs Carelse said, peacefully. 'Fred told us you are interested in politics, Mr Cathcart.'

'Jamie'. He tried once again to get Fred's parents to call him by his first name. Mrs Carelse smiled at him, but he guessed he would still be 'Mr Cathcart'. 'Well,' he said, 'I think it's almost impossible to live in South Africa and not be concerned politically, isn't it?' Fred had rather shame-facedly warned him how conservative he would find the household.

'We don't hold with politics in this house,' Mr Carelse said.

'You don't, Pa,' Fred answered.

'What Fred's father means,' Mrs Carelse said, 'is that we don't hold with party politics. All this scratching and biting, this personal nastiness, this demeaning of other people, well, it doesn't seem very Christian to us.'

Mr Carelse joined in. 'I'll tell you what we think: if you took all the politicians of every kind, English, Afrikaans, white, Coloured, Bantu, Nat, SAP, Unity Movement, whatever, and locked them up on Robben Island, this country would be a better place. Why we can't just let people be … just let them get on with their lives peacefully … It beats me, man, and so we have no politics in this house. Or we shall all end up in Canada.'

'Do you know that our eldest boy has emigrated to Canada, Mr Cathcart?' Mrs Carelse said. 'We didn't want him to go, but he's very happy there. He's married a Canadian girl, and they have a baby. He has a good job too.' She gestured to the sideboard and the youngest daughter reached for a photograph in a silver frame of a cheerful replica of Fred with a pretty white woman sitting next to him, a small baby in her arms.

'Is she a Catholic too?' Jamie asked.

'Charlie met her in church,' Mrs Carelse said. 'She's a good girl. Her father and mother run a hardware shop and she helps there. They want Charlie to work for them, but he's too proud, he says.'

'Are you tempted to emigrate? To join your son?' No sooner had he asked the question than Jamie regretted it. The whole family other than Mrs Carelse seemed to be staring down at the table and the empty coffee cups.

'One is often tempted, Mr Cathcart; but we must try to resist temptation.'

'Our family has been in this country for at least three hundred years ...' Mr Carelse began, and Fred added, 'Some of them for longer, Pa.'

'Shush, Fred,' Mrs Carelse said firmly, and her husband went on with what was a speech he had clearly made before: 'I have worked hard; I have used my own hands to make a good business; I have built good, strong houses and I cheat no one; I even employ a white accountant; my workmen do what I say, and when I say so, because they need the jobs and because I pay them decent wages and treat them right – tough, but right. Is this reason to leave my own country? Leave me alone, and my family and I will get on with our own life.'

'I didn't mean to be rude, sir.'

'No one thinks you were rude, Mr Cathcart,' Mrs Carelse said. 'Mr Carelse isn't angry with you; but you will see why we don't respect politicians in this house.'

Walking back to the railway station with Fred a little

later that afternoon, Jamie apologised for what had been – he said – clearly a bloody silly and indiscreet question.

'No, man,' Fred answered, bleakly. 'It was a bloody good question. It's our big debate, you see. If you took a vote, the family would split half and half. My big brother really wants us to go; he says we'll all get better jobs there and won't be pushed around like we are here.'

'Your mother?'

'Oh, I think she wants to go. Little Joey – Charlie's son – that's her first grandchild, see, and he can't come here because his mother is white and his father … Well, he isn't, is he?'

'Can't she just visit?'

'She won't go without Pa, and he can't go because he can't get a passport.'

'Won't they give him one?'

'He won't tell us, but I think he applied once and was turned down. I think he might have been in trouble before he met Ma; they don't talk about it. But she won't go any-where without him. So, you see, if they go to Canada, it'll be forever – exit permits; and Pa's right: he's worked so hard for his business. Why should he give it up just be-cause he's a *kleurling*?'

They walked on in silence towards the station. When they got there, Jamie reached out and shook Fred's hand, very formally. 'Thank you for inviting me,' he said. 'It was a lovely meal, and I really like your family.'

'My mother likes you too, I think,' Fred said, then grinned. 'She'd like you even more if you were a Catholic.'

'No chance of that, Fred, I'm afraid. What little religion I have is strictly Protestant.'

* * *

Looking back at his first two years of university, Jamie was always astonished at how fast the time had gone. He had passed his exams – getting Firsts in the subjects he really enjoyed, and Seconds in the rest. He knew the central parts of Cape Town and some of its suburbs really well – there is nothing like walking to discover a city. He was a minor but steady member of the university orchestra, and had a set of friends there entirely separate from the crowd in the men's residence who were sufficiently like the boys in his old school for him to rub along with them peacefully enough, though he had few real friends there. He was one of the few white students who moved easily with the black and Coloured students. He had had several girl-friends, none particularly serious or steady, partly because it was expected in those days that boys paid for every-thing when they 'took girls out', and he simply couldn't do that very often. His friendship with Fred was a genuine one, despite the difference in their colour, and he was a regular visitor to Athlone. Sometimes when the holidays came near he was tempted to stay on in Cape Town because there was so much he wanted to do, so many people he wanted to be with, but simply hadn't had time for; but Peter was still at home and he could get holiday jobs in Grahamstown to eke out his term-time allowance a little, whereas in Cape Town holiday jobs were very hard to come by. So, when the men's residence closed for vacation, he packed a suitcase and a haversack, and hitch-hiked his way up the Garden Route and on to Port Eliza-beth, and then on to Grahamstown.

Meeting Jenny a third of the way through his third year at the university changed most things. First of all, he wanted to be in Cape Town whenever she was there – and she could afford to be there even when the women's resi-dence was closed for vacations. For instance, when there were commitments at the ballet school – which was where she spent most of her free time (although she was at the university to take an arts degree, her real love was ballet) – she stayed on to dance, and took a room in a little hotel in Rondebosch for as long as she needed to. Her home was in Johannesburg, but her parents were divorced and she had for years lived very independently of either; while her allowance wasn't enormous by the standards of wealthy Johannesburg, she was never short of pocket money, and her father seemed happy to pay her bills. Jamie became adept at scrounging a bed or a sofa or just a space on a floor for a few nights from one or other of his friends who lived permanently in Cape Town so that he could be there with Jenny, even during holiday time.

Secondly, his place in the orchestra became even more important to him, partly because it was from there that he had first set eyes on Jenny. She was dancing in the *corps de ballet* in a modern ballet written specially for the university ballet school to perform at the opening of a new university theatre, rather taller than most of the other dancers (and the reason, said Jenny, she was either going to have to be a star or would have to become a teacher, because she stuck out of the *corps de ballet* like a beanpole), and he had taken one look and that was it, and he knew then it was for ever and ever, so much so and so obviously so that the man who shared the third row of the second violins with him had, during a few bars' rest, poked him in the ribs with his bow and mouthed jokingly to him, 'Pay attention to the music; you are drooling.'

At the party after the performance, Jamie had gone straight up to Jenny to introduce himself and to ask her out – he had no idea where, he hadn't even thought of a place he might take her, but he had asked with such con-fidence, such certainty, that Jenny had said, grinning at this tall, blonde and skinny man clutching a violin case, 'Yes, of course I'll go out with you. You'd better tell me when and where, though, hadn't you?' So they had gone from the party to have coffee at a students' café in Ronde-bosch, and later he had walked her back up the hill to the women's residence, getting her in just as the doors were being locked for the night. He found, to his surprise, that he was still carrying his violin; he usually locked it up in the music school after playing, but he had clean forgotten.

So, when he met Jenny next day after lectures and walked her down the hill to the ballet school where she had a rehearsal, he was still carrying it; and while she was dancing he went to practise, and then he waited for her afterwards.

That became the pattern of most of their days: they would meet after lectures and walk down the hill to the ballet school; she would go in to dance, and he would go to the music school.

One of the side-effects of the love affair was, Philip Whitehead told him, that 'You're becoming quite a serious musician, Jamie Cathcart, now you're practising a bit more.' However, he would practise only long enough to make sure that, before her rehearsal finished, he would be waiting for her outside the ballet school. Then they would walk somewhere, or go to have coffee in a café, or they would catch a bus into Cape Town to go to the cinema, or go to listen to Frank Harris's 'easy listening' sessions in the lounge of the Alhambra, or merely go walking in the Gardens or sit on a bench in the sun or the shade – to talk and to listen and to talk and to listen. They talked so much, and listened so much, that they scarcely noticed that, whenever they came into the lounge at the Alhambra, Frank Harris would abandon the tune he was playing to slide easily into some or the other love song: *People will say we're in love* or *True love* or (left hand syncopating, right hand running the rhythms over the ends and beginnings of each phrase) *I want to bounce the moon /Just like a toy balloon* or …There is no happiness like first love, and nothing will ever match that ache and longing, that extraordinary muddle of certainty and uncertainty, that rolled-up sweetness.

Politics now took second place to Jenny. While he still talked to his political friends on campus, he had less time to go to their meetings or their discussion groups; though he took Jenny with him to one or two gatherings, she said she hadn't much interest in what she called 'abstractions' – and that she wanted to talk to him, and to listen to him, not to hear other people going on and on about boring things. Of course apartheid was wrong, and of course it wasn't going to last for much longer; anyone could see that, she said, and getting there might be quite nasty, but she wasn't so interested that she wanted to spend time on it. It was, Jamie realised as he got to know her better, almost inevitable that she would not be wrapped up in ideas; although she wasn't as anti-intellectual as some of her fellow dancers, who seemed to spend so much time dancing that they didn't do anything like thinking, she was utterly committed to dance and saw her future as a dancer, not as a student or whatever being a student might lead to.

Oddly enough, however, he was now asked by Barney to do something practical to help and Jenny was included in the request. 'It'll look less suspicious if a nice young white couple do this together,' he said. He wanted Jamie and Jenny together to open a post office box at the Diep River Post Office. 'I need somewhere quiet I can get things sent to from overseas,' Barney told them. 'You can use your own names, or you can make up false ones if you want to. They don't usually ask for identification papers – not from *witmense*. Then you give me the key and forget all about it, including the number. You'll never hear anything again about it – but you'll be helping, I promise.' It seemed so little to do – and Barney was right: no sooner was it done than it seemed forgotten.

While they were standing in the Diep River Post Office (the 'Europeans Only' side), trying for all the world to look like a nice young couple, Jenny asked the woman behind the counter for an application form for a passport.

'I thought you had a passport already,' Jamie said. He knew that Jenny had been to England with her mother for Christmas the year she left school and before she came to the university. Moreover, because her father had been born in England, she was entitled to hold – and actually held – a British passport.

122

'This is for you,' Jenny said. 'I want you to get a pass-port.'

'Are you planning to take me somewhere? There's no way I can take you anywhere,' Jamie teased her. 'Anyway, I have to have a South African passport. We've been in South Africa a long time; we're not recent immigrants like the Diceys.'

'I just want you to have a passport. Please.'

So her gentle nagging prevailed, as usual. He was per-suaded to get from his mother an official copy of his birth certificate; a friend took two passport-sized photographs and Simon du Plessis, as a qualified doctor, signed the declaration one Sunday morning that this was a true like-ness, though Jamie said the passport photographs made him look like a 'straw-haired half-wit'. Jenny sent the doc-uments off and, in due course, Jamie had his shiny new South African passport, though no means of making any use of it.

'Since it was my idea,' Jenny said, 'I'll look after it for you. It'll be safer with me, and I'll feel safer knowing we can leave whenever we want.'

'I'm not leaving,' Jamie said. In recent weeks, there had been several well-publicised cases of students and univer-sity teachers who had been refused passports but offered one-way 'exit permits', acceptance of which would mean that they could never return to South Africa – at least under its present regime – and the regime knew full well that it would last forever.

It was probably no coincidence that, at much the same time as Barney asked Jamie and Jenny to open the post office box, Jamie found that he was beginning to be regarded generally as something of a figure on campus, perhaps not yet a leading light of the left, but at least a proponent of radical views. Rather to Jamie's own sur-prise, he had spoken several times at meetings of the Students' Union and, as a result, was then invited to pro-pose a motion at a Debating Society meeting: 'That this

House supports sportsmen and women overseas who refuse to play against racially selected teams'. Irate rugger players invaded the meeting to howl down any speaker who dared support sanctions and to cheer those who spoke against boycotts and, afterwards, Jamie found himself so unpopular in the men's residence that he began to think he would have to move out at the end of the year if he could find a cheap enough room to rent. Then, when Dr Liebermann was banned from setting foot in any school or university in the country, Jamie found himself, along with Barney Jacobse, one of the main speakers at a lunchtime protest meeting in the Jameson Hall. 'You were brilliant,' Jenny told him afterwards as they made their usual way down to the ballet school. 'I had no idea that you could talk in public like that; I mean, Barney was very funny and very clever, but you were so passionate.'

'I hate this kind of bullying of people the government doesn't agree with, Jenny – I really hate it. And that's really what it is: they are trying to bully people into acquiescence.'

'I think you should be a bit careful, all the same, Jamie darling. One of the other girls said that there were security policemen there, taking notes.'

'Oh, there are always security policemen at everything now – and if it's not Special Branch there'll be a police spy reporting. I am not going to be bullied by them or anyone.'

'Can I bully you, Jamie?' She had stopped him under the trees on the steep path down near the tennis courts above the ballet school, and now turned him around to look at her.

'Anything you want,' he said. 'Anything at all. I'm putty in your hands.'

She pulled his head down to kiss him, and touched him as she did so. 'This,' she said in a whisper, 'this doesn't feel much like putty to me.'

* * *

For five days, no one came near him, except that, three times a day, a plate of food was pushed through the door; It was hard to tell the hours because the light in the cell was kept on all the time, and his watch had been taken away. He tried at first to count the chiming of the church bells, but there were too many to hear clearly. The muezzin chanted at dawn and dusk, and that helped, if only for familiarity. Some time after daybreak there came a tin plate of porridge and a tin mug of what might have been either tea or coffee; some time later there was another plate of samp mixed with beans and a minute quantity of stew made mainly out of vegetables; and in the evening a thick slice of bread and another mug of something tepid. On the first day he ate nothing except the bread but then, thinking he must either go on a hunger strike properly or not at all, he forced himself to eat what came through the door. There were two buckets in the corner, one holding what he hoped was clean water. On the second morning, thinking it might be emptied, he left the second bucket next to the cell door; but it stayed there all day and so he moved it back again to the far corner. There was a mattress on the floor and two blankets so revolting that, until he got very cold on the first night, he lay on top of them.

On the second day, he remembered some exercises he had once been shown to keep the fingers supple and strengthen them: you kept three straight and bent the fourth at right angles, then bent another at right angles, then a third; then you alternated the fingers, faster and faster, and then you went back again, slowly, until the muscles and tendons began to ache. The right hand didn't need the same exercises, but he did them all the same. Then he set himself to remember as much music as he could. He imagined he was actually sitting in an orchestra, and he closed his eyes and hummed his line to himself, bar after bar after bar, holding the beat of the metronome or the conductor's baton firmly in his brain, though, towards the end of each phrase, he allowed himself the luxury of a rallentando. For two days he managed to occupy the hours like this and was surprised at how much he could remember; his *teachers had always criticised him for relying too much on the score in front of him instead of learning by heart so that he could play entirely from the heart. 'But I want to play from my head, too,' he would tell them, even though he knew he should have enough confidence to do without the crutch of a score in front of him. On the third day, as he was working his way through some tricky phrases in the third movement of a Schubert sonata, he was interrupted by a voice calling his name from somewhere outside. He jumped up from the mattress where he had been sitting, cross-legged, and shouted back. 'Ja, man, it's me, all right. Who are you? I'm all right.'*

He waited for the person to call back, but there was nothing. After a while, he went back to his mattress and began the third movement again, but again was interrupted. This time he stayed on the mattress and didn't reply. Nothing broke the silence, until he began to hum again; he had got only nine or ten bars into the first phrase when the voice called again. This time he did not stop though the steady beat of the metronome faltered. He forced himself to continue, even as the calling grew more continuous and louder, until there was nothing to do but stop.

It's only three days, he said to himself. It's only three days, and it's as bad as this already. We were warned, but this is worse. I must find other things to do. I'll take the alphabet, and for each letter there will be a name, and for each name a story. So there is ... Alan? Adrian? Arthur? Oh yes, Arthur. I remember Arthur; that must be three years ago now. That was something new, all right. And there's B for Barney, but I may not think of Barney here; I must put Barney out of my head. So C is for Charlie, who used to be my friend, until we fell out because he cheated – that's another C all right: C for Chea – or should it be Ch for Cheat? In some alphabets C and Ch would be different letters, I guess. And then there's D. Who do I know who is called D – for David? For Daniel? He who went into the lions' den and came out safely. Not me, I'm afraid, not me.

On the fifth day two security policemen came to collect him for questioning. One drove, and one sat in the back of the car with him. On the way, he tried to see people he knew in the streets; but though they drove through Salt River and Woodstock he saw only strangers. When I walk here, he thought, I do not go ten yards without a friendly greeting. Have they locked all my friends away too? Is that why the streets are empty? Have they thousands in detention, then? And if they have why do they want me too? At the Caledon Square Police Station the car was driven into a courtyard at the rear of the building and then he was taken up several flights of stairs to an office with the curtains drawn. There were two chairs in there and a little table. When he made to sit, one of the policemen jerked the chair away from him. 'You don't sit, kaffer,' he said. 'You stand.'

He replied in Afrikaans: 'Ek is geen kaffer nie, meneer.'

'Fokken' hotnot,' the policeman answered, and slapped him across the face, twice, back and forth, as hard as he could, so that he nearly fell with the force of it.

When he could speak again – there was blood on his handkerchief, he noticed – he said, 'I want a lawyer.'

'There are no fokken' lawyers here, kaffer, except the ones we've got locked up too.' The other policeman thought this was a marvellous sally, too, and they both laughed uproariously while he stood, waiting.

After four hours, during which he had kept silent, except when he repeated his request for a lawyer, the two policemen who had brought him in and who had been shouting questions at him went away. Two more came in and sat watching him for several minutes without asking any questions until they were joined by a third man, a younger, rather tubby man wearing a smart blazer and blue trousers which so nearly matched the blazer that it might have been a suit. The younger man gestured to the policemen and, grinning, they stood up, one on each side of the prisoner. The man in the blazer asked a question; when there was no reply, he stood up, stepped forward and, as the policemen held the prisoner's arms, hit him as hard as he could in the solar plexus. He stepped back. 'Now,' he said, 'now I will ask the question again.'

'I want a lawyer.'

This time there were two punches, the right to the solar plexus, the left lower. The policemen let go of his arms and he fell, holding himself and trying not to make too much noise. The man in the blazer lent over him and said, almost gently, 'I'll tell you what, man: I'll make a deal with you. Each time you don't answer, I give you one extra.' He stood again, and the policemen lifted the prisoner up. 'Now, let me ask you again,' and the man in the blazer repeated his question. When there was no reply after a moment or two, he stepped forward and grabbed the prisoner by his hair, forcing his head back. 'That's number three,' he said. 'Perhaps you are one of those moffies who like a bit of the rough stuff,' and, still forcing his head back, he punched him three times in the balls. This time the policemen left him lying on the floor.

After six hours he was dragged by his arms to a cell somewhere else in the building and dumped on a mattress. After a while he must have slept; it may have been an hour, it may have been six. He had no idea. When he tried to stand, there was too much pain. There was a toilet in this cell, rather than a bucket, and he managed to get to it, though he was too swollen to use it. He slept again and woke only when the man in the blazer and two other policemen whom he hadn't seen before came into the cell. The man with the blazer said to them, 'This is the one I was telling you about. This is the moffie who's had so many cocks in his mouth he's forgotten how to answer questions.'

Because he still couldn't walk, the policemen dragged him into the middle of the floor while the man in the blazer got the bucket of water from next to the toilet. The policemen forced him to kneel with his head over the bucket. The man took his blazer off and laid it carefully on the mattress, then rolled up the right sleeve of his shirt. Once again he asked his question and, before there was time for a response, forced the prisoner's head down into the water and held it there while he counted. 'Bloody hell,' one policeman said as they struggled to hold the straining body still, 'this is wet work. Hou stil, kaffer.'

'There's something else we can do if this is too wet,' the man with the blazer said. 'There are his hands. He'll be worried about his hands.'

Chapter 6

Because her mother was going to England and her father to Durban with a new girlfriend, Jenny had asked Jamie if she might spend Christmas that year with his mother, Peter and himself in Grahamstown. While he had been a little worried about how his mother might react to Jenny, the prospect of not being separated for the holidays was such a relief that he had said yes before even consulting his mother.

In fact, the visit had been altogether a success. Of course, his mother had moved a spare bed into Peter's room for him, and had put Jenny in his bedroom. But, the first night home, as he had lain awake waiting for Peter to fall asleep so he could get into bed with Jenny next door, Peter had said quietly to him, 'There's a torch in the bed-side table, Jamie. I don't want you falling over the cat and waking Mum.'

'How did you know?' he asked, smiling to himself in the dark. There were no cats in their household; their mother said she was allergic to them.

'If, brother, you could see your face when you look at that girl, you'd know. Actually, one can see it's pretty mutual – lucky boy you are.'

'Is it that obvious?'

'Well, I hope you're planning to marry her, otherwise there'll be trouble. For God's sake don't wake Mum; and you'd better take my alarm clock so you wake in time to get back here in the morning.'

So he had been able to sleep with Jenny every night for the ten days they were home and, if his mother had realised, she hadn't let on. To Jenny, she was charming, cheerful and often great fun. 'I think your mother is wonderful, Jamie,' Jenny told him soon after they had hitch-hiked up from Cape Town together (as Jamie told Peter, when you hitched with a pretty girl it was amazing how easily you got good lifts). 'I don't see why you were worried I wouldn't get on with her; she's nothing like as sad as you said.'

'Well, she isn't sad now,' he said, defensively and even guiltily. Was it the fault of Peter and himself that she didn't usually enjoy herself as much as she seemed to be doing now? For instance: out of the blue his mother had suddenly suggested that they might play some duets together – they hadn't done that since he was about thirteen.

'Mum, I've left my fiddle in Cape Town; I couldn't hitch with it.'

'I knew you would, so I've borrowed one from the school for you to use this holiday.' She was triumphant at her forethought.

So, that evening after supper, while Peter and Jenny listened, his mother had opened the piano and he had tuned the borrowed violin, and then they had played together for nearly an hour: some quite tricky Schubert first, then Vivaldi, then an arrangement of some Handel tunes, then – getting still simpler – some Christmas carols and some popular tunes. 'You two could get a job playing at the Alhambra,' Jenny told them, laughing. 'Frank Harris couldn't compete.' So she had to explain who Frank Harris was, then who their other friends were, and their work and their entertainments.

At the end of the evening, Mrs Cathcart kissed Jenny on both cheeks and said, 'My dear, I've learned more from you this evening about the way my elder boy lives in Cape Town than I have in three years of letters and holidays; and thank you, Jamie, for playing with me – I guess I should thank Jenny for that, too, because you've become a real musician since I last heard you play. And now I'm going to bed, and you three mustn't sit up too late, talking.'

131

She was being heavily arch with them and, later, in bed Jenny whispered to Jamie that she thought his mother knew that they were sleeping together.

'Oh, I don't think so,' said Jamie, sleepily.

However, when his mother said farewell to them early in the morning before they walked down the hill to the road where they might pick up a lift to Port Elizabeth, she spoke to Jenny as if she were already an affectionate mother-in-law saying farewell to a new member of her own family. 'Now, make sure you stop in a hotel overnight if you don't get a lift straight through,' she said. 'Have you enough money for that, or shall I lend you some? Are you sure? I know Jamie, you see; he's quite stubborn, and he'd stand all night on the roadside just on an off-chance.' She kissed Jenny warmly and added, 'And there's always a room for you here, with or without my son – though mainly with him, I'd guess.'

Having taken his degree at the end of his third year at the university, Jamie had decided he might be able to live more cheaply while he did his teacher's diploma – which he was committed to doing as part of the deal with the scholarship donors – if he left the men's residence and took a room in Rondebosch, down the hill from the university. He would, after all, be spending a substantial part of the year getting practical experience as a teacher in various schools in the Cape, and travel from Rondebosch would be easier than it would be from campus. Jenny would – for once her father had insisted – stay on in the women's residence; but they both knew that if he had a room of his own it would be easier for her to come to him. They could not take advantage forever of the generosity of Simon and Adrienne and, anyway, that was only for weekends; what about Monday, Tuesday, Wednesday and Thursday? Jamie's new landlady – the manager of a shop in Claremont, single, she said, divorced – would provide Jamie with tea and toast before she left for work in the morning. Once she had gone, he could use her bathroom, though there was a hand-basin in his room and a pot under the bed for emergencies. If he wanted to make himself supper, he could use the kitchen in her flat between six and six-thirty, but he wasn't to cook downstairs because of the risk of fire. He could have visitors, but no one overnight: that was a rule, she said – definitely no one overnight. The room smelled damp – it was effectively a cellar in the block of flats – but it had its own entrance out at the back, it was cheap, and it was just across the road from the music and ballet schools.

Mrs Cathcart had very much wanted them to stay in Grahamstown for New Year's Eve, and so had Peter; he knew Grahamstown was boring, he said to Jamie, but it was even worse when Jamie wasn't there. However, Simon and Adrienne had invited them to a party on New Year's Eve, and Jamie had arranged with the landlady that he could have the room from before the New Year. So they hitchhiked back on 30 December. 'The longest we waited,' Jamie grumbled ironically to Jenny, 'was when you went to the lavatory behind those bushes. Three cars passed me then; you came back, and the next car drove us all the way to George. I remember last time I hitched down the Garden Route I stood for twelve hours outside Mossel Bay.'

The women's residence didn't open again until late January. For form's sake, and to pacify her parents – though they seemed to show so little interest in her doings that pacification hardly seemed necessary, Jamie thought – Jenny took a room at her usual small hotel in Rondebosch, though in fact, despite the landlady's overnight rule, she moved in almost entirely with Jamie except when she went back to the hotel to change her clothes. Many of their usual friends were away from Cape Town, and both the music and ballet schools were closed for the holiday.

They soon fell into a pattern of sybaritic laziness. When the landlady knocked on his door in the morning with his tea and toast, Jamie shouted out, 'I'll get it, Mrs Peters; I'm just dressing,' and leapt to collect the tray before she tried

133

to enter the room. He and Jenny shared the breakfast in bed until they heard the landlady leave the flat for her work. First he, and then Jenny, would sneak upstairs to the lavatory and the shower. Then, a little before midmorning, with an old khaki haversack containing suntan oil, bottles of water and books, they would catch a bus along Main Road into town, sitting upstairs at the front so they could see the sights and the people. They would then transfer to another bus to take them through Sea Point and further along, on to Clifton's Fourth Beach.

There, having found themselves a peaceful corner in the rocks, they would sunbathe and swim all day and, when the sun came abruptly down in the evening, wander off the beach to a hotel bar. Jenny would have a glass of white wine, Jamie would have a beer, and then they would make their way back, either to stop at a cheap Italian restaurant in Sea Point or in town, or to eat bread, cheese and ham in Jamie's room, or to risk cooking a pot of spaghetti on an electric ring they had smuggled into Jamie's room. By eleven, they would be sound asleep in Jamie's bed.

At first, Jenny tried to avoid getting suntanned – 'I'll be in trouble with the ballet school if I go back all sun-burned,' she said – but, by the end of January, they were both very brown from the sun – except for the even more interesting bits of each other that seemed emphasised by being still so white.. Both were also very skinny from eating so little and very fit from swimming each day in the cold Atlantic rollers. The world had been rolled up into just two people and they were too happy even to realise they were happy.

*　*　*

When Willem Bearer was detained towards the end of January, Jamie and Jenny – like almost everyone they knew or who knew Willem – at first assumed this was either the typical mistake of a police state ('They've prob-

134

ably got the wrong Willem Bearer,' Jenny said. 'It's a common name, isn't it?') or possibly something to do with his sexual habits.

'Has he fondled a policeman?' Jamie wondered lewdly to Jenny.

'I do hope it's a joke, Jamie darling,' she replied. 'It'd be awful if it wasn't.'

Then all sorts of rumours began to do the rounds, of what Willem might have been up to. Perhaps he wasn't so apolitical after all; perhaps all that was a front. Jamie began to worry about the post office box they had opened for Barney. Had he involved them in something dangerous – dangerous for Jenny, especially, as she never seemed to understand that there really were political pitfalls, especially for the unwary? A few months earlier, there had been a series of mysterious explosions in the Cape, mainly – it seemed – of a symbolic kind (statues of famous South African leaders of the white variety were blown to pieces) rather than actual industrial sabotage or guerrilla warfare: no one had claimed responsibility though some newspapers had suggested this was probably the work of the banned ANC and its military wing, *uMkhonto weSizwe*. Was this what Barney and his fellow conspirators had been up to?

No one seemed to know where Barney was and, when Jamie tried to find out from others in the group, all he got was a shrug. He couldn't get Fred on the telephone, either at home or at the builders' yard. He asked Frank Harris if there might be a point in his going to see the vice chancellor of the university to try to get a protest about Willem's detention from him; after all, Willem was a very distinguished student. Or at least he might see the director of the music school. Jenny thought he should talk to Philip Whitehead first, which he did; Philip seemed very evasive on the telephone, but promised he would have a word with the director. Nothing happened. Jamie telephoned again, and this time Philip Whitehead was so distant as to seem merely a ghostly voice. Yes, he said, he'd gone with Frank to talk to the director, who had talked to the vice chancellor, who had made some telephone calls, and whose advice was to keep well clear of a very dangerous situation that could rebound most unfavourably on the university and the music school.

'Jamie,' Philip said plaintively, 'I'm simply not in a position to take risks. You know how fond I am of Willem, but I suspect he's been up to something very foolish.'

Jamie put the telephone down, fuming. He had left Jenny on the beach to go up to a telephone box on the main road, and he went back down again, to throw himself on the sand next to her, muttering, 'Gutless bastards, the lot of them.'

'Philip?' Jenny asked.

'Of course,' Jamie said. 'He's scared shitless. Even worse than Frank.' He mimicked Philip's slightly precious tones: 'I spoke to the director; the director telephoned the vice chancellor; the vice chancellor telephoned his friend, the head of the police who is a fellow Rotarian; and the head of the police warned the vice chancellor about Willem's vice ...' He lapsed into his own voice; he was not a good mimic, he knew. 'And Philip knows all about vice, you see, and doesn't want a scandal.'

'It's a bit odd, isn't it?'

'Yes,' said Jamie. 'I feel very helpless. I wish I knew where Barney is. I'd like to do something.' He jumped up. 'Shall we swim?'

They skipped going to the hotel bar that evening and instead, on their way home bought a bottle of cheap red wine, some sausage rolls and fruit for supper in Jamie's room. 'I feel a bastard sitting in a bar or a restaurant with Willem locked up,' Jamie had said as they were leaving the beach. They were back at the room just after nine and, as Jamie put his key in the lock, Fred Carelse stepped out of the shadows behind the dustbins. 'Jamie, Jenny,' he said. 'Thank God you're back. I've got terrible news.'

136

'For goodness' sake, Fred, we could have kept you waiting hours. What's the problem? Come in, but we'll have to be quiet.' Mrs Peters might just about cope with finding a girl in his room, Jamie knew, provided they weren't actually in bed together; but finding a Coloured man there would probably be too much to bear.

'Willem's dead.'

Jenny put her arms round Fred, who had begun to cry, noisily.

'Hush, Freddie, hush,' she said. 'It's all right now. Just tell us what's happened.'

'The security police went to Willem's mother and they said he had committed suicide. They made her go with them to look at him in the police morgue.'

'Willem wouldn't kill himself,' Jamie burst out. 'They must have murdered him.'

'They say he hanged himself by a blanket from the window.'

'Bullshit,' Jamie said. 'That's bullshit. They've murdered the poor bastard. Willem wouldn't kill himself. He just wouldn't.'

His voice was raised. 'Jamie,' Jenny warned him, gesturing upwards to where Mrs Peters might be listening.

'Where's Barney?' Jamie asked Fred.

Fred broke away from Jenny; he had stopped weeping, though his face was still contorted. 'That's why I've come to you, Jamie. I've come from Barney.'

'Where is he?'

Fred shook his head. 'That doesn't matter,' he said, 'but Barney sent you a message. He says: can you borrow a car to drive him out?'

'You mean across the border?'

Fred nodded. 'He says he's got to get out in a hurry. I think I'll go with him too.'

'What's going on, Fred? You'd better tell me.'

'No, Jamie, man; I'd better not. Do you think one of your whitey friends would lend you a car that could get us out?'

'Tonight?'

'It's too late now.'

'Tomorrow night? I know someone who might lend us a car, I think.'

Jenny interrupted. 'Who, Jamie?'

'Simon?'

'To run someone out of the country?'

'No. I'd tell him something. I'd tell him your father was ill and you had to get to Jo'burg, and that I was driving you. He's got that big Rover in the garage; they use Adrienne's little car mostly.'

Jenny looked doubtful. 'I don't like lying to Simon.'

'Nor do I. But it would involve them less. It's safer.'

'I'll come with you,' Jenny said.

'No.' Jamie tried to sound adamant.

'Then, if they stop us, I can say I'm with you, and that we gave Barney a lift, or that he's a servant or something.'

'And Fred. Fred, did you say you would come too?'

Fred looked desperate, but nodded fiercely. 'If Barney's going, then I'm going too. Especially after this business with Willem.'

Jamie had almost forgotten Willem's death in the knowledge that there was now something real, something active, something dangerous to be done. 'Poor bloody Willem. Listen, Fred. Tell Barney I'm sure I can get a car. We'll go as soon as we can tomorrow night. I can get you to the border in the very early morning if we drive fast, and you can walk across before dawn. There are bound to be dirt roads the farmers use. Then Jenny and I will be away from the border by daytime.' He had already accepted that she would come too; she squeezed his arm in recognition of his agreement.

'I can drive too,' she said; actually, she had had a licence longer than Jamie had and had probably driven more miles than he had. Uncle Hamish in England had paid for Jamie to have driving lessons when he turned eighteen, but because the family didn't own a car he hadn't had much practice, except when he borrowed friends' cars.

'We need to get some maps of the border area. There must be dirt roads there. We'll need to avoid the towns when we get close to the border area.'

'Where'll we meet you and Barney, Fred?' Jenny asked.

'You mustn't come to us or to where Barney is. We think the police are looking for him already; they've been asking around. We'd better come here. I'll get one of my brothers to drive us here.'

'Fred, I'm sorry to say this, but you'll have to bring some money for petrol. I'm broke, as usual.'

Jenny butted in: 'I've got money. I'll get some tomorrow.'

'You don't have to worry about money, either of you. Money's not our real problem. We could have hired a car, but Barney can't drive and I haven't got a licence yet.'

'That's fine, anyway. Tell Barney we'll meet here, after dark tomorrow, say at about eight. Then we drive ...' He grinned; this was scaring, but it was also an adventure.

In fact, most of the adventure turned out to be almost dull. Fred and Barney arrived promptly at eight. Whoever dropped them had already driven away before Jamie answered their quiet knock at his door. Barney had a small navy-blue holdall, but Fred was lugging a large suitcase. 'For goodness' sake, Fred,' Jamie said. 'How on earth are you going to lug that through the bush? You may well have to walk about six hours as far as I can tell from the map. You'll have to get right clear of the border.'

'I couldn't find anything else,' Fred said miserably. Barney looked scornful, but said nothing, and Jamie guessed that Barney would probably have preferred to be travelling alone.

'I'll tell you what,' Jamie said. 'I've got an old army haversack you can take. You may have to leave some things behind. Fill the haversack with the essentials and leave the rest in the suitcase under my bed.'

With Barney and Fred sitting as low as possible in the back, Jamie drove Simon's big Rover through the hours of darkness over the Boland mountains and then north-east on the main roads to Kimberley, gradually driving faster as he gained confidence in the powerful machine, and then for an hour or two on dirt roads over the flat distances of dry savannah towards the border. Jenny's suggestion that she might drive for a while to give him a break was stubbornly refused until in his weariness a bush on the side of the corrugated road turned into an apparition about to launch itself at the car, when he handed over to her – and, quickly realising that she drove most competently, he slept for nearly an hour. Barney and Fred were both sound asleep for most of the time; Barney had confessed to total exhaustion after several days of constant moving. Every now and then, one would wake to ask, 'Where are we now?' and whoever was driving would answer as best he or she could.

There was a bad half-hour while Jenny was driving; someone in a large car seemed to be following them, just out of the range of the dust, and they feared it might be a police car. First, Jenny woke Jamie, and then he woke the others; they peered into the dust behind them, but could see nothing but the headlights. When Jenny speeded up, the car behind did so too; and it slowed when she slowed. Eventually, she swung the car abruptly off the road and into a picnic spot, turning off the lights as she did so. The other car swept past; there seemed to be only one person in it. 'I guess it was someone just using our tail-lights as a guide,' said Jamie.

Half an hour further on, awake now but still content to let her drive, Jamie said suddenly, 'Jenny, slow down; there's something in the road.' Fortunately, even though she hadn't seen anything, she did as she was told, because suddenly out of the grey light there emerged, standing solid and silent right in the middle of the road, a huge kudu bull.

'My goodness, it's lucky you saw him, Jamie; we would have killed him,' Jenny said.

'And he would have killed us, too, most likely.'

Barney and Fred had woken again. The bull was still standing calmly in the road. 'My God,' said Barney. 'What's that?'

'He's a kudu bull; isn't he magnificent? There'll probably be some kudu cows and calves in the bushes nearby – unless he's a solitary chap who's been chucked out after a fight with a younger bull.'

'Why does he stand there?' asked Fred. The bull showed no sign of moving, so Jenny had begun to manoeuvre the car around behind him.

'It's maybe a bit warmer there. He has been here a lot longer than we have.' Jamie knew where he'd seen that bull before; he was the same as the god-kudu in the Bushman's painting that Peter and he had discovered above the pool, and he was here to tell them that Africa existed before any of them and would still exist after all this nonsense about borders and politics had disappeared.

Fred giggled from the back seat. They were back on the road again and Jenny was accelerating. 'I tell you what, man,' Fred said. 'He'd make a helluva lot of biltong.'

'Fred, are you never not hungry?' Barney asked, and Jenny said, as if in reply, that Jamie would find in the glove compartment in front of him some sandwiches she had made that afternoon when they were collecting the car from Simon's and Adrienne's house.

When dawn approached, Jamie took over the driving again; they stopped several times to check the map but it was so vague and the area so large that, in the end, they had just to guess. 'We could probably just drive you over the border,' Jamie said. 'I think it's about a mile further on, on this road and I don't think it'd be manned here; but there may be a patrol, so I think you'd better get out and walk. You've got the compass Jenny bought. Just take a bearing north and walk. I think you should pick up the road again in about four miles, and then you'll just have to walk until you are well clear of the border. You may want to rest up for the hot part of the day.'

Jenny gave them the rest of the sandwiches and made sure the bottles of water in the side-pockets of the haversack were full and tightly closed. Jamie had been more worried about Barney, physically at least, but he seemed calm and confident; it was Fred who seemed nervous and worried, though he was a strong and fit young man. Barney said that he knew there were people in Botswana who would look after them. 'Moenie worry nie, Jamie,' he said as they shook hands by the side of the car. 'Everything's fixed up the other side. There's a lot going on that you know nothing about.'

So, while Jenny found a turning place a little way up the road, Jamie saw the two men off, once again making sure that they understood what he had meant by taking a bearing north. Barney didn't even turn to wave, though Fred looked back several times in the clear dawn light before the bush hid them both. Back in the car – and hardly noticing that Jenny, having turned the car round, now stayed at the wheel – Jamie said, 'Oddly enough, I'm much more worried about Fred than Barney; I thought Barney would struggle physically, but he's fine.'

'I suspect that he's much tougher than he looks.'

The journey back to the Cape was entirely uneventful. They stopped in Vryburg for a late breakfast and then in Kimberley for a few hours' sleep; the outside of the Rover was very dusty now and, when they reached the outskirts of Cape Town, they had the car cleaned as well as once again filling up with petrol. By late afternoon the car was back in Simon's and Adrienne's garage, and by eight Jamie and Jenny were sound asleep in Jamie's room.

* * *

Since the new academic year was beginning, Jamie and Jenny had now to abandon their long beach holiday so that they could settle back into much the same daily routine as the year before, except that now they had Jamie's room to go to after they returned from the ballet school. However, the first day was immediately disrupted because on his pillow was a note from the landlady, Mrs Peters: 'Please call upstairs as soon as you get in.'

Jamie left Jenny downstairs and went to knock on the door that separated his room from Mrs Peters's flat. 'Mrs Peters,' he called, 'it's me – you left a note.'

Mrs Peters appeared, still in her work clothes, and look-ing flustered. 'Mr Cathcart,' she said very formally (she had taken to calling him Jamie most of the time), 'your brother telephoned from Grahamstown. He says he needs to talk to you urgently; but I have to say to you that I really don't want to have to take messages for you, and will you tell your brother not to telephone here again? I don't like it that you gave him my number.'

'Mrs Peters, I did not give him your number. He has my address – that's all. I don't know how he got your number. It must be an emergency. Did he say my mother was ill or something?'

'No, nothing like that – just that he needed to talk to you urgently.' Mrs Peters's tone had softened. 'I hope it isn't that your mother is ill. You can use my telephone if you want to.'

'No, Mrs Peters, I wouldn't dream of it. I'll telephone from the box on the corner; it's only a few yards down the road.'

And a good thing he had done that, too, he thought, as he listened to his brother. 'The police were here today, Jamie; they said they were looking for you to answer some questions. Mum is in a panic.'

'I'm sorry. Tell her it's nothing. It probably is nothing.' Had Barney and Fred been picked up on the border? he wondered. They wouldn't have given names, surely. What else might it be? The post office box? He had no idea, but did his best to reassure his brother. When his mother came on the line, tearful and wanting him to come back to Grahamstown at once, he was thankful he was in a telephone booth where he could claim to be running out of change so he could cut her off.

Back in his room, he found that Mrs Peters had taken Jenny upstairs for a cup of coffee; as he went up the stairs he heard her saying, 'Well, I have to say I find your boyfriend a very nice quiet lodger. You know, I take him a pot of tea and some slices of toast every morning for his breakfast, and he's so shy he never lets me come in.' Jenny was, he saw, struggling to keep a straight face since she had been consuming half that breakfast for weeks.

Jamie motioned to her to drink up, but told Mrs Peters, as cheerfully as he could, that there was no emergency. No, his mother wasn't ill. There was just some family business that needed to be settled urgently. Downstairs, on their own again, he told Jenny the truth.

'Do you think we'd better go away?' she asked.

'Where to?'

'Well, across the border too. Or to my mother in Johannesburg.'

'Actually, you know, I don't think we've done anything illegal. We merely drove a couple of friends to the Northern Cape. It was they who crossed the border illegally, not us.'

'That post office box?'

'We don't know that was anything illegal either. Look, this is probably nothing – there are so many raids now, so much intimidation. It's probably a way of trying to stop me making speeches on campus.' He was, he knew, putting a brave face on the business.

'It could be something to do with Willem. You were friends. He might have implicated you.' Jenny's voice tailed away. She knew it wasn't likely.

'In what? I hadn't done anything. Sweetheart, I don't know why Willem was murdered, if he was murdered.' He was silent; the reality of Willem's death had still not taken complete hold of either of them. There had been some talk

144

in the car going north, some pity, some sympathy for old Mrs Bearer, but it was almost as if they had needed to put Willem's death to one side because it hadn't happened where they were a part of it. Jamie had suddenly thought of something else, however, and now he said it. 'All the same, darling, I don't think you had better stay here tonight. Just in case the police come.'

So, after a small argument – 'Well, if they do come, I want to be here with you,' she had said stubbornly, until he managed to make her see how it would seem to an outsider – he had walked her back to the little hotel in Rondebosch. 'It's a good thing your clothes are in the wardrobe,' he tried to joke as he kissed her goodnight and watched her let herself in the front door. 'They've probably forgotten they rented the room to you.'

'That reminds me: I must book out tomorrow,' Jenny said from the doorway. 'I suppose I should really have gone back into res today. Most of the other girls did. Last year seems such a long time ago, doesn't it?' She hesitated, then waved and closed the door, though he stood waiting on the pavement for several minutes for a light to go on upstairs before he walked slowly back down the road to his own empty room.

The police came for him at six in the morning, not to his own door, but to Mrs Peters's. She came downstairs in a pink towelling dressing gown, righteous in her indignation. 'I thought something was going on yesterday,' she said over her shoulder as she led him up the stairs to where two policemen in plain clothes waited. He had wrapped a towel round his waist and pulled on an overcoat to answer her knock at the inside door.

'Are you Mr James Cathcart?' the elder of the two policemen asked.

'Of course,' Jamie replied. 'What can I do for you?'

'You will accompany us to answer some questions.'

'Dressed like this?' Jamie answered. 'May I at least put on some trousers?' To his relief, he found he was not afraid; his battle was out in the open now and his mood was excited, almost exhilarated.

'We wish to search your room anyway,' the policeman answered. 'You can dress while we search.'

'Am I allowed to make a telephone call?'

'No,' said the older policeman.

The younger policeman spoke for the first time. He was rather tubby and wearing a blazer. 'Who do you want to telephone?' he asked. His accent was not nearly as Afrikaans as the other man's, indeed, he might be English-speaking, Jamie noted.

Jamie wanted to telephone Jenny, though he knew he shouldn't; but how was she going to find out otherwise? She would be going straight from the hotel to the women's residence, he knew, probably by taxi since she would have suitcases. They had planned to meet as usual after morning lectures. What would she do when he simply didn't turn up? He spoke to the younger policeman: 'Can you tell me this? I have important lectures this morning for my new course. How long will these questions of yours take?'

'That depends on you, Mr Cathcart.' The younger policeman seemed amused. 'All the same, if I were you, I wouldn't plan to attend many lectures today.'

'Are you detaining me?'

'We are going to ask you some questions, Mr Cathcart.'

They were downstairs now in Jamie's room; the older policeman was searching the room, with meticulous efficiency: each drawer was taken out, emptied on the bed, turned over, refilled, and replaced. He's looking for documents, Jamie thought; he thinks they may have been taped to the bottom of the drawers. The policeman took out each book in turn from Jamie's meagre bookcase, held it upside down, shook it in case anything was concealed in its leaves, and then checked that the book inside was what the dust cover said it was. I'd never thought of that, Jamie noted. Brown-paper covers, yes, but not the wrong cover on a book. The possibilities are endless. The policeman

146

came across something that clearly excited him; he called the younger man over, then said to Jamie, 'Is this your book, Mr Cathcart?' It was a thin paperback copy of Lenin's *What is to be Done?* published by an East German publishing house. Barney had lent it to him months ago; he had read it in a desultory fashion over several weeks and had forgotten to return it.

'A friend lent it to me.'

'Are you aware it is a banned book?'

'Is it?' Jamie answered. Of course he knew it was a banned book, and neither he nor Barney should have had a copy. However, if this were the limit of his guilt, it wouldn't be too bad. 'Someone lent it to me,' he repeated. 'I didn't know it was banned. I haven't read it; it's very boring.'

'It's boring, but you haven't read it,' the man in the blazer said. He took a plastic bag from his briefcase and put the book in that and then into his briefcase before making a note in his pocketbook. 'Who was the friend who lent it to you, Mr Cathcart?'

'Oh, I can't remember. Someone up at the university. Reading a book doesn't make you a communist.' Jamie had managed to dress now, turning his back on the police-men as he did so. 'Am I allowed to go upstairs to shave and wash?' he asked.

'Wash in this basin here,' the man in the blazer said.

'Do I have to piss in that basin too?' He was beginning to resent this. 'I want to use the lavatory upstairs.'

'I shall have to accompany you.'

In the event, the policeman let him use the lavatory on his own, though he checked the window first, presumably – Jamie thought – to make sure he couldn't climb out, and then stood outside the door. To Jamie's relief, Mrs Peters was nowhere to be seen, though she was crashing about in her bedroom.

Back downstairs, Fred's suitcase was open on his bed. Jamie had forgotten that. 'Is this your suitcase?' the police-man asked.

'A friend left it here.'

'Which friend?'

'Oh, one of my university friends; he left it here because he was going away on holiday.'

The other policeman went over to the bed and together they rummaged through the case. There didn't seem to be anything of significance in it, but still they closed it up and made it clear that this, too, would come with them. 'Now,' said the younger policeman, 'now, Mr Cathcart, you can pack yourself a little bag – wash things, pyjamas, towel, a clean shirt, socks and so on.'

'That means you are detaining me.'

'It means nothing, Mr Cathcart. Just pack a bag, and then we will go.'

* * *

In later years, looking back on the five weeks of his detention – all of them in solitary confinement (though it seemed to be policy that the police moved prisoners from one set of police cells to another every fortnight or sooner, so that they should build up no routine nor relationships with gaolers), with no access to a lawyer nor to visitors, with no books nor paper nor pencil and with actually not that much time spent in being questioned by the security police – Jamie would always claim that they were the most significant part of his South African education. Everyone remotely involved in political activity had heard something of the pressures which being locked up induced in the prisoner and his or her resources, and there had been plenty of advice about what to do.

For instance, Jamie vividly remembered a lecture he had heard in his first year at the university which purported to be literary criticism, but was in fact a discussion of the effects of solitary confinement, taking as example ('exemplar' the lecturer said) Martin Decoud in Conrad's *Nostromo*, a man most civilised, sophisticated even, well educated, but without any 'inner resources' – not Conrad's words, but the lecturer's – to help him cope with being left alone on an island to guard a cache of silver. Decoud ends up weighting his body with silver ingots so that, when he turns himself adrift in the rowing boat that has been left with him and then shoots himself, he sinks without trace.

Everyone in Jamie's circle of political friends knew of local examples of apparently strong-willed and powerful people who had cracked up so badly – and so quickly – in police custody that they had given evidence for the state against former allies, even against people they had themselves recruited for illegal activity. There were however things to be done by prisoners to protect themselves against quick collapse: routines to be followed that would create an illusion of business, if not the reality; activities to be undertaken and games to be played; particular dangers to be avoided or ploys used by the security police to beware.

To be feared was torture, which Jamie knew now was sometimes used even against white prisoners, though most commonly against blacks: simple beating up with fists, boots or truncheons; more sophisticated forms, like near drowning by forcing a prisoner's head repeatedly into a bucket of water or – horrible variation – by strapping a prisoner upside down to a kind of trapeze, so that he could be lowered head first into a tub of water, or by electric shock. Jamie wasn't sure what he would do if they attached an electrode to his penis, apparently a favourite of one particular torturer in the security police. There was much less moral repugnance and more sympathy felt towards those who 'sang like dickeybirds' in police custody if they were in fact submitting to torture, though that sympathy was not extended to those who gave evidence in court for the state against their friends and allies, even when they had been tortured into telling.

One of those who had talked in Barney's 'discussion

group' had been an older man, a devout Moslem, who had been detained for more than three months in police custody, beaten up, threatened, but eventually released without being charged. 'Everybody cracks up a bit,' he had said. 'You can't help it; and when the Boere are beating the shit out of you and you know something, it's crazy not to tell them something so that they'll stop the beating. All you can do is to crack up as slowly as possible and tell the Boere as little as you can. Then they put you back inside and leave you while they check up; so it's best to give them a little bit of the truth rather than just lies. But everybody is going to crack a bit; it's mos human nature ...'

Having Simon du Plessis brought into the office where they were questioning him on the second day could have been bad; in fact, from the police reaction to Simon, he guessed they had expected someone by the name of Du Plessis to be an ally, and thus to be angry with Jamie for the deceit he had practised to get hold of the car. Perhaps Simon had given them that impression merely so he would be able to see Jamie himself. In fact, Simon was at first apologetic to Jamie ('I'm terribly sorry I had to tell them but I didn't know what was happening; I thought you'd been speeding, or something, and Adrienne was a bit scared, too'). Towards the police he was angrily sarcastic, so much so that the police hustled him away after he had spoken barely a few sentences. 'I'm really terribly sorry I had to tell them, Jamie,' Simon said, 'but they were pretty threatening towards Adrienne when they came round.'

One of the security policemen said abruptly to Simon: 'Dr du Plessis, you told us he drove your car to the border without permission.'

'No, I didn't,' said Simon. 'I said I lent him the car, but thought he was going to Johannesburg. You will have to ask him yourself where he went if he didn't go to Johannesburg. It was you who said the border.'

'This is a serious matter, Doctor.'

'Since you are holding my friend without giving a reason, I should hope so.'

'Doctor du Plessis, I am surprised at your antagonistic attitude. We're talking about a danger to the state.'

'And I'm talking about the danger to individuals of detention without cause or charge.'

'Your car was used for an illegal purpose.'

'Then you had better charge me,' said Simon, 'though I don't think you could make anything stick for long before the court started laughing.'

'This interview is terminated,' said one of the policemen, angrily.

As Simon was shepherded out, he said over his shoulder, 'Adrienne sends her love.' Jamie grinned at him; he was feeling much more cheerful, especially as Jenny had not been mentioned.

Jamie was on his own for the rest of the week. Food and a bucket of tepid water were pushed through his door three times a day, but no one came to his cell and he was given no exercise, not even the hour a day prisoners in detention were supposed to get. He used the toilet in the corner of the cell and washed himself as best he could using the bucket of water. Though he had his shaving kit, the razor blade had been taken away when he had been signed in at the desk, as had the belt of his trousers. At the end of a week – Jamie was keeping a careful check on the passing of the days and nights by scratching a calendar low down on a wall with a nail he had found in a crack in the floorboards – he had a visit from a magistrate; this had been one of the legal concessions when the ninety-day detention legislation came before the parliament. Jamie decided, on the spur of the moment, that any kind of protest in principle to the magistrate would be futile, so he made his complaints as specific as he could: first, he had nothing to read, not even a Bible – he thought all prisoners were allowed at least Bibles. To his surprise, the magistrate was cross about this; when he spoke in Afrikaans to the sergeant who accompanied him, it was clearly as a reprimand. Encouraged, Jamie continued his complaints. Second, he would like paper and a pen or pencil. No, said the magistrate, you are not entitled to those.

'Surely I am entitled to cleanliness,' Jamie continued. 'I'm wearing the clothes I was arrested in, and I haven't had a shower.' This wasn't quite true: he had brought his little bag into the cell with him and it had contained a spare shirt, socks and underpants. Using his shaving soap and some of the water from his bucket, he had managed to wash the collar and underarms of a shirt and his underpants and socks when they had begun to stink. It had taken hours to do – which he knew was an advantage – and waving the shirt around his head to dry it had been another lengthy chore.

Again, the magistrate was clearly cross; words were spoken, notes made.

'Any more complaints?' the magistrate asked. It was apparent he was by no means on Jamie's side, but he was a stickler and rules weren't being obeyed.

'I've had no exercise,' Jamie said. 'I thought I was entitled …' He continued, but the magistrate was already speaking to the sergeant.

'You will get two half-hour periods of exercise every day from now on, Mr Cathcart,' the magistrate said.

Mr Cathcart, thought Jamie to himself; I'm a human being again. So he decided to push his luck. 'The food is disgusting,' he said. 'It's barely edible.'

'Have you not had food brought in from outside?'

'I didn't know I was allowed to.'

Again, the magistrate spoke to the sergeant, then turned back to Jamie. 'You will have to pay for it yourself.'

'I think my friends will probably manage that.'

'I will see to it that you get a Bible; that clean clothes are given to you every day; that you are allowed to shave yourself in the yard – under supervision; that you can have a shower in the yard – also under supervision; and that your friends can supply you with food more to your taste.'

Jamie decided to risk a tease; if he was being treated as human, perhaps the magistrate was human too. 'I don't suppose you can arrange for me to be released,' he said.

The magistrate allowed himself a grim smile. 'Now that, Mr Cathcart, that lies well beyond my limited powers. I would however advise you to answer the questions the police are putting to you.'

But that is what I'm simply not going to do, thought Jamie: at least not until I bloody well have to – not until they beat me up or attach an electrode to my cock or duck me in a bath of water. I'll chat away like mad; I'll make all the conversation they want; I'll tease them by trying to convert them to my own way of thinking; but there will be no names mentioned, and nothing about a trip to the border, and even less about a post office box in Diep River.

That night, the police moved him to another police station, he wasn't sure where, but he thought it might be Sea Point because it was in that general direction and he could smell the sea and thought he could hear breakers. The cell was cleaner than that at Caledon Square had been and there was a Bible on the floor next to the mattress. Next morning, there were some clean clothes in a neat parcel and he knew Jenny must have brought them because, on the collar of an otherwise very clean shirt, there was a lipstick kiss. So she was all right too. During the course of the morning, a food parcel was delivered too: again, he knew it must be Jenny's doing because among the various goodies there was the kind of chocolate she knew he liked and – even better – a bar of the sandalwood soap she always used and which her body smelled of. From then on, there were clean clothes and a package of fruit or chocolates or fruit juice or some luxury to supplement or even, some days, to replace the tepid porridge and the tough stew and overcooked *samp* which were still served to him three times a day. Perhaps even better than all this was the simple fact that, by standing on the lavatory seat and pulling himself up by the bars on the small window high in the cell wall, he could just catch a glimpse of the sea.

He had managed to bring the nail from Caledon Square police cells and used it now to scratch another calendar, low down on the wall behind the lavatory; he was a little nervous that he might have lost a day during the move, but he was fairly sure it was Tuesday now. Next to the calendar, he scratched a shorthand list of the daily routine he had begun to establish in Caledon Square. No matter what the temptation to do otherwise, he stayed in bed until his breakfast was pushed through the door. He would eat what he could of that; though he had never liked porridge much, he made himself eat that first because the bread could be saved for later. Before dressing he – who had loathed physical education at school – would work his way through a routine of exercises, stretching, press-ups, jumping on the spot, until he was sweating and panting. Then he would wash and shave; at Caledon Square he had managed, by putting two razor blades into his razor at once, and handing back only one to the policeman, to keep a blade in his razor, and so could shave in a cupful of water from the bucket. Without a mirror it was difficult, but he used the bottom of a metal talc bottle to see his face, and with his fingers he could make sure all the stubble had gone, even if he had to shave three times over. Then he would wash his hands and face, and comb his hair. He would dress carefully. Then came bed-making and clothes-folding; he made his bed like a hospital nurse had once done for him and then he unpacked his holdall and folded everything from scratch again, ordering it carefully before re-packing.

He had brought shoe polish and a shoe brush with him, and next in the routine came shoe cleaning; his father had taught the boys to clean their own shoes when they were young, but it wasn't until now that he became as meticulous as their father had been. He had read somewhere that 'spit-and-polish' meant literally that, so now he shone his shoes as if he were a sergeant in a Guards regiment, until he could see his face in the toecaps. Then he would sit on his bed and read a chapter of the Bible; he had begun with Genesis and read a chapter each day, no matter how long, how short, how enthralling, how dull. If he found himself skipping or speeding up, he would make himself go back to where his attention had slipped and read aloud; when he came to lists of names, reading aloud helped. Next came music practice: he had found himself missing his violin more than he had thought possible and remembering what he might have been practising was a poor substitute; he therefore set himself to remembering as much as he could of each piece he had regularly played in the university orchestra. It was, he knew, a fundamental weakness in his musical abilities that he had a poor aural memory; when he had taken grade exams, it had always been the aural tests that he had hated – and neglected. So, to remember anything was a struggle, even when he managed to visualise the notes on the page.

With any luck, round about this time, a policeman would come to let him out of his cell. He would grab a towel and his bar of soap, and would strip to wash himself under a cold shower in the corner of the prison yard, and then, for the rest of his half-hour, he would walk round and round the yard, as fast as he could. He would have preferred to have had the shower at the end of his walk, but the policemen who came had clearly been instructed not to talk to him nor even to answer basic questions, and he learned that he couldn't rely on any of them to tell him time was nearly up so he could have the shower last. On his first day in the Sea Point cells, he had said to the young policeman, 'Look, I want to shower before I go back inside. Will you tell me five minutes before my time is up so I can walk first and then shower?' The policeman hadn't told him but had merely, with an unpleasant smirk, locked him sweatily back in his cell.

That didn't matter; in a sense, it helped because he knew he needed never to fall into the trap of either liking or trusting a policeman. The old Muslim at Barney's gathering had told them that clearly: 'You have to remember that each Boer is a Boer. Maybe some of them are less filled with hate than others, but assume always that each one is your enemy.' And that helped, particularly when they took him for questioning. Often, one would leave the room on some pretext and the other would say, 'Ag, man, Jamie, my boy, you'd make all this so much easier if you'd answer the questions,' in the friendliest possible fashion, and then – even when you knew what the ploy was – there was such temptation to regard this as really friendly advice, and begin to slip. So, he would be prepared to talk about anything, but there were questions he would not answer: he knew nothing about Barney Jacobse at all except his name from the university and he really couldn't remember any other names – he had always, he claimed, been hopeless at remembering names, particularly if they were African or Afrikaans – or where discussion groups had been held, or who had addressed them. And, yes, he couldn't deny that he had been in Simon du Plessis's car that night, and he had had two men in the back, but he didn't know their names, and the girl with him was just a girl from the university he was friendly with and went out with sometimes, and he had dropped the men where they asked to be dropped and he didn't know what they had been carrying. And, yes, the suitcase did belong to Fred Carelse, whom he had met somewhere and who had asked him to look after it, but he didn't know anything about a letter that had been in the suitcase and he couldn't remember who had lent him the book by Lenin, and perhaps he should have realised it was banned, but he hadn't. And, yes, all right, if they were going to charge him under the Suppression of Communism Act, they were welcome

156

to do so, because he wasn't a communist and would happily say so in court, but they would have to charge him and get him to court first.

Eventually, the police would tire of him and he would be sent back to his cell. He knew he was fortunate; if he had been black or Coloured or Indian, he would almost certainly already have been tortured, or merely beaten up out of frustration, or even worse. There was hardly any pretence any more about those who died in solitary confinement from a 'heart attack' or from 'falling over in the shower' or 'slipping while going down stairs'. Until the rules were changed, he was going to be stubborn; he had always been stubborn, he knew – his mother had told him that often enough – but now it was going to become a virtue, as long as he could manage it.

Back in his cell, he would force himself to resume his routine at the particular point for that day, even if the session of questioning had interrupted it. After the meal served him at lunch time – the main meal of each day, such as it was, usually some sort of stew, with potatoes or *samp* and overcooked vegetables – he would force himself not to lie down; if he slept then, he knew that the night would be interminably bad. Instead, he would play some game he had invented for himself, or adapted: on the floor under the mattress he scratched a set of squares on which he would play what he called 'mini-chess' – he cut all the major pieces from cardboard, though did without pawns, and then played left hand against right hand; or he would play a dictionary game, which required him to think of a verb beginning with each letter in the alphabet in turn, then a noun, then an adjective, then an adverb – and he would fine himself one point for each word he missed, and then do press-ups to pay for the points; or he would take a mental journey, say from Cape Town to Grahamstown, and remember each town one went through, and then the different aspects of the scenery.

The difficult time was the evening, particularly when it

became dark outside. There seemed to be no time pattern when the light would be switched on or off – it couldn't be done from inside the cell and Jamie suspected it was done deliberately at random. Indeed, on one or two nights it wasn't switched off at all. The point was not to get riled; if one decided it was being done deliberately to disturb and disorientate, one could cope with it better. So the evenings became time for remembering. He sent himself back to school and worked his way round a room full of his classmates, repeating their names and foibles; then he did the teachers too. Then he started on those he knew at the university. Then, briefly, he allowed himself a conversation with his mother before summoning up his father to try to remember everything about him: how he looked, how he spoke, what he wore, the things he said. Then it was Peter's turn and that was easy: he would say to himself, 'We'll do a bike ride down to the Bushman's cave on the way to the Kowie,' and he would take the pair of them on their bicycles slowly up from Grahamstown, over Stone's Hill, past the turnoffs and on to the pool, the cave, the magical figures. Lastly, before he put on his pyjamas – he had given up pyjamas because of Jenny, but had packed a pair in his holdall when he was detained – he would allow himself to think of her: every part of her, every detail of her face and body, every mannerism, every speech she had ever made to him, every moment he could remember. And then, with luck, he would sleep.

Occasionally, the police would put someone else in one of the other cells; he always hoped it might be someone else political, but it never was. He guessed that, if they did, it might be a trap of some kind; the old Muslim had warned them: 'Never trust the Boere. If they put someone in the cell next to you, it's probably someone they're paying, and they will be trying to get you to tell something – they probably have a tape recorder on you anyway.' However, one night, the police put in the cell next to his a cheerful drunk, an English seaman off a merchant ship in the Duncan dock, obviously plastered out of his mind. Jamie shouted out to him, the drunk shouted back, and they exchanged names and details; Jamie tried hard to get some news of the outside world out of the man, but he claimed never to read a newspaper – 'too bloody depressing, anyway,' he said, 'especially with all this politics. Did you say you were in for politics? More fool you, then, old son; I'm in for being pissed out of my mind. And disorderly. I told the barman he was a hairy cunt, and then said the bar-girl had great tits; turned out she was his wife – they both got a bit cheesed off with me. Shall I tell you a joke about a politician?' And he told Jamie a series of jokes, mainly so lavatorial that, ordinarily, Jamie would have been revolted, but that night he was glad to listen and to encourage the man to continue until, at last, one or the other of them had fallen asleep. When Jamie woke next morning, the drunk had gone, presumably to a magistrate's court, or perhaps back to his ship.

He was moved again, somewhere about an hour's drive inland. He had no idea where it was, but suspected it might be somewhere like Bellville, because the police station was new and built in brick rather than cement. However, the move could not have been communicated to those who usually brought him clean clothes and extra food because for two days nothing came other than the standard prison meals. Nor was there any sign of a visit by a magistrate. Instead, the questioning began to get rougher; it won't be long now, Jamie thought, before they begin to lose patience and beat me or pretend to drown me or hitch me up to a generator. I wonder how much longer I can hold out now. It was the fourth week now; though the routines still held, and he knew they helped, he was also aware that, if he slipped even for an hour, he might slip forever. There were things happening that he couldn't explain: voices calling, shadows appearing, horrors emerging. Even Peter and Jenny weren't entirely reliable now; they would get hazy and speak with the wrong voice, or not be there when he needed them. Even his dead father couldn't be summoned up. Suppose ... suppose Peter had been telling the security police things about him; would Peter try to explain to the police about their father, or about Chief Gadla, or about Makana coming over the horizon? Might they have arrested Jenny too? Might they be spying on her, or doing things to her? He found himself saying out loud one afternoon: if anyone harms a hair on her head, I will buy a gun and I will blow his brains out.

Someone new came to question him – well, not new, because he was one of those who had arrested him, the tubby young man in the smart blazer. Until now, Jamie had always been questioned at the headquarters of the security police, at Caledon Square; and he had always been questioned by at least two policemen at the same time, often working in relays. Now, the new man came to him at wherever it was he was now being held, and he came on his own.

'Well, Jamie,' he said when the policeman who had unlocked Jamie's cell and led him into an office in the main building had left, closing the door. 'We meet again.'

'I don't know your name,' Jamie said firmly. He didn't bother to ask when there were two policemen present.

'Ah, yes,' said the man. 'You are the one who's not good at remembering names. Well, my name doesn't really matter, Jamie, but you can call me ... let's see ... Peter – the same as your brother.'

Jamie looked at him in silence. Was this a threat of some kind? 'No,' the man said. 'Genuinely. My name is Peter. Peter Maasdorp. Not Pieter; Peter, in the English form. Maasdorp because my family was Afrikaans, but became English-speaking a long time ago. And you are wasting our time, Jamie Cathcart.'

'I think that's a bit rich, coming from you; it's you who are holding me in detention. I didn't put myself here.'

'I think you did, Jamie, I think you did.' Peter Maasdorp

– if that was his name – rocked back on his chair and sighed. 'Today's my day off. I was going to go fishing. Do you like fishing, Jamie?'

Jamie shrugged. When his father was alive, he and Peter used to fish with him, but they hadn't done so with anyone else since his death. 'I haven't done any for a long time,' he answered.

'I love fishing,' Maasdorp said, stretching. 'Sometimes in the sea, but mainly in a river, or just in a well-stocked dam.' He stood up to look out of the window into what Jamie thought must be the car park of the police station. 'I'll tell you what I really like about fishing. When I've hooked something, and got him up into a net, and have landed him, and he lies there on the bank, panting, and I know: now I can throw him back in, now I can keep him. And sometimes I throw quite big fish back, just to see them begin to breathe in the water again – and they are quite still sometimes, and I wonder if maybe I've kept them out just a bit too long, and they are going to turn belly-up; but usually they begin to move, and suddenly they seem to realise, and – whoosh – they are gone. And I wonder if I'll catch them again.'

'Do you eat the fish you catch?' Jamie asked.

'Funny you should ask that, Jamie. No, I love fishing, but I'm a true Afrikaner in one way: I'd rather eat meat than fish, if I have a choice.'

'The Xhosa are like that, too,' Jamie said. 'They don't like eating fish, even when they live on the coast.'

Maasdorp turned back from the window. 'Are you trying to rile me, Jamie Cathcart? You're right, though, you know. There's much more similar between the Afrikaners and the black people – what I'm instructed to call 'Bantu', though actually I think they are right to want to be called 'African' like the Afrikaner, really – than between the English and the Afrikaners. I'm both, you see, so I know.'

'Then why treat them so badly?' Jamie asked.

'Jamie Cathcart,' the policeman admonished him like a

161

schoolmaster. 'We don't treat black people badly. Most of them we treat very well; you compare them with their brothers in the rest of Africa and you will see how well off our black people here are.'

'That's an invalid comparison,' said Jamie wearily. One had heard this kind of crap so often, and he hadn't much interest in debating this kind of point with a security policeman.

'No, you are wrong,' Maasdorp said firmly. 'The great majority of our black people want nothing more than to continue to live peacefully. If it was otherwise, we couldn't contain them. No, the truth is that there are only a handful of troublemakers who want to change things. Do you hunt, Jamie? Back there in the Eastern Province?'

'No,' Jamie said.

'In the Transvaal, where my father's people come from, we hunt baboons – there are too many of them, and they come down to raid the mealie lands. So we wait a while, and then we put up a trap, either one of those cages with a door that falls when a baboon grabs the bait or the one I really like: you take a pumpkin and hollow it out, with a hole just big enough for a baboon to get his hand in; then you nail the pumpkin down into the veld with some long spikes or you put it on a chain and you put some pumpkin pips inside. Man, baboons love those pips. Now most baboons are scared, and they keep away from human beings; but every now and then, along comes a big baboon, very important, and he smells the pips, and he puts his hand into the hole, and grabs a handful of pips.' Maasdorp began to cackle with laughter. 'But, then, you see, with his fist full of pips, he can't pull it out of the hole; he can get his hand in, but he can't get his fist out – and he doesn't know enough to let go of the pips. And you can walk right up to him, and he gibbers and jumps up and down, trying to get free, and he pretends to bite you, but he won't let go of the pips, and he can't get his hand out. Oh man, I laugh so much I nearly wet myself.'

He came over to lean on the table and to look into Jamie's face, so close that Jamie could see where he had nicked himself shaving that morning. 'And then we shoot him, right in the gut. That takes him a long time to die, and he makes so much noise that the other baboons, the ones that aren't so foolish as the one with his fist in the pumpkin, the others run further and further away, and they don't come back there for a long time. I tell you, I've seen one of those big baboons tearing his whole gut out, everything, all the insides, and picking up grass and stones to stuff inside to try to stop it hurting – and he still won't let go of those pips.' He stared into Jamie's face. His breath was clean and smelled of toothpaste, Jamie noted: this was the kind of man who bothered to clean his teeth after meals. 'Don't make me do this to you, Jamie. You're just an ordinary South African boy. These people you are mixed up with … they're communists, they hate the whites, they want to run this country for themselves, not for other people. They'll make use of you until you are no use to them and then you'll have nothing.'

Jamie stared back. He had been afraid before, but it had been as much fear for others – for Jenny, for Barney, for Fred, for poor dead Willem, for his beloved Peter – as for himself: but now he was afraid for himself. This was a horrible, sick person staring at him, and he was helpless in front of him, and the man knew: he had a little smile on his face. He was enjoying this. Jamie closed his eyes and dropped his head; he could not bear to go on looking. What was he going to do?

Maasdorp stood up from the table where he had perched and went back to his chair. Picking up his briefcase from the floor, he took out a typewritten page and laid it neatly on the desk. Then he took out a pen. 'Now, Jamie,' he said, 'to speed the process up, so that maybe I'll get a bit of my day off actually off, let me read you a statement. If you will sign this statement, I will take it back to my superiors, and then we shall see what we shall see, but I think – and

I would recommend – that you be released with a warning as to your future conduct. Or you can decide to go on being stubborn.'

'Am I allowed to read the statement?'

'Of course, Jamie, of course.' Maasdorp turned the document so that Jamie could read it and pushed it towards him.

Jamie read in silence, then looked up. He was, he realised, having the utmost difficulty in concentrating; at first glance, the words seemed entirely random, almost without syntax. 'Am I allowed to change anything?' he asked.

'Well, if you must, you must,' Maasdorp answered. 'I don't know when I can get a typist again. But here's a pen.'

Jamie tried to read again, and this time made more sense of it. The statement was made by him, James Frederick Cathcart, at the Bellville Police Station (so it is Bellville, Jamie thought), on a blank day and blank date, 1966; and it was made of his own free will, not under coercion (as if detention in solitary confinement isn't coercion, thought Jamie). The statement admitted that he, James Frederick Cathcart, had become involved with a group of subversive students and others, including trade unionists, who were plotting to overthrow the state by violent means, and that he had assisted that group by a) opening with Miss Jennifer Dicey on 7 November 1965, at the Diep River Post Office, post office box number 695C, in the name of Mr and Mrs Frederick Cathcart, of 11 Langlaan, Newlands, said post box to be used for the receipt of, among other things, subversive material from abroad and b) by driving the leaders of that group, Messrs Barnato Jacobse and Frederick Bryan Carelse, in a car borrowed from Dr Simon du Plessis, on 3 February 1966 to a point at which they could cross the South African border illegally into a neighbouring territory. Then there followed a list of people whom Jamie was supposed to have met at Barney's discussion groups: Willem Bearer (deceased), Barnato Jacobse, Frederick Bryan Carelse, 'Sonny Boy' Adonis, Rupert Zanzile, Shadrack Kobe, Khotso Lamani, Phakamile Mtirara, Fikile Sethwala, Sophia Zewene, Muhammed Verlaten, Ezekiel Bosman, Clive Ashley, Ahmed Singhal …

Jamie looked up from the list. 'Most of these names mean nothing to me,' he said. 'I mean, this wasn't the kind of thing we did; we didn't start by saying, "Hi, I'm Jamie Cathcart, and I come from Grahamstown." The most we ever heard were first names.'

'These are all people who attended those meetings,' Maasdorp replied.

Yes, thought Jamie, and I wonder which were in the pay of the security police. 'I can't sign if I don't know the full names of people who were there.'

'Well, who do you know? Put lines under the names you know.'

Jamie looked at the names. It was obvious that Willem had been more involved than he had let on – and, anyway, the poor bastard was dead; no further harm could come to him. He took the lid off the pen and underlined Willem's name. (If he had looked up he would have seen Maasdorp smirking.) Then he underlined Barney's name, then Fred's. If they had got safely into Botswana, they were safe; if they hadn't, there wasn't any real need for him to try to protect them. The old Muslim: the police knew all about him anyway – they had held him for five months in solitary. The others had called him Ahmed; he must be Ahmed Singhal on the list. Jamie put a line under his name, then a query. 'Look,' he said to Maasdorp. 'I'm really not very sure about these other names; I think this may be one I met, but I've put a question mark there too.'

Maasdorp nodded, as if to confirm that he was content, though Jamie knew it didn't much matter. One name, twenty names; it didn't matter. What mattered was that Jamie gave them something. He underlined two more names he thought he recognised: Ezekiel must be Zeke, and he thought Khotso Lamani was the small, skinny black man who had been so unfriendly when he first started attending meetings. He paused over the list a moment longer, then handed the page back to Maasdorp. 'May I ask how you know about the post office box?' Jamie asked. As far as he knew, there were only two people in the world who knew about the box: Barney and Jenny.

Maasdorp looked steadily at him, still half-smiling. 'We know much more than you ever realise, Jamie. We put things together and we add them up. We are professionals, remember.'

And we, Jamie reflected bitterly, we are just bloody amateurs. 'I'll sign,' he said to Maasdorp. 'But just for those names I underlined, not for the others.'

'All right.' Maasdorp took his pen and carefully crossed out the names not underlined. He wrote something in the margin, filled in the day and the date, and handed the paper back to Jamie. 'Please,' he said, 'please feel free to read it through again. Then sign in the margin for the day and date, and sign for the amendments – just initials will do – and then sign the bottom, and I will witness your signature.'

Jamie signed, his head bent over the paper. He couldn't bring himself to look up at Maasdorp when he handed the signed statement back.

'When will I be released?' he asked.

Maasdorp feigned astonishment. 'I didn't say you'd be released, Jamie. I just said I would talk to my superiors. I'll do that – and I'll show them the statement. Then we shall see.'

* * *

Back in the cell, Jamie lay on his bed, unable to bring himself to return to the routine he had managed to continue since he first established it. He was appalled with himself for signing the statement that Peter Maasdorp had prepared for him.

166

He had stood up for weeks without answering those questions, yet now – under the most ridiculous and perverted pressure – had capitulated without struggle. Fish out of water and wounded baboons – was that all it took to break down his resistance? Where was all that much-vaunted stubbornness? What would Peter think of him? And Jenny? What would his father have said if he had been there?

How had the police discovered about the post office box? Had it been a trap? Had the post office officials spotted that half the information he and Jenny had supplied was phoney? Had they been collecting and copying whatever had been sent there anyway? Who had infiltrated Barney's group? Who had given all those names to the police? And where did poor Willem fit in? Why had he underlined those names? Why hadn't he just kept to his vow of silence? All these questions and not a single answer; and he had signed the statement, thinking he would be released – and now even that seemed just a temptation he had succumbed to. Maasdorp hadn't even promised release; he had merely said he would talk to his bosses. So now (Jamie thought) I've sold my soul and I haven't even got out of detention. I've been done.

Some time later, he forced himself to clean his shoes; he had scuffed them slightly when he had been led to Maasdorp, and they were dusty too. So he rubbed and spat and rubbed and gradually the sheen was re-established, and the fact that he had made the statement reverted to something of no great importance. After all, there was little enough use that could be made of it. If they had the names already, the fact that he had confirmed the presence of a handful of them wouldn't have any great significance at all. They seemed to have known about the post office box all along. They already knew that he had driven Barney and Fred towards the border. Perhaps they could charge him with something – being a member of a banned organisation (but he had never become a member of anything) or furthering the aims of a banned organisation or of

167

international communism – but he was quite prepared to stand up in public to avow that he was not in any shape or form a communist. No, the only thing that had been hurt was his pride in his own strength, his own invincibility.

He slept and there was a new dream: he, brother Peter, farmer Ted Impey and policeman Maasdorp were on the Bedford farm and they were hunting. At first he wasn't sure what, but then there was a crashing and thundering in the bush ahead, and it was a huge kudu bull, standing six foot at the shoulder, with horns four foot high, spiralling upwards. We can't shoot him, Peter said in the dream, and the policeman and the farmer lifted their rifles, as if in answer. Then the kudu was gone, racing ahead somewhere, and they were all running after him, in and out of the thorn bushes. Someone fired a rifle, and the kudu was injured, running on three legs, trailing a hind leg, and there was blood on the ground for them to follow. Suddenly, they came up against a huge, closely meshed fence, like a border fence, with razor wire on the top, and it was clear that the kudu bull must somehow have jumped the fence, despite his injury.

And then Jamie was on his own, not in the bush any more, but somewhere near the seaside, and he was running down a narrow sandy track towards the sea below. Someone was drowning there, but if he was quick enough he might be able to save him. He could hear his father somewhere nearby too, calling him; at first his words were garbled and then they reconstituted themselves as: come back, come back. I can't come back, he shouted, and his father became visible, a half-dissolved ghost, and he said: you're beginning to forget me, aren't you? You don't care that I'm almost gone for good now, and that I'll disappear forever soon. That's not true, Jamie answered, Dad, that's not true. I'll never forget you. But when he woke he was still crying.

* * *

After the second round of beatings, the two black policemen threw him in the back of a van usually used for transporting police Alsatians; it stank of dog still, though someone else seemed to have bled on the floor before him and that smelled bad too. The white man hadn't actually joined in the beatings, as far as Khotso could tell, but had merely stood to watch, making jokes and encouraging the black men. Khotso didn't know his name, though he thought he had seen him before at meetings; he heard him call one of the black policemen 'Eric' and the other 'Duiwel', but there were no other names. He had resolved, when the beatings had started, that he would remember all he could for as long as he could; he had never stopped believing that, in the end, they would win the struggle – and, if he was still there for the victory, he was going to be one of those who saw to it that justice was measured out as it should be. Whenever he could, he looked hard at the white man's face to remember it, even if he didn't know his name.

It was hard to remember such things when you were being beaten; then, it was easier to lie in a corner of the yard with your knees closed up hard against your chest so it was more difficult for them to kick your private parts, and with your arms locked tight around your head and with your eyes closed. They stopped kicking and hitting when they thought you were unconscious, so it was best to be as still as you could. It seemed too that there was nothing they wanted from him, no talk, no information; they asked no questions, they just beat him. Sometimes, one of them would say something to him, but it was generally a curse. Someone must have told them about what he and Willem had done; Willem was the clever one, and he had found out in a book how to make the explosions, and Khotso had helped him. The police seemed to know everything and now they were punishing him – as he guessed they had punished poor Willem. Anyway, whatever they did, he wasn't going to talk: they might be asking no questions, but there weren't going to be any answers either. Sometimes, when they kicked him especially hard, as when they got the kidneys, it was hard to keep silent – and he knew he had wet himself. He

169

must smell of piss as well as blood. He could taste his own blood; when he swallowed he knew it was blood from his own mouth he tasted, where the policemen had hit him with their fists first, before he fell down.

It was cold in the cage on the back of the van. As far as he could tell from where he lay on the floor of the cage in the back, all three men had squashed themselves into the front seat – the white bastard driving, the other two next to him. He had no idea where they were taking him; it seemed a long way, but because he was unconscious some of the time he wasn't sure. They had started the beatings in Roeland Street, but then they had moved him somewhere else in a car; they had put a sack over his head so he couldn't see where they were taking him. He didn't think it was a police station; it seemed more like a private backyard. At first, as they went there, he had tried to count minutes and to remember turnings, but after a while he had lost track, both of time and direction. Then, he had still been hurting in particular places: his mouth, his nose, his ribs on the right side, his ankles – one of the policemen had a trick of kicking your ankles away suddenly so that you fell. 'Who said you could lie down, kaffer?' the white man would shout and, as soon as he got up on his feet again, the black policeman would kick his ankles away. He must have done it five times before Khotso stopped getting up; that was when they began to kick him where he lay on the ground. Now, he hurt so much all over he didn't know which part didn't hurt; he seemed to be hurting inside too. It was hard to breathe; very shallow little breaths seemed to be easier but the movement of the van made that very hard to do.

He woke when the van stopped. It was still quite dark and they seemed to be in the veld somewhere. He was very cold now. He could hear the men talking, and then he heard a match and smelled tobacco. I could do with a cigarette myself now, he thought. A glass of water would be welcome, too. He tried to move a little, but stopped when he heard Duiwel say, 'Is the little kaffer awake?' Perhaps it was best to be still.

After a few more minutes, the cage was opened and one of

the men grabbed hold of his shirt to pull him out onto the road. 'Sis, man,' he heard the white man say, 'he stinks like a public toilet. Has he shat himself?' Khotso was afraid he might have done though he wasn't sure.

He had managed to get his feet under him as he was pulled from the cage, and so now he could crouch in the dust; he thought it safer not to try to stand yet. He could see from their boots that the men were standing around him. Better not to look up, he thought: better just to stay here. He could hear them talking but it seemed a long way off and he guessed the beatings had hurt his eardrums too.

They had him by the shirt again and they were making him stand up. 'Come on, kaffer,' the white man said. 'Stand up now. You're not that badly hurt. Come on, stand up, or I'll tell them to hit you again.'

Slowly, he forced himself upright. When the pain in his back almost made him vomit, he staggered once, and a hand caught him roughly to steady him. 'Come on, man, stand up,' the white man exhorted him again. Khotso managed to open his right eye to look at the man. His left eye wouldn't open; Khotso guessed it was swollen too much. 'So now, kaffer,' the man said, returning his stare, 'you see me, and I see you.'

Khotso tried to say something, but there was only a croak. He tried again, and managed to say what he wanted. 'Jou gat,' he said, you arsehole.

The man smiled at him. 'The little kaffer still wants to fight, eh?' For a moment Khotso thought he was going to be hit again, but nothing happened. He closed his eye again, concentrating hard on standing upright; perhaps he should concentrate on the pain rather than trying to ignore it. Perhaps that would make it easier.

'Now, little kaffer,' he heard the white man say as if from a distance, 'you are going to take a walk – on your own. We are releasing you, see. You're free to go.' Hands turned his shoulders so that he was facing away from the van, and a hand pushed him in the small of the back to make him begin walking.

It was hard to walk; he thought one of his ankles might be broken as it seemed to buckle when he stepped forward, but one step became another and he was moving. He was going into the veld, away from the policemen, away from the van. He knew what was going to happen; he supposed he had known it from the moment the van had stopped in the early dawn somewhere in the veld, with no houses near.

'Run, kaffer,' he heard the policeman shout. 'Come on, man, you're free now. Run.'

Khotso stopped. It's going to happen, he thought; you knew it happened to other people, you read stories about it, you heard people talking about it, but you never thought it would happen to you. It was going to happen to him, all right. And, no, he was not going to run. He was not going to make it easy – for them or for himself. He turned, very carefully, to look at where the three men were standing. He was right. The white man had a gun. Khotso hesitated, then began to walk, step by slow step, back to where he had come from.

Chapter 7

Four days after his release from detention, Jamie and Jenny were in London, installed in a tiny flat on the edges of Pimlico that belonged to a rich Johannesburg friend of Jenny's mother. 'Sarah says you can stay virtually as long as you like,' Mrs Dicey had told them when she met them off the flight from Cape Town. 'She says she won't be coming to London again until July; I suspect she uses it only to have affairs in, and her present man has a ranch in Bechuanaland.' Indeed, judging by the size of the bed, the flat did seem to exist mainly for sexual purposes and Mrs Dicey (a pretty and well-cared-for woman who looked very young to be Jenny's mother, except that her hair was too perfectly blonde) seemed completely unfazed (her sort of word, Jamie noted) by the fact her daughter would be living with a young man to whom she wasn't married.

'Mum asked me,' Jenny said, 'if you are a good lover.'

Jamie looked at Jenny in astonishment. He had never thought that these things might be a matter of comparative merit. He loved her, and he made love to her whenever there was the opportunity, or whenever she hinted that she might like to be made love to. Indeed, it was still a matter of astonishment – as well as delight – to him that she did want him to make love to her, and that she seemed to enjoy what happened as much as he did, indeed, that she sometimes suggested that they might try something she had heard about from one of her friends or read about in a book. Indeed, the straightforward way was still so strange and wonderful that the other things didn't matter very much, though they made Jenny laugh.

'What did you say to your mother when she asked you that?' Jamie asked.

'Well, I didn't tell her I cut my nails short now, just because of you.' Early on, after they had started sleeping together in Simon's and Adrienne's house, she had discovered one morning that her nails were bloody from having clawed his back as she came under him. He had had to wear a T-shirt under his ordinary shirt for several days until the wounds healed. Jenny told him that that kind of thing didn't always happen and he had helped her cut her nails from then on. It had been wonderful, but also very sore.

London wasn't easy, all the same. For one thing, it was grotesquely expensive. Jenny's father was giving her an allowance from a bank account he held in London, and Jamie still had his monthly allowance from his mother, though it translated into very little in English terms. For another, the weather was ghastly: he had supposed that spring might be beginning by the middle of March, but it was bleakly cold and drizzling. Weather forecasts said there was snow in Scotland and in the north, and he hoped that they might have snow in London too – he had never seen settled snow, even in the Sneeuberge – but the one night when it did snow what had fallen had turned to sludge by eight o'clock next morning. Especially when Jenny enrolled herself in the Chelsea Ballet School and started to disappear there every morning, he felt cooped up in the flat, and desperate for space to move in, for his eyes to move over. One Sunday, even though they couldn't afford it, even though it was a miserable day, he insisted that they take a train to the seaside, just so he could feel there was a horizon somewhere that wasn't buildings. Paradoxically, he still felt safest within four walls, and some days he hardly ventured out of the flat. Jenny persuaded him to walk with her along the embankment to the ballet school each morning, and then he would walk along the Thames for an hour or two. Even getting soaked through was preferable to staring out of the flat window at nothing other than roofs.

Worse than being poor and confined was that, every night, he would have nightmares; the details varied, but the constant theme was that a policeman had come into their room and he was helpless to fight back. Even locking the bedroom door wasn't an antidote; somehow the man would still be there at the bedside, wearing his blazer, carrying a gun, speaking reasonably but threatening horrible things, too horrible to remember when he would eventually wake, struggling and shouting. Jenny would hold him, restraining him first as best she could, weighing him down, hugging him, cuddling him, cradling his head, stroking his back until he was calm again. He would get out of bed, check that the front door of the flat was still chained and locked, check the windows, and would then come back to bed, locking the bedroom door too. 'I know, darling, I know. It's entirely irrational; nobody's coming for me here – but tell that to my nightmares. It's that man, Maasdorp; you know, I think it was he who murdered Willem. I think that story of his about the fish turning belly-up was to do with Willem. I think they murdered him, perhaps not meaning to, but still …'

Several times when he was out walking, Jamie formed an impression that he was being followed by someone. He would duck sideways into the entrance of a building to wait for the follower to catch up and pass him so he could check; but then he remembered he was only an amateur and these were professionals. If they didn't want to be seen, they probably wouldn't be seen.

He decided the flat in which they were living must be bugged and spent hours crawling around the floor when Jenny was away from the flat, trying to trace unexplained wires. It was clear that the letters that came from home were all being opened before they left South Africa; one could tell from the state of the glue and the messiness of the envelopes. They were reading his mother's letters and Peter's too.

He wanted to be on his own, and yet he couldn't bear

being on his own. If for any reason Jenny kept him waiting outside the Chelsea Ballet School, or if he hadn't gone to meet her and she came home to the flat even twenty minutes later than he had been expecting her, he would be cold and distant with her, knowing that he was being silly, yet unable to do anything about his own silliness. And she, in love with him, but also impatient, bossy, independent, would flare back at his cold silence: 'You don't own me, Jamie Cathcart. I'm not your possession. I'm not a toy.'

There seemed no point in trying to explain, so he wouldn't answer. He would go to sit on the sofa in the minute sitting room, or would lie on their bed and pretend to read, or he would clean his shoes again. In due course, one or the other would relent: Jenny would come to sit on the sofa with him, putting an arm around his shoulders, or would lie on the bed next to him, or he would walk up behind her where she was – say – washing her underclothes in the sink in the kitchen, and he would put his arms around her to cup her breasts, and she would lean back, and peace would be made.

'I'm sorry,' he would say. 'It's that bloody cell again. What do you think people are like when they've been inside for – say – eleven months? I was there for only four weeks.'

'Five, really,' Jenny would answer. 'And I guess they are pretty mad.'

'Do you think I'm mad?'

'Yes,' she said, turning to him, arms around his waist, but looking up at him. 'Yes. I think you are, a bit.'

Oddly enough, it seemed to help, being told he was a little mad. It explained the nightmares, even if it didn't stop them. It explained why he thought he was being followed when he went walking. It explained his ambivalence about the flat: he wanted to be safely inside the flat, yet he couldn't bear being cooped up in it.

The security police had held him for another five days

176

after he made his statement. He had begun to think that Maasdorp had lied entirely. There hadn't been any intention of releasing him if he made the statement; it had merely been a trick. They were (he convinced himself) going to hold him until he broke completely, or until he could be brought before a magistrate and charged – under the Suppression of Communism Act – for having been a member of a banned organisation, for having a copy of Lenin's book (why hadn't that been included in the statement or were they going to deal with that illegality by prosecuting him?), for helping Fred and Barney to the border; and by making the statement he had helped no one but the police themselves. Almost all his careful prison-cell routine had been abandoned: he cleaned his shoes still, he kept himself clean, he shaved, but there seemed no point in doing exercises or in walking around the yard for half an hour at a time. He had read the Bible the whole way through, twice; he picked over it periodically now, looking up this story, rereading this psalm.

Maasdorp never came back. When, eventually, Jamie was released, it was without explanation. Two policemen he hadn't come across before collected him from Bellville and drove him back into town where they kept him standing in the charge office at Caledon Square while they completed various bits of paperwork. Nothing was said about release, and he was certain that the paperwork was something to do with a charge. Even when they returned to him the possessions that had been taken away from him when he was first detained – his wallet, his keys, his belt, his pen, a diary – he did not believe them. This was still pretence. Eventually, one of the policemen turned to him to say, 'Well, Mnr Cathcart, to where do you wish us to take you?'

'What do you mean?'

'Mnr Cathcart, we are releasing you. We will deliver you back to your house. Where is that?'

'Aren't you charging me?'

The other policeman guffawed. 'No, Mr Cathcart, no – not unless you tell us something special you want us to charge you with.'

He was still not at all sure it wasn't a trick, a game to break him down further. 'Well, if you are going to release me, you'd better take me back to where you took me from,' and he gave the address of his room.

However, when he got there, he discovered that Mrs Peters had changed the lock on the door; peering through the window, he could see that the bed was not made up. 'I think my landlady has slung me out,' he said to the policemen; he felt helpless, standing there in the yard outside what had been his room. Where were his things, he wondered? He looked at his watch. Jenny might be at the ballet school now, he thought, but he couldn't turn up there with his little holdall, looking no doubt like a ghost. The policemen were still there waiting. Even they were looking nonplussed. 'Could you drop me up at Dr du Plessis's house?' he asked. He had got out of the habit of making decisions for himself.

Simon was at work, of course; Adrienne wasn't there either. 'Madam has gone shopping,' the servant, Madelie, told him, clutching to her bosom some washing she had been doing, and clearly terrified by the presence of the policemen. 'But Master can wait for her here, if he wants. Can I make Master coffee?'

He hated being called 'master', and Madelie knew quite well what his name was; it is the police who make her behave like a slave, Jamie thought. Oh, damn this country and the way it corrupts us all. 'I'll stay here,' he told the policemen. 'Mrs du Plessis will be back soon. She'll know what has happened to my stuff.'

The police drove off and Madelie became human again. She clutched his hands, then told him they were all so pleased to have him home again, and that Mrs Du Plessis and Jenny would be so pleased to see him. 'Those police, hey, man, they scare me, Master Jamie,' she said, and he knew that, even if he was still 'master', he was Jamie too. Madelie scurried off to make him the first decent cup of coffee he had had for weeks and, with a mug of coffee in his hands, he walked in the garden, still half-expecting the police to come back again to rearrest him, though he was exulting in even temporary freedom, bright flowers, lawns, shadows under trees and the mountains in the near distance.

Jenny had been with Adrienne; she had moved in there soon after Jamie had been arrested because she couldn't bear being on her own, she said. Adrienne and Simon had been marvelous: it was Madelie who had done all his washing and ironing, so he always had clean clothes, and Adrienne had driven her (Jenny, not Madelie – her words were tumbling over each other as she circled him in the garden, almost like a puppy welcoming him home again, so dark-haired and beautiful in her pink shirt and blue jeans that he could hardly believe that he deserved such approbation) to the various police stations each day so she could bring the food to him. That's where they had been that morning; they had driven out to Bellville to deliver some clean shirts and underpants. Had Jamie noticed the lipstick on his shirt collars? It had been Adrienne's idea; Jenny didn't like the kind of lipstick that came off, so she had borrowed Adrienne's to send those messages. Anyway, they handed the stuff over at Bellville, and then the dimwitted sergeant had said to them that 'the detainee in question' was no longer there, but had been taken away, and he wasn't going to tell them where, even if he knew. 'They all treated us, everywhere we went, as if we had just walked in a dog's mess in the pavement,' Adrienne said. 'You should have heard the things Jenny said to them. A couple of times I thought she'd get herself arrested too.' So they had driven to Caledon Square to find out where Jamie was and had been told he'd been released, but the bloody security police didn't know – or wouldn't say – where he was.

Yes, it was true (Jenny answered his questions, a little less breathless now). After his arrest, when Jenny went round to his flat to collect some clean clothes for him, Mrs Peters had told her that she was cancelling Jamie's tenancy of her room with immediate effect, and would she be so kind as to pack all Jamie's stuff up at once because she didn't want criminals living in her flat? Had she really changed the lock? Jenny laughed. My goodness, what a cow Mrs Peters had turned out to be. She had done more than just hint that she knew Jenny had been spending nights there, but Jenny had fought her and had managed to get back not just the deposit Jamie had paid, but the whole of that month's rent, in return for her clearing the room. Jamie's clothes and books – and his violin, which she had fetched from the music school – were waiting for him in Simon's and Adrienne's spare room, which was where she herself had been sleeping while her Jamie was in detention. Later that afternoon, after he had telephoned his mother and Peter to tell them he had been released, and as he lay next to her as she slept naked on the bed in that same room, he knew that he should be unutterably happy, yet could not shake off the sadness that had settled on his heart like a vulture. Whatever happened, he was going to die. He knew that now. He was going to die, she was going to die, everything had an ending.

If Jenny noticed the sadness, she did not let it deflect her. She had made some decisions for them both while he was in detention, she said. They were flying to London on Sunday night. She had already bought the tickets with money her father had given her, and she had used his connection with the airline to get them seats, though their names wouldn't appear on the passenger lists. Through her mother, she had arranged somewhere for them to live in London while they sorted themselves out. She had a reference from the ballet school which should enable her to get a place in a ballet school in London; South African dancers were apparently very welcome there still. She had talked to his mother on the telephone about his English uncle, Hamish, the lawyer, and they were going to visit him some time after they arrived in England. Hamish had been making a very English fuss about his nephew's detention without trial; apparently he had been to see a British cabinet minister and had written to the South African ambassador in London, as well as writing to the *Times*. Jenny had a copy of that letter to show him. His mother had sent it on from Grahamstown. No, neither Jenny nor his mother thought it would be sensible for Jamie to go to Grahamstown en route to Johannesburg and a flight to London, even though they knew he would want to see Peter – and his mother too, of course; the crucial thing was to get him out of the country while he still had a passport. Yes, of course Jenny had his passport: why did he think she had kept it in the first place? It was tucked away somewhere very safely with her own. If he had been keeping it himself, wouldn't the bloody security police have found it when they searched his room, and did Jamie think they wouldn't have confiscated it? And he wasn't to worry about money; she had enough money for the time being, enough for both of them, and they would worry about a job for Jamie when they got to England. He had his degree already, even if he didn't have a teacher's diploma yet and, if he didn't want to teach, surely his uncle would fix him up with something.

Jenny and Jamie went to have lunch with Hamish Cathcart during their second week in London. 'Will you be coming by taxi or tube?' he had asked them when he invited them to meet him at his club on Pall Mall at noon the next Wednesday. 'I hope you won't think this impertinent of me,' he said on the telephone to Jamie, 'but you'll need to be wearing a tie and a jacket – and of course I don't know your fiancée, but could she please not wear trousers? The club is rather old-fashioned about these things; women at all are something of an innovation.'

'I'm not sure I'm going to cope with this,' Jenny told

Jamie as they walked down from Piccadilly to Pall Mall and the club. They had avoided the temptation to tease Uncle Hamish – whom Jamie thought he remembered from his father's funeral, but wasn't sure – by having Jenny wear her shortest possible miniskirt ('so short,' she said, 'that if I bend over you can see my neck') and she was demurely dressed in a pinkish-brown tweed coat and skirt which she had bought the week before. Jamie wore his university blazer and tie. 'At least my shoes are shining,' he said.

In fact, Hamish Cathcart turned out to be thoroughly unstuffy. For one thing, though he was in his late fifties, there was no mistaking that he and Jamie were blood relatives, could in fact have been father and son, so similar were they in their spare frames and height. They had the same wide-spaced eyes and beaky noses, though what hair Hamish Cathcart still had on his head was grey, unlike Jamie's blonde mop. It was clear too that he had not entirely given himself over to Englishness; when he saw Jamie on the steps of the club, he had at first held out his hand and then, with a great grin, had hugged him. 'I'm sorry if a hug embarrasses you,' he had said, 'but, first, you look so like my brother – your father – and I have to say it seems pretty parsimonious to greet someone out of gaol with a handshake. So welcome, dear boy, and congratulations. It's about time someone in our family stood up to those bastards who have taken over what should be the greatest country in Africa. I've been saying rude things for years, but you're the first in the family actually doing things.'

'Honestly, I did very little,' Jamie answered.

'Well, that's not what the Foreign Office said to me.'

'What did they say?'

'Well, they never say very much, but they implied you were a dangerous revolutionary. I told them stuff and non-sense: it's the British have got apartheid so wrong. We should have been the first to stand up to say, "No more". Now, we may be too late.'

Just then an elegant old man in a dark pinstriped suit walked past. 'Ah, Ralph,' Hamish hailed him. 'Just the man. May I introduce to you my nephew and his fiancée? Jamie Cathcart has just been released from gaol. Jamie, Jenny, this is Sir Ralph O'Dowd – otherwise known as Mr Justice O'Dowd.'

'I've read about you, young man,' said the judge. 'I don't myself think it's completely accurate to compare detention without trial to a gaol sentence.' He shook hands with Jenny, then with Jamie. 'What are your plans now?' he asked Jamie.

'I'll need to get a job – if I can get a work permit, that is,' Jamie said.

'As what?'

'Eventually as a teacher. I have a degree, but I'm not qualified.'

'Teaching what?'

'English … Latin … History, I guess, though I don't know that much British history, except the Tudors.'

'Games-player?' The interrogation was brusque but pleasant.

'Not really; I mean, I play most things badly: cricket, tennis, rugby. I do play the violin too.'

The judge fished in his jacket pocket to produce a pair of pince-nez which he perched on his nose; Jamie had read about them, but had never seen a pair before, much less seen a pair in use. The judge looked quizzically over the top of the glasses at Jamie. 'What sort of level?'

'Competent amateur,' Jamie replied. 'I passed Grade 8 at school.'

'This is a very fortunate coincidence,' Sir Ralph said. 'Extraordinarily fortunate, possibly. It happens that I am Chairman of Governors of a certain prep school in South London, and it happens that last week, in the middle of the term, we had to get rid of the so-called Director of Music in a hurry – for the usual sort of reason. Clearly this wouldn't apply in your case.' The judge smiled appreciatively at

Jenny; Jamie had no idea what he was talking about. 'The headmaster told me yesterday he was desperately searching for a temporary replacement. Give me your telephone number and I'll arrange that you are seen – probably tomorrow.'

'I don't have a teacher's diploma.'

'Immaterial,' the judge said. 'If you can teach, you don't need one. This is not a state school.'

'And I don't have a work permit.'

'I imagine we should be able to get you one without too much difficulty. Latin, English, some History, young enough to blow a whistle on the games field, and a musician to boot: you may be exactly what the school needs. I play the fiddle myself, a bit; we must talk more about that one day soon.' He looked at his watch. 'I must go. It's been very good to meet you, young man,' he said as he shook hands with Jamie, 'and you too, young lady.' He bowed to Jenny and left them.

Jamie looked at his uncle who was finding it hard to contain his amusement. 'And to think,' Hamish said, 'all I was intending was a bit of a tease of an old friend who happens to be a High Court judge.'

'Is he serious?' Jamie asked. 'About the job, I mean?'

'Good God, yes. Fairlawn is one of the best prep schools in London.'

'Is that what it's called? He didn't say.'

'No, he didn't. It's another reason I know Ralph O'Dowd. My firm acts as the school's solicitors. Oh, you may not realise this, but when he said he "used to play the fiddle a bit" he meant that, when he came down from Cambridge, he had to choose between being a barrister and a concert violinist. He still plays in one of the best amateur orchestras in London.'

'Is that how things usually work here?' Jamie asked his uncle as he led them into a large dining room with panelled walls.

'No, not usually. Just occasionally, I suppose. And I

don't always approve, but one has to admit it's quite use-ful when one is a lucky recipient. For all its failings, the old-boy network does often help the talented. On the other hand, despite what newspapers say, it quite quickly stops helping if it turns out you don't have the talents after all.' He gestured with his head towards the corner table where Sir Ralph O'Dowd was already in intense con-versation with another distinguished-looking and elderly man in exactly the same sort of suit. 'D'you know who he's lunching with?' Jamie thought he might have seen the man's face in a newspaper somewhere, but couldn't remember a name. 'Well, it's a former government chief whip, a minister, a privy councillor, and so on; they must be plotting something. Ralph does an extraordinary amount of wheeler-dealing for a High Court judge.'

After what Jenny said afterwards was one of the best plain lunches she had ever eaten, Hamish took Jamie by the elbow to steer him to a reading room where they would have coffee. 'While the young lady is not with us,' he said to Jamie, 'there's something else I want to ask you – a bit impertinent, really, but I am your father's elder brother, and I guess sort of head of the family, if such a category still exists. Are you planning to marry Jenny? I hope you don't mind my asking, Jamie.'

'Not at all, Uncle Hamish.' Jamie stared down at his cof-fee cup. 'I feel I've somehow got out of the habit of mak-ing decisions. The answer is yes, probably, when I get round to asking her. I mean, we are living together, after all. I suppose that means you think I should marry her.'

'I'm presuming nothing, Nephew Jamie. What I'm try-ing to say to you is this: if you want to marry Jenny, I would be delighted – no, I would be honoured – if you wanted to marry her from our house. There's a nice church next door to the house, and I know the local clergy-man, and you could have the reception in our house; it's big enough for quite a big party.'

'I don't think we know enough people for a big party.'

'To tell the truth, Jamie, I always feel a bit guilty about your mother, your brother Peter and you; I didn't do enough for you when my brother died. I'd like to make up for that now. I'd get your mother and Peter air tickets to come over.'

'My mother's quite tricky about money.'

'But if you were getting married ...?' He left the question in the air because Jenny was making her way across the Turkish rugs to join them; but, soon afterwards, as Jenny and Jamie were leaving, he took Jamie by the elbow again to say, 'What I was saying: I meant it, you know. Do think about it.'

'Of course I will; I'm very grateful to you.'

'What was your uncle saying to you while I was in the loo?' Jenny asked as they walked back up towards Piccadilly.

'Oh, we were talking about this job at the prep school and our plans and so on,' Jamie said vaguely.

'Are we going to spend a weekend with them soon?' Jenny asked. During lunch Hamish had pressed them to come as soon as they could to meet the rest of the family in the Old Rectory near Beresford.

'As soon as you want, my Jenny.'

* * *

Was it possible, Jamie wondered later, sitting on the sofa in the tiny sitting room of the Pimlico flat and looking out at the grey light of the early dusk of what still wasn't quite spring, was it possible to get a disease of the will? As one could get a disease of the joints like arthritis, or a disease of the intercostal muscles? Since the security police had arrested him, he had made hardly a decision for himself; even the one decision he had made – to keep his silence about Barney and Fred – had been overturned by Maasdorp. The stringent routine he had imposed on himself in detention had in a way been a substitute for the exercise of will; because everything had to be done in order and to a particular pattern, decisions had been removed. He had contributed to his own destruction. Since then, Jenny had decided everything and he had decided nothing. Even today, it seemed possible he might have found a job without lifting a finger, and might merely nod his head and could be married to Jenny – which, as far as he could say that he wanted anything, he wanted with all his heart, except that all his heart no longer seemed capable of anything so decisive.

What Ralph O'Dowd said would happen did: there was a telephone call from the headmaster's secretary of Fairlawn Prep the next morning. He was interviewed by the headmaster (a lively and elegant man wearing a double-breasted blazer with quantities of silver buttons and a pink tie), shown round the school (which didn't take much time because its site seemed tiny to someone used to space and games-fields) and – before the end of the afternoon – offered a temporary post until the end of the summer term. He was to teach music to the senior classes, and English and Latin to ten-year-olds, to coach some rugger for the rest of this term (his disclaimers of any skill were met with a knowing wink from the headmaster who had 'played a bit of rugger himself' and so was knowledgeable about South African standards) and some cricket in the summer, and to do various duties. But it wasn't a boarding school, so he wasn't required to live in, and they didn't work weekends. Jamie had no idea whether the salary offered was reasonable or not; daily travel from Pimlico to Wimbledon was going to soak up some of it, certainly, but he and Jenny couldn't stay for ever in Sarah Witney's flat, and a flat south of the river might be affordable in due course, given that Jenny was still getting an allowance from her father. Jamie hadn't said anything to the headmaster about his living arrangements, but had merely said he was 'single, but engaged' (though he still hadn't asked Jenny to marry him), partly because he guessed that even a school in the metropolis might not approve of one of its young masters 'living in sin'. If things worked out, there was a good chance the job could continue and even become permanent – and if that happened, there was a small flat in the main school building which (the headmaster told him) was sometimes rented to a young member of staff for a nominal sum in return for a modicum of weekend care-taking duties.

To Jamie's surprise, the headmaster wanted him to start the very next day. 'I'm a bit short of tidy clothes,' Jamie confessed. 'I thought I'd better spend tomorrow shopping for a sports jacket, flannels and things.'

'You'll be fine as you are,' said the headmaster. 'However, may I ask if a small advance on salary would be appreciated?'

'Well, it really would be,' Jamie confessed. 'At the moment, I'm scrounging off my uncle and my fiancée.'

'Come into the accounts office,' said the headmaster, 'and we'll sort something out. Would fifty quid be enough to tide you over?'

'More than enough.'

Jamie was astonished, but realised that the generosity had a point when the handing over of ten five-pound notes was accompanied by a hearty, 'Well, see you at eight-thirty tomorrow morning, Mr Cathcart.'

Actually, working in a preparatory school suited Jamie's present state of mind very well indeed. Most of the teaching was old fashioned and undemanding, very similar to that which Jamie had experienced during his own schooldays; the Latin textbook guided him through the work almost on a daily basis, and whatever was happening to English teaching in the outside world obviously hadn't been communicated to the elderly head of English who gave him the following advice: of the six lessons of English his ten-year-olds were allocated a week, one was for spelling (lists were provided), one for punctuation, one for comprehension, one for composition, one for the reading of a class novel, and the last should be spent catching up on any area which he felt hadn't gone that well during the previous week. 'Myself,' the head of English (who, Jamie decided, must have taken his degree well before his own father was born) boomed, 'myself, I nearly always use the extra period for a bit more spelling and punctuation. By the time they get to Common Entrance, I want Fairlawn boys to have a reputation in their public schools as never making a grammatical error of any kind.' Very quickly, Jamie decided he would devote the extra lesson to reading poetry with the boys and getting them to try to write poetry; but he judged it sensible otherwise to do what he had been advised.

As far as the music lessons were concerned, however, there was no guidance of any kind. There was another teacher of music in the school, who played the hymn during morning prayers and loud recordings of opera in her classroom lessons, mainly – Jamie realised after the first week – to try to muffle the mayhem of the boys' behaviour in her classes. When Jamie tried to find out from the senior boys what they had done in lessons with his predecessor, there was such leering and nudging that he resolved never to raise the topic again. Instead, he brought his violin to school, found some simple sheet music of folk songs and jigs, spent laborious hours copying it out onto Roneo paper which he ran off on a copying machine, and set about teaching his classes – he saw two classes for three periods a week each – to read music. It transpired, quickly enough, that some of the boys were already learning instruments, and that in fact there was considerable musical talent in the school, though it found most of its expression not within the school itself but in lessons taken and commitments undertaken outside the school. So he encouraged them to bring their own instruments to class and to play them, and before the end of his first term had the beginnings of a chamber orchestra, admittedly with an odd combination of instruments. But for Jamie himself and for some of the boys this was rather more exciting than standing around half-frozen outside, pretending to play or to coach a game he had never found very interesting.

The other duties – supervising a daily lunch queue, once a week taking a class of boys whose mothers couldn't collect them until well after five o'clock and who therefore did some of their considerable quantities of homework at school, correcting exercise books (a never-ending chore, this), and seeing that the so-called library monitors did their work of tidying and re-shelving the books in the small school library – were in fact sufficiently mindless in their routine as suited the helpless passivity he had fallen into since his release from detention. These were things that were laid down as the duties of a young schoolmaster in a well-run and somewhat unimaginative school. Only the music made him think of anything remotely new.

The boys themselves were mainly very pleasant and generally well behaved. The fact that Jamie had been locked up in South Africa so recently gave him extraordinary credibility when it came to discipline – the boys seemed to think he was what they called a 'really hard man', and it took no more than a raised eyebrow to produce silence, even with boys he didn't actually teach. They all seemed very young to him – especially the ten-year-olds – and, though he got to know some of the older musicians better, his attention was still focused mainly inwardly. In the staff room, too, he did his work dutifully but somewhat abstractedly; when his colleagues tried to draw him out about his South African experiences, he refused, as politely as he could, to respond. Not being able to make sense of it himself made it hard for him to explain to outsiders what he was feeling.

Arranging something as apparently simple as the visit to his uncle's home in the Oxfordshire countryside turned out to be much more difficult than getting the job at

Fairlawn. The Cathcarts appeared to be busy every week-end for months in advance, usually because they were attending a wedding or visiting friends in Scotland – and the one weekend they were free turned out to be one that their sons couldn't manage after all. 'And, of course,' Sarah Cathcart said in what seemed to both Jenny and Jamie a very languid drawl, 'half the point of your coming to us is to enable you to meet the cousins.'

'I wonder if they don't want us to come to stay because we aren't married?' Jenny asked Jamie after the third attempt to fix a suitable date had foundered.

'I'm sure it's not that,' Jamie said. 'Anyway, even if it was, they could just put us in separate rooms. Uncle Hamish said they had seven bedrooms. No, it's just their being English, isn't it? I mean, the English just don't drop in, as we do at home. Is it something to do with over-crowding? Or just to do with good manners?'

In fact, when the Cathcarts tried again to get their nephew and his girl to spend a weekend in Beresford, Jenny and Jamie were busy themselves since they had been invited to a gathering of some of the South African political exiles in North London. They really wanted to go, especially as Jamie had heard a rumour that Barney Jacobse was some-where in London, though he had no idea where he might be found. Even if Barney were not at the party, someone there might have an address or a telephone number. Having got themselves a little lost on the underground (they caught a train going towards Edgware and not High Barnet, so had to backtrack, and then had trouble with the *A-to-Z* before they by chance turned into the right street, but still had to work out which side of the street the house was on) they arrived very late at the party. By then it was well under way and spread over the whole house – all sorts of groups and cliques in fierce discussion or animated flirtation or passionate determination to get plastered, while upstairs a variety of couples had begun to firm up diplomatic relationships. Jenny and Jamie deposited their

191

contribution to the feast – a bottle of Spanish red wine – on a table that held quantities of similar bottles, the better-quality wines mainly empty, the rest half full, and a motley array of dirty glasses, then worked their way through the various darkened rooms, introducing themselves to their hosts, greeting a few acquaintances, meeting other people they had heard about but not met, picking up snippets of conversation and slices of propositions, all the while looking out for Barney Jacobse and Fred Carelse in particular.

Eventually, abandoning Jenny so that she could continue a conversation with a tiny but beautiful young man she remembered from the Cape Town ballet school, Jamie found Barney in the kitchen. He was holding forth as usual, left hand cupped over his heart, right hand emphasising each point made, and his court gathered around – two rather plain young white women (quite obviously English), a black man whom Jamie hadn't seen before but who he guessed was South African, another very tall black man whom Jamie guessed was West African, and a very glamorous Indian woman in a silk sari with gold edging. Spotting Jamie, Barney rushed over, grabbed him by both hands and dragged him into the group. 'Now, my friends,' he said loudly as he introduced Jamie to each person in turn, 'what I was saying about white liberals doesn't apply to this man because he's my friend; he's the one who took me to the border when I escaped. This is an honourable white man.'

'Come on, Barney,' said Jamie, embarrassed as well as flattered. 'You'll be elevating me into an honorary Coloured next.'

'You are, Jamie, you are. You've served your time in detention; you are now one of the oppressed.'

'Barney, four or five weeks in detention is hardly a prison sentence, and I'm one of the privileged, not one of the oppressed.'

Barney looked at him; he had been showing off, but he was being serious now. 'Four weeks was too long for Willem

192

Bearer,' he said. He took Jamie by the hand and drew him away from the group to a corner of the kitchen, saying as he did so, 'Sorry, my friends, I need to talk to the whitey.' When they were alone in the corner, he said quietly, 'Did you make a statement?' There was no accusation in his voice.

'I signed a statement they had prepared. They wanted me to say I knew the names of everyone in the group, but I wouldn't.' Jamie's voice was miserable. He was ashamed of what he was saying, and even more ashamed of what he wasn't saying. 'Where's Fred? Is he here?'

Barney shook his head. 'No, he's gone straight off to Canada. One of his brothers is there. Fred's much more interested in business than in politics.'

'I'm sorry I made any statement at all.'

Barney was matter of fact. 'Nearly everybody makes a statement in the end. Five weeks is longer than most people manage. You say they prepared the statement for you?'

'Yes.'

'They already knew what they wanted you to say?'

'I think so.'

Barney dropped his voice even lower. 'Are you still with that girl, Jenny?'

'Of course. She's here, next door. Come and say hello; she'll want to see you.'

Barney shook his head vigorously. He was finding it hard to look at Jamie. 'No, man, no. Listen, Jamie, this will be hard for you, but you know that people are saying she made a deal with the police to get you out of detention.'

'That's simply not true.'

'I'm afraid it may be true. Jamie, we have very good contacts; I really shouldn't be telling you this.'

'Barney, this is bullshit. She wouldn't do it. It's just a smear. Anyway, why do it?'

'To get you out. People are also saying now she told the police about Willem.'

'But that's crazy – and impossible. We thought Willem wasn't involved; we thought he despised politics.'

'He did, but he's dead now. Jamie, all I'm saying to you is: be careful of that girl. She may be an informer now.'

Jamie looked at Barney, no longer seeing anyone he admired, much less someone he liked, but a man so twisted by conspiracy that he would believe anything, no matter how absurd. He shook his head. 'No,' he said. 'No. I don't have to be careful; she didn't do a deal with anyone. She would have told me.'

Over Barney's shoulder Jamie saw Jenny coming into the kitchen, clearly looking for him. He pushed past Barney, saying as he did so, 'Look, there she is. I'll get her – you can talk to her yourself.' He walked over to Jenny and put the back of his hand very gently against her cheek. She was smiling at him and he felt his whole heart go out to her; he bent suddenly and kissed her swiftly.

'That's nice,' she said. 'What's that for? I've not been away long.'

'I love you,' he said. 'Come and talk to Barney.' But when he turned Barney was not there. 'Where's Barney?' he asked the group he had been talking to.

The black South African indicated the other door of the kitchen with his head; 'he went out,' he said. Beckoning Jenny to come with him, Jamie tried to follow Barney but could find no sign of him anywhere. Systematically, he searched through the various rooms, but Barney was nowhere there. Was he in the lavatory? he wondered. He didn't think Barney would be one of those cavorting in bedrooms upstairs. Eventually, he sought out the hostess of the party; she told him, vaguely, that Barney had had to leave early: 'We think he got some sort of message he had to go somewhere.'

Going back, Jamie found Jenny standing on her own, a half-empty glass of wine in her hand. 'Are you all right?' he asked.

'I don't know why, but I'm not terribly enjoying this. It seems to be very cliquey.'

Jamie nodded. He didn't like this at all; there was something unpleasant happening, a scratchiness, a mood of snide backbiting. Barney's departure had dismayed him; did he really believe what he had said about Jenny? Jamie had been warned – even in Cape Town – about the politics of the exile community. Political exiles – and not only of the South African variety – mostly felt guilty at having removed themselves from the place of real danger and into a safe place where, in effect, position and influence became substitutes for activity and organisation. More time was spent honing metaphoric knives for the backs of powerful colleagues and co-conspirators than on learning to use real rifles. Still, how extraordinary to find someone as clever – as wisely wide-ranging – as Barney had always seemed to him to be, wasting his time spreading lies about someone as loyal and good-hearted as Jenny. She wasn't in any way anyone's political rival. What conceivable good would besmirching her do anyone? What would Barney gain from spreading rumours?

'Yes,' Jamie said. 'I've had enough too. Let's go.' Without bothering to say farewell or thanks to their hosts – the husband seemed to have disappeared anyway, probably upstairs, Jamie guessed, and the wife was swaying from room to room, moving dirty glasses from one place to another and slurring her inconsequential speeches – Jamie and Jenny collected their coats from the pile in the downstairs lavatory and slipped out into the chilly London evening.

When they were safely in the almost empty underground train going back towards Pimlico, Jenny turned to Jamie to ask, 'What upset you at the party?' She looked very pale in the stark light of the compartment and there were shadows under her eyes that he did not think he had noticed before.

'I didn't enjoy meeting Barney again,' he said, brusquely.

'Is that why he rushed off like that? I saw him talking to you one moment, and then he was gone.'

'He said something to me.'

'What?'

'About you.' She was pale, he noted, though there were two patches of red on her cheeks now.

'What did he say about me?' Jenny asked fiercely.

'I don't want to tell you. Anyway, they're lies.'

'What lies?' She was still fierce, but there was something else in her voice now that made him take her left hand into the grasp of both his own hands.

'Jenny, he said you did a deal with the security police to get me out of detention.' He stared at her, and she stared back, her pale face very still. Her chin, tilted up a fraction so she could look at him, did not wobble, but her mouth tightened and then, suddenly and mysteriously, almost magically, two huge teardrops appeared and rolled down her cheeks. She stuck out her tongue to catch one, but the other fell from her chin on to the back of his hand. She said nothing, but looked at him still. 'Jenny, it's not true, is it? You didn't do a deal with the ... with those people, to get me out of gaol. Did you?'

Carefully, Jenny took her hand out of Jamie's grasp and turned to look ahead of her down the carriage at the rows of almost empty seats. There were two other couples up ahead of them, both middle-aged, neither talking to each other. The train roared and rattled its ungainly way into London, and the cold wind whistling into the compartment made one glad of an overcoat, though this was meant to be spring.

'Jenny,' Jamie said quietly. 'I think you'd better tell me.'

She did not turn to look at him, but said very quietly, 'I thought they weren't going to let you out. There was a rumour going around that you would be charged with ... oh, all sorts of things, and then another rumour that you were being so stubborn that they were going to hold you until they broke you completely; they have done that to some people, Jamie. I kept on thinking of Willem and what they'd done to him.'

'I know,' said Jamie. 'What did you tell them?' He

should, he thought, be angry, but he wasn't: what he felt was something else, something enormously protective, almost – he guessed – what a mother might feel towards a child.

'I telephoned Caledon Square, and I said who I was, and could I talk to someone? And they picked me up after ballet one day and drove me to a parking place in Hout Bay.'

'Who's "they"?'

'I don't know the driver of the car, but the man who sat in the back to talk to me was Captain Maasdorp. Jamie, he was horrible; I was so scared.'

Before he could stop himself, Jamie burst out, 'Did that shit ... did he touch you, or anything?'

'No, he just looked; he stared – at my breasts, at my legs. He was ... lascivious. He kept on asking things.'

'What things?' Jamie demanded.

'He wanted to know if we slept together – things like that.'

'If I ever see him again, I think I'll kill him.' Jamie was almost astonished at the sudden rage of his own jealousy. He had not, he thought, been a jealous or even possessive lover. At parties, for instance, when other men gathered round Jenny, or even when he saw that she was flirting with someone, or when she was on stage, dancing, he hadn't minded particularly, indeed, was invariably proud of her lithe beauty, not least because he knew she would soon enough be with him again, and their intimacy was such that it could not easily be loosened. But now, imagining Maasdorp leering at her made it seem that he could almost taste his own rage. 'What did you tell him?' he asked

'Not very much, Jamie. I am sorry now I told him anything.'

'What?'

'Just about the post office box we opened, and about the discussion group, and about driving Barney and Fred to the border.'

'Did you give names?'

'Well, just Barney and Fred, and maybe one or two others in the group, but I didn't know many names. It was nicknames, really.'

Jamie was silent. So that was why Jenny's own name hadn't been in the statement. 'And then what?' he asked.

'They drove me back.'

'Where to? The ballet school?'

'No, they dropped me near the women's res. I don't think anyone saw.'

Well, Jamie thought, it seems likely someone had, unless Barney's people had a plant inside the police force, which seemed pretty unlikely. 'Did Maasdorp ask you about Willem Bearer?'

'Yes, he did, but I said he was only a musician and had hated politics. They knew about him; they kept calling him a "moffie". Maasdorp was gloating.'

'Did he say anything about seeing you again? When they dropped you?'

'No, but I asked them when they were going to let you out. I'd said I would tell them things only on condition.'

'And you trusted them?' He tried not to let bitterness affect his speech. He leaned forward to rest his forehead on the seat in front of them.

'I was doing it for you. That was why I wanted us to leave so soon. I was frightened of what he might do. He questioned you too, didn't he?'

'Yes,' he said. 'Yes.' He took his forehead off the cool metal in front of him and sat back silently as the train buffeted through North London, seeming to rush furiously from one station to another, slowing down inexplicably sometimes, then rushing ahead again. Jealous rage had fallen away. He turned to look down at Jenny, sitting next to him, head slightly bowed, hair covering her cheeks so her eyes weren't visible, hands folded in her lap. Gently, he pulled her hair back so he could see her; she was crying still, very quietly, staring ahead. He felt his own eyes filling with tears. 'Will you marry me?' he said.

She seemed not to hear at first. He reached over into her lap, took both her hands in his, and said again, 'I said, will you marry me? Must I say "please"?'

Her eyes were very red; the mascara had run, and her nose was running. 'You don't have to marry me,' she said. 'I would still have done it.'

'Do you want to borrow my hankie?' he asked.

'Is my nose running?' she asked, staring at him. He nodded. 'Yes,' she said. 'Yes. I want to borrow your hankie – and, yes, I will marry you. Are you sure you want to? You're not just being kind?'

'I'm not kind. I hadn't realised how much you love me – or how much I love you. Yes, I want to marry you. If we don't get married, I don't know what I'll do. Die, I think.'

'You're not cross I told the police?'

'Not cross; I wish you hadn't, but that's not the point. It's done. You did it. I know why you did it. We'll have to live with that. I have to live with the fact that I made a statement to the police. We both have to live with that. Barney can think you're an informer if he wants to. I know you're not. None of that's important any more. You really will marry me? Promise.'

'Actually, I think I'm probably married to you already, aren't I?'

* * *

When he telephoned his uncle, Hamish Cathcart, to ask if they might take him up on the offer to be married from the Old Rectory in Beresford, probably in the summer, perhaps June or July, so that Jenny's mother and father and his own mother and Peter might be able to attend, the reaction was so warm, generous and instantaneous that Jamie was able, afterwards, to reassure Jenny. She had wondered why they didn't simply go off to find a priest who would want to get them out of a state of sin and legally into bed together (they were in bed at the time, intertwined – as lovers should be, Jamie said – unable to distinguish mine and thine), or even to a registry office. Did they really need to go through a proper wedding with flowers and things, especially as she wasn't sure that Jamie's aunt and uncle were really as hospitable as all that? They were so happy as they were; all they wanted now was to be legal – especially because of passports and things. (Jenny had come into the country easily on her British passport; Jamie had had a harder time persuading the immigration officer that he was merely a tourist visiting his English family with his girlfriend. But, fortunately, the prep school had managed to pull enough strings to get Jamie a proper – albeit temporary – work permit, and his status in the country was thus more settled.) Jamie however wanted a proper wedding, though without too many frills; though he didn't tell Jenny, he also wanted the exile community to know that he regarded the rumours about Jenny as merely vicious.

Moreover, he wanted his brother there, and his mother too, and he was worried that they wouldn't be able to afford the journey without Uncle Hamish's help with the fares. With a pocket full of coins – though the flat had a telephone, they tried not to use it – he had gone to a telephone kiosk in a local pub to telephone Grahamstown with the news of their engagement. His mother had been so pleased, she said, so thrilled that they were going to settle down – and settle down, she hoped, in England; South Africa was becoming a hateful country, she said: no one had any respect for each other any more – English, Afrikaans, black, white. Peter, having heard his mother's end of the conversation and realising the cost, was more laconic, but even over that distance and despite the time delays in transmission, Jamie could hear his brother's unfeigned delight.

'Are you happy, brother?'

'Yes.'

'Then we'll try to come over. Give us a date as soon as you can.'

Having agreed on the telephone that Jamie and Jenny would marry from their house in the summer, Hamish Cathcart telephoned two days later. It would be sensible, he said, if they could actually meet in London somewhere to talk over details; the young people might not realise this, but organising a wedding required much planning and Sarah was giving him a hard time over arrangements already. He (Hamish) had a suggestion: he and Sarah had four tickets to the City Opera production of Gluck's opera, *Orfeo & Eurydice*, the following week. They had been planning to take one of Hamish's partners and his wife, but at the last moment they had dropped out – family illness. Would Jamie and Jenny like to come in their place? It was very short notice, he realised, and the production had had very mixed notices, to say the least, but they might enjoy the experience. He would take them out to dinner afterwards, to his favourite Italian restaurant, and they could at last sort out a weekend for a visit to Beresford, and then settle the preliminary details of the wedding.

Jamie knew the music of the Gluck opera, though he had never been to an actual opera before; nor, it transpired, had Jenny, though she had been so often to the ballet. 'We'd love to come with you,' he said. 'Do we have to dress up? I don't have a dinner jacket.'

'Well, some people will be "black tie", and I probably will myself – mainly to please my dear wife, who thinks these things must be done properly. But if you haven't got a dinner jacket, don't for goodness' sake go out and hire one; just wear a suit. Jenny will dress up, presumably. Shall we say we'll meet outside the theatre, then, for a drink at seven? Will that be convenient?'

Jamie didn't actually own a suit – when she packed for him in Cape Town, Jenny had decided that his old school suit had better be given to the Salvation Army – and wore to work either the sports jacket and flannels he had bought with Mr Philips' advance on salary at the prep school or his old university blazer. Jenny didn't have a problem, of course; she had a knack with clothes, inherited from her mother, and she made the oddest garments seem special, just by combining or contrasting colours, or tying a scarf round her hips. Watching her dress one evening, before they left to meet some English friends Jenny had met at the ballet school at a local pub, Jamie had said, 'I suppose the reason it doesn't matter what you are wearing is that most blokes spend their time mentally undressing you.'

'Most women look better dressed than undressed.'

'Not you,' Jamie said lazily.

'You're biased,' she said. 'Are you sure you want to go to this party?'

'I know what I'd rather do.'

She crossed to the bed to kiss him. 'We've just done it,' she said. 'And we can do it again when we come back. Don't be so lazy.'

The question of the suit was solved by Jenny's reminding him that, if he wanted to get married in a church and have a reception in a grand house in the country, he was either going to have to hire morning dress ('I'm not hiring anything,' Jamie said firmly) or he was going to have to buy a decent grey suit.

'They are expensive, aren't they? I looked when I bought that sports jacket for school and they seemed either tatty or exorbitant.'

'I have a plan,' Jenny said. 'I saw a place near Leicester Square that sells suits people have ordered from proper tailors but haven't collected. People your shape tend to go to tailors anyway and don't buy things off the shelf. Let's try that first. It'll be my wedding present to you.'

An hour in the shop under Jenny's critical eye had accomplished the finding of a dark grey suit – 'with a waistcoat,' she insisted: 'I won't marry you in a church if you don't wear a waistcoat' – made by a famous tailor from Savile Row for someone who had, for some reason, not collected it. With some lengthening of sleeves and trouser-legs, some nipping at the waist of both trousers and jacket, it fitted Jamie almost as well, said Jenny as she surveyed him before they set off for the opera, as if he had actually gone to the Savile Row tailor himself, and had paid ten times as much as she had paid. She had even per-suaded Mr Lipmann to throw the alterations in free.

'You look wonderful – sort of Spanish,' Jamie told Jenny in the lift. She was wearing a black skirt, very full, and a dark blue blouse, with a man's white silk scarf (also found at Lipmann's, in a grubby cardboard box in a corner, and thrown in by Mr Lipmann as part of the bargain) tied round her waist.

'Thank you, kind sir,' she said and, as they left the lift, she did a pirouette for him so that her full skirt flew up round her.

'If you do that in the theatre lobby, various old men are going to have heart attacks,' Jamie said.

* * *

The opera required even more than the usual suspension of disbelief. Jamie was glad they had seats at the very front of the upper circle. From there he could watch the violin-ists when he wanted to take his eyes off the hero and heroine, whose voices were clearly superb but who seemed to him both too middle-aged and too portly to be entirely convincing as desperate lovers. He did however notice, with interest and also with pleasure, that his aunt, despite her very English manners, dress and languid voice, took firm hold of Hamish's hand as the lights went down; it seemed reasonable therefore that he should take Jenny's too. She seemed entranced, leaning forward against the rail; it was, he realised, not entirely an artistic interest when she whispered to him, 'Every time Orpheus takes a breath I think the buttons of his waistcoat are going to pop.'

'And what about Eurydice's bosom?' he whispered back.

'I thought you said you didn't like big boobs.'

He smiled back at her. 'Concentrate on the music,' he mouthed, and turned his own attention from the stage to the orchestra pit as the conductor, small and round with a bald patch almost like a tonsure, but as energetic as an athlete, enticed the full gloomy passion of the first two acts from orchestra and singers.

When the dancers came on, Jenny turned to him, smiling brilliantly. 'This is more like it,' she whispered and turned back to the stage. When, during Act Three, Orpheus finally submits to Eurydice's pleas that, if he doesn't look at her, she will think he no longer loves her and then, when he does, collapses (rather carefully, given her age, shape and costume) back to the floor of Hades for ever and ever, Jamie gave Jenny his handkerchief, partly because he needed to use it himself. Love however intervenes and – in the best eighteenth-century manner – death is overcome and Orpheus and Eurydice are reunited. Love has triumphed – and the dancers celebrate accordingly.

'I hope you enjoyed that,' Hamish Cathcart said to them as they worked their way through the West End crowds towards the restaurant.

'It was marvellous,' Jenny said. 'The costumes especially, and the music is so romantic, isn't it? Almost Gothic. I'm not sure I like the happy ending, though; it seems a bit tacked on, doesn't it?'

'The eighteenth-century poets and playwrights often did that – they rewrote Shakespeare tragedies to have happy endings: Cordelia isn't really strangled, Lear doesn't really die and so on. It was the way they saw the world – or the way they thought the world should be,' Jamie said, trying not to sound too pompous in his learning.

'I do wish,' Sarah Cathcart drawled, 'it were possible to have slim singers. I guess to be able to have voices big enough for opera requires big frames too, but they really were rather plump, weren't they?'

'I thought you would approve of middle-aged lovers, darling,' Hamish smiled at her.

'My dear,' she said, dryly, 'it was their figures not their age I was commenting on.'

'If I ever have to go down to Hades, Jamie, will you come to fetch me?' Jenny kept tight hold of his arm, every now and then skipping to keep up with him as he followed his uncle's and aunt's briskly English pace down the pavement.

'Not if you get as fat as that Eurydice,' he answered, laughing at her as she danced along the pavement beside him. 'I wouldn't be strong enough to carry you back.'

Hamish Cathcart was clearly not only a regular customer in the restaurant, but a favoured one. Though it was very crowded, there was a good table reserved for them, and the owner himself took their order at once. Hamish spoke to him in what sounded to Jamie like fluent Italian; Sarah leaned towards Jamie and Jenny. 'He loves showing off his Italian; I gather it sounds very good but is actually rather ungrammatical.' She looked affectionately across the table at him.

'When did he learn Italian?'

'We've been going to the same villa in Tuscany every summer for years. I think we should probably buy it. We pay out more in rent than we would to a bank, but it is perfect for us and the children, and as grandchildren come along it will be even better. You must come to stay.'

'That would be lovely,' Jenny said. 'I've always wanted to go to Italy. Is that why you like opera?'

'I suppose there's a connection. Now Hamish is going to tell us what to eat.' The conversation with the owner seemed to have ended.

'Yes,' said Hamish. 'Now, though it may seem rude to

start with me, let me tell you that I'm going to have a proper Italian meal: I'm going to have a plate of pasta to begin, then veal – Mr Traversi here tells me it's very good, not the nasty white stuff, but proper meat – and then a real Italian pudding. And I think you should have the same, though of course you can have what you want from the menu.'

'Hamish,' his wife said firmly, 'you know that if I start with spaghetti, even a small plate of spaghetti, I'll eat nothing else. Of course, you children must eat properly, but, Mr Traversi, would you think me very rude if I began with a small salad, then had a small piece of veal with your usual wonderful vegetables, and then had some of your homemade ice-cream?'

'Very good, Lady Sarah,' the owner said, making a note of her order.

'I didn't know you were "Lady" Sarah,' Jamie said. He had called her 'Aunt' once, and she had told him very firmly that she was to be called 'Sarah' and on no account 'Aunt'. 'Uncle Hamish hasn't become Sir Hamish without my noticing, has he?'

'Good heavens, no,' Hamish joined in. 'Sarah has the title, not me.'

'We don't make a fuss about it,' she answered. 'My father was – well, still is – rather grand, that's all.'

'A duke?' asked Jenny.

'Not a very important one,' Sarah said, clearly wanting no more discussion of the subject. 'Now, my dear, choose your own food, and then may we talk about more serious matters? For instance, now I have set eyes on you, I can ask whether you might like to think about wearing as your wedding dress my own. I had hung on to it in case we had our own daughter, but we had sons only, and their wives weren't the right shape. You are – and though I say so myself, my wedding dress is very beautiful too.'

'Wait until you see it,' said Hamish. 'It was made in Paris, and is mainly pearls. I was jolly glad I didn't have to pay for it. Sarah looked wonderful; there was a portrait of her wearing it in *Vogue*.'

'It sounds fabulous,' said Jenny. 'I'm longing to see it. I thought I'd probably have to make my own dress.'

'You really don't have to wear it if you don't want to.'

'I'm sure I shall, but I had better try it on, hadn't I?'

'My dressmaker will alter it if needs be, but you look the right size to me. Now, other matters: dates and caterers.' She got a black notebook out of her handbag, and then a silver pencil.

Mr Traversi coughed politely. 'Oh goodness, I've stopped you ordering. I am sorry,' Sarah said. 'How rude of me; it's just that I am, if I may say so, very excited about this wedding – not having a daughter of my own, you see. If I get bossy, you must say so.'

'You are always bossy, my darling,' Hamish smiled at her. 'Jamie, Jenny, order. Jenny first.'

'Well,' Jenny said. 'I think I want exactly the same as you.'

'Me too,' said Jamie.

'If we can order a meal in an Italian restaurant as peacefully as that, we should be able to arrange something as simple as a wedding without any trouble. Mr Traversi, I think we shall have a bottle of champagne to begin with, and then a bottle of that house special of yours, the one from Montepulchiano.'

And so they ate and drank, and Lady Sarah took them efficiently and firmly through the details of their wedding, noting decisions in her book, and telling Hamish firmly what he would be required to do, though she was going to do most of the work herself. At the end of the evening, when she took Jenny off with her to powder their noses, Hamish leaned across the table to say to his nephew, 'Well, young man, you and your fiancée have clearly made a huge hit with Sarah. It's not everyone she likes, either,' he said, grinning wryly. 'She's quite choosy, Sarah; I've never quite worked out why she chose me – just my luck really.'

Looking at him, Jamie remembered his own father with such vividness that he still seemed almost alive. 'Didn't her family approve of you?'

'A poor South African boy in a London solicitors' office? You're joking.'

'But you had a Cambridge degree ...'

'Brains are dangerous. I've heard Sarah's father say approvingly of someone impossibly stupid, "At least one knows where one is with her".'

'How did you persuade them?'

'I didn't – Sarah did. She told them she was pregnant.'

'Was she?'

Hamish grinned naughtily. 'We hadn't even been to bed together, but Sarah had made up her mind. I think her father knew she'd win; her mother was the tricky one. She and Sarah fought all her childhood, apparently.'

'I'm not sure I'd fight with Sarah.'

'From experience, I wouldn't advise it; but even dukes' daughters are human. You'd be surprised how many people assume they aren't.'

'Do you get on with her family now?'

'Oh, very well: I've grown into their shape, I suppose. I'm a sort of chameleon – actually, a stick insect is a better description. I suit myself to my surroundings, really. Sarah's father and I are very good friends these days; and her mother has learned to keep the peace now she's old.'

'You are both being very generous to us: it's so kind of Sarah to offer Jenny the wedding dress,' Jamie said.

'It's a great pleasure. If I may tell you what you clearly know already, Jenny is a stunner: beautiful and funny – a rare combination. Her parents will come to the wedding, presumably?'

'Oh, I should think so. They are divorced, but I think they'll both come.'

'I'm afraid divorce is the new condition of our times,' Hamish said. 'It's one of the reasons I can afford restaurants like this: I do much of my business helping people to get divorced. I don't somehow think you're the divorcing kind, are you, Jamie Cathcart?'

'No,' he answered. 'Like you and Sarah, I guess.'

'Oh, Sarah would never let me divorce her, even if I wanted to,' Hamish smiled. 'But yes: "for better or worse …"'

Jamie replied, ' "Till death us do part." I'll mean it when I say it.'

'Of course,' said his uncle as he rose to greet Sarah and Jenny. 'Now it's time for me to put you two in a taxi and for Sarah and me to remind the head porter at the club that we have taken a room there for the night.'

'It's been a wonderful evening,' Jenny said, kissing first Hamish and then Sarah. 'I am so happy to be marrying into your family – and I'm longing to see the wedding dress. You are incredibly kind.'

* * *

Ten days later, coming back to the flat in Pimlico from the Chelsea ballet school, but having made a detour to buy vegetables for supper and a big bunch of flowers to take with her and Jamie as a thank-you present for the Cathcarts (with whom they were due to spend the weekend in the Old Rectory, Beresford, West Oxfordshire), Jenny Dicey had just stepped from between two parked cars to cross Lupus Street, when a white Ford car, stolen an hour earlier from south of the river, and driven by an otherwise unidentified white man – thought by one passer-by to have been in his mid-thirties, stockily built, with short hair – sitting next to another man, also unidentified but of Indian or dark Italian or Spanish colouring, and moving at a speed variously esti-mated as forty, fifty and sixty miles an hour, had knocked her down and had then sped on, not stopping. Even though a taxi tried to follow it, the car got clean away and was found next day, again south of the river, burned out in a run-down housing estate.

Neither the driver nor his passenger was ever identified by the police. One senior policeman told Hamish Cathcart ('off the record, of course') that there was something very peculiar about the whole business – 'almost professional' was the phrase he used – though Hamish, after consulting Sarah, decided that he wouldn't pass the comment on to Jamie.

After a week, the senior registrar of St George's Hospital, to which Jenny had been taken by ambulance after the accident, told Jenny's parents and her fiancé that there was simply no chance of her ever regaining consciousness. Even if by some miracle he was wrong and she did, her spine had been shattered by the force of the collision and the brain damage was such that consciousness would be an unkindness. Nevertheless, even after all the support systems had been turned off, her heart and lungs were so powerfully trained that they kept working for three more days before the doctor finally pronounced her dead and released her body for burial.

At Hamish's suggestion, she was buried in the church-yard of St Agnes's Church, next to the Old Rectory in Beresford.

PART TWO

Chapter 8

One of the effects of the lecture which Huston Stillman had arranged for Jamie Cathcart to give in the Department of Inter-Cultural Studies on the work of the Sturrock Foundation and on his ideas about the future funding of education in a post-apartheid South Africa was a general awareness that he was back in existence. Some contemporaries clearly didn't know he had ever been away, but had merely assumed he had dropped out of public view after his release from detention – something which often happened, and which was clearly part of the intimidatory purposes of solitary detention. Some hadn't realised he had become a prohibited immigrant or, more accurately, that he was one of the few people carrying a British passport who was required to have a visa in order to enter South Africa, and that requests for visas from dangerous people like him were routinely refused – usually not immediately, but long enough after the application was made to make even application seem futile. Planning to visit therefore became a pointless exercise since every visa application demanded a reason and the reason had usually disappeared long before the application was refused.

In part, his disappearance from the communal memory had been the result of Jamie's own decision, after Jenny's death, to break almost all his ties with South Africa and with things and people South African. Friends who had heard of Jenny's death and who tried to commiserate face to face were met by Jamie's stony-eyed disapprobation, particularly if he thought they might have been among those who believed – or who had spread – the rumours that she had become a police

211

informer. Even people who had been as close to Jenny and Jamie as Simon and Adrienne du Plessis had their letters of agonised grieving acknowledged weeks later, with a laconically formal note.

Of course, he had kept in touch with Peter and with his mother too, when they had returned to Grahamstown after the funeral but, for the first few years, he had neither the funds nor indeed the desire to go home. And then it seemed sensible to keep away because more people like him, some even less politically involved than he had been, were being picked up by the security police and treated more and more roughly, in detention and elsewhere. Less pretence was maintained that there was no torture in detention. Despite protests locally and internationally, ninety-day detention became one-hundred-and-eighty-day detention to save the police even the farcical need to release and re-detain. When his South African passport expired, it took him several months to bother to send it to the embassy for renewal. More months passed, during which time he heard only that his request had been referred to Pretoria. Nearly a year later, a letter came to inform him that renewal of his passport had been refused; no reason was given. He was in effect stateless; but he wasn't going anywhere, and even the requirement that he report occasionally to his local police station, which had originally been imposed when he had first been given a work permit, was officially allowed to lapse.

After he had been in the country five years, he gave the correspondence he had had with the South African authorities to Hamish Cathcart; Hamish spoke to what he called 'friends in high places'; Jamie was called to a meeting with someone from the immigration branch of the Home Office; and, shortly afterwards, with very little fuss and formality, James Frederick Cathcart became a British citizen. Even though he still didn't plan to travel anywhere, he applied for, and was granted, a British passport.

Perhaps only those who have been stateless, or who have crossed a border without documents, or who have learned to regard government as enemy rather than as protector, friend and ally, will understand why Jamie used to say that, of all his (still quite meagre) possessions, his passport was the most precious. Some years later, at a dinner party at the Cathcarts' house in Beresford, there was a conversation about what object one would take with one, if one were told one's home was on fire and one had time to choose a single item only. When his turn came, Jamie didn't hesitate. 'My passport,' he said firmly and then amplified his remark by adding, 'My British passport.'

'But it's so easy to replace,' said one of the guests. 'I mean, I lost my passport when I was on holiday in Portugal, and it made not a blind bit of difference. I just got a bit of paper from the embassy in Lisbon. Surely you'd take something precious, Jamie, like that violin of yours.'

'I hardly play it now,' Jamie answered. 'No, it'd be my passport, all right. I like knowing where it is just in case I need it suddenly.'

Now, back in Cape Town, old friends he hadn't thought of for years, and some whom he scarcely remembered, sent messages to Peter for him, or telephoned the house, or invited him to visit them in their big and luxurious houses, or to have dinner at smart restaurants. White South Africans felt – Jamie realised – extraordinarily isolated; being the political pariahs of the world was not pleasant, and almost the first question anyone asked him was whether he thought it right that they should be so persecuted internationally. Jamie accepted a few invitations but, when one was drinking a man's wine, or standing under the old vines on his verandah looking up across Constantia to the mountains beyond, or sitting on eighteenth-century yellowwood chairs in a Cape Dutch farmhouse in Franschhoek, it was hard to answer – particularly when these were old friends who lived decent lives and loved their children – that one thought they had got every scrap of disapproval they deserved, and were likely to get a great deal more if they didn't change their ways. 'But it's not our fault,' they would wail. Only the very honest or the totally cynical would admit how well they had done – and were still doing – out of apartheid, even when they said they abhorred it and looked forward to its ending. The very few who were still deeply involved in active politics, particularly in the activities of the United Democratic Front – the UDF for short – and the Black Sash, were too busy to see him except fleetingly, and anyway not very interested except possibly in what he might be able to contribute financially (though the sending of money to South Africa for political purposes had been made an offence by law) and some were trying very hard to keep entirely out of sight, even of visitors from overseas.

There was also still attached to Jamie – not least because of the old rumours about Jenny which neither her death nor gossip that she had been assassinated, either by those who thought she had become an informer or by those who had tried to employ her as one – just a modicum of … well, 'suspicion' would be too strong a word, so 'dubiety' might do. Was Jamie what he seemed to be? Was he tainted in some way? When the stakes included one's own personal liberty, one was not inclined to take chances with trusting other people unless one really had to.

Jamie had himself deliberately made it quite difficult for other people to tell what he was. He was temperamentally inclined to be dependent on only a very few people, and one of the effects of Jenny's death had been to make the English Cathcarts very important to him. Hamish and Sarah became almost surrogate parents, and Hamish in particular – with his ability to assimilate himself in his surroundings and to his fellows almost to the point of

214

invisibility – became a role model nearly as significant as his father had been.

When the police had tracked him down at school, and the headmaster had broken the news to him in his sitting-room-cum-study, Hamish and Sarah were the people Jamie had turned to. Hamish had come straight from his office to meet Jamie at the hospital, and Sarah had arrived soon afterwards. It was Hamish who summoned Jenny's mother and father from South Africa and who paid for Peter and their mother to fly over for the funeral. It was Sarah who cleared the flat in Pimlico of their possessions because Jamie said he could not set foot there again. Jenny's clothes went to what Sarah persisted in thinking of as 'a home for errant girls', though she tried to remember to call it by its proper name when she chaired the committee which ran it. Sarah herself packed Jamie's suitcase and books and transported them to the Old Rectory. It was Hamish who arranged that Jamie should take over the small flat at Fairlawn School in return for some care-taking duties at the weekend, and Sarah who had it cleaned, bought curtains for it, chucked out 'the quite ghastly tat which passed for furniture', and sent to the school for the flat a lorry-load of a few essential pieces of furniture – a decent bed, a glass-fronted bookcase, two armchairs, a proper desk, a kitchen table and four sturdy chairs – which she had taken either from the Old Rectory or from one of her family homes. 'Nonsense,' she had told Jamie when he wondered whether he shouldn't be paying for some of this. 'We have far too many possessions anyway; my brother was glad to give me that desk and those chairs – said he needed the space.' It was understandable, given Jamie's deliberate isolation of himself from his old South African life, and given their instinctive appreciation of everyone's need for privacy – growing not out of upper-class coldness but out of the need to be sensible about one's passions – that he should idealise both Hamish and Lady Sarah –

Hamish because he was so like his father, Sarah because she was so unlike his mother

Most weeks, usually on a Monday or Tuesday, when, for work's sake, Hamish Cathcart made a habit of staying in town, Jamie would join him for a quiet dinner at the club. There he would hear Hamish's insider version of the latest noble divorce, and tell him in return the latest gossip from Fairlawn Prep. Occasionally, Sarah Cathcart would override Jamie's objections and insist he come to the Old Rectory for a weekend. Together, they would walk over to the churchyard where Jenny's body was buried, and Sarah would – according to the season – weed or plant some violets or put a bunch of flowers on the grave while Jamie prowled around the graveyard before coming back to where Sarah was working. She would talk in her matter-of-fact way about the village or her charitable work or the antics of the latest appalling clergyman whom the bishop had foisted on St Agnes', and never say a word about the person whose body decayed below the gravestone she had chosen herself because Jamie had said he really didn't care what was there or what was on it. Sarah didn't need to be told that Jamie's way of dealing with grief was to hedge it round and then put up notices at every entry reading 'Private – Keep Out'. That would be, she knew, precisely her own way of dealing with such unpleasantness. Woe betide trespassers. There were things it was better not to discuss: you showed what you felt by the way you behaved, not by anything you said.

However, after a year had passed, Sarah thought it reasonable and decent that, when Jamie came to stay, she should invite some sensible and attractive young woman to dine with them too, or even to stay overnight if she seemed very promising. Once – fifteen months after Jenny's death, when Jamie came to stay in Tuscany with them for a week – she managed to find a young woman whose fiancé had just ditched her most cruelly (though, in

Sarah's private view, it was probably a good thing he had because he was manifestly unsuitable for her god-daughter). To Sarah, Samantha Dalrymple seemed a real candidate for Jamie's devotion; but after three years of Jamie's courteous disdain of all her matchmaking efforts she accepted, with a rather sad shrug – because she did (as she said to her husband) 'so want to see that young man settled and happy again' – that there wasn't much point in getting even someone as beautiful, sad and lonely as Samantha to stay. She would have to leave Jamie's heart to heal in its own slow way, if it was ever to heal, and she introduced Samantha to a cousin who married her within six months and lived happily ever after.

Working – and living – at Fairlawn suited Jamie very well. The boys had treated him with deep and respectful sympathy for a few days after the funeral and his return to work when Peter and his mother had gone back to Grahamstown. But very soon they were cheerfully back to addressing him normally as 'Mr Cathcart, sir' to his face and 'ol' Carthorse' or 'Cathy the Cart' when they thought he couldn't hear. Although he was still the youngest member of staff, he was distant enough from – and with – them to retain the respect he had had as a 'recent gaolbird' when he began teaching; they quite liked him, but said that he could be very scary, and it wasn't sensible to get him riled.

Because he was now living on premises in a small flat made out of what were once the servants' quarters of the huge Victorian townhouse that accommodated the main part of the school, he did more and more of the mundane duties of schoolmastering. The headmaster once described him to a visiting colleague as a kind of 'junior assistant headmaster-cum-caretaker'. When the numbers in the school rose yet again, and another temporary classroom was added to the back of the building, the headmaster appointed a properly qualified music master, and Jamie rather thankfully relinquished his classroom teaching of music to do more History with senior boys, though he continued to run the chamber orchestra, rehearsing twice a week after school, and performing on speech days and similar occasions. Nowadays, he hardly ever took his own violin out of its case, except to augment the string sections of the orchestra.

Some of the mothers, realising he was lonely and heterosexual, made genteel passes at him, and one in particular invited him home for supper on a night when she had quite forgotten her husband had to be away, out of the country on business. When she had made it quite plain that she was not in the slightest thinking of divorcing or being divorced, but wouldn't mind a discreet fling, Jamie had astonished her with the desperation of his lovemaking. Thereafter, when the coast was clear, he would occasionally again be invited for supper and (when the children were asleep) sex. Even more occasionally, over weekends, when her husband had taken the children out to a show or the park or a skating rink, she would slip out of the house to do some last-minute shopping and find herself calling in at Jamie's flat at the school for sex without supper. What existed between them was not, Jamie acknowledged to himself – for no one else was privy to the affair – morally admirable, but, for both of them, it was probably better than the alternatives. Nobody was ever going to replace Jenny, he knew.

England suited him well, too – or at any rate that part of England he chose to inhabit, which was narrowly defined by class as well as by place and situation. England was in its own way another secret place, and Jamie could make it even more secret; people didn't intrude unless they were invited, and even then they were diffident. If someone or the other asked you a question you didn't want to answer, you didn't answer or you changed the direction of the conversation, and no one would be so rude as to press for a reply. He wanted to be private; he wanted to be a stick insect, like Hamish Cathcart; he wanted to move very slowly and carefully, and he liked it best when no one took too much notice of him.

After Jamie had been at Fairlawn for nearly five years, Sarah's father, the duke, mentioned to Hamish that the Sturrock Foundation was looking for an assistant secretary – preferably someone who knew a bit about education because the secretary (actually, he was a Secretary very much with a capital S, because before he became secretary he had been an ambassador and not an especially successful one, retiring a little prematurely after a rather unsteady royal visit to the country he was meant to nurture, but still of course with a knighthood), though someone of considerable consequence, was perhaps a little ignorant of education in its widest sense. This was a pity as the Sturrock Foundation devoted about half its enormous – and increasing – income to education of one kind or the other. The duke had taken over as chairman of the Foundation some twenty years earlier, following the death of the last surviving member of the Sturrock family, which had been considerably better at making money than at breeding children – the last member of the family having left the fortune he had made quite independently of the other Sturrock money to the Foundation because he had no descendants to speak of. Most years, the duke would have to take one of the charity commissioners out to lunch to explain, yet again, why the Foundation was finding it so hard to spend all its income. 'Ronald Whatisname' – the duke had never been good at names – 'is very competent with admin, but quite sticky about only giving grants when we are satisfied that they will be properly spent. We really need someone much younger and more energetic, still scrupulous of course – it's not our money, worse luck' – for the duke was grander than he was rich – '...but someone who will want to spend the stuff. Not a show-off, of course: no statements to the press or anything like that.'

'I think I might know someone,' Hamish said. 'In fact,

you've met him too. Do you remember my nephew, Jamie Cathcart? Tall, skinny boy with rather a lot of blonde hair? Lost his fiancée in tragic circumstances just before they were due to marry, and very reserved ever since then.'

'Good Lord, I remember perfectly well. Sarah's very fond of him. Hardly says a word, but very sensible. Where's he now?'

'Rather a dead-end job in a prep school: Fairlawn – I expect you know its chairman of governors, Ralph O'Dowd. It's a good school, but the present headmaster is going to go on for years. I think he's training my nephew up to succeed him, but it could be ages.'

'I'll have a word with Ralph. We shall see.'

Knowing that the duke invariably did as he said he would, Hamish made double-sure that Jamie came to dinner the next Monday so he could warn him that there might be stirrings. Jamie – who was occasionally conscious that his duties and responsibilities had increased much more rapidly than his salary (he was paid a pittance, even by schoolmasterly standards, and even though his accommodation was free) – said he was content where he was, but would of course consider a move, if the duke really did want him.

An advertisement appeared, references were taken up, interviews were held. Very skilfully for a man who took pride in his own claims of intellectual dufferdom, the duke led the other trustees to the decision he had already reached well before the meeting, even though he seemed not to remember what the candidates' names were but had to refer to each by what he had determined as a leading characteristic: thus Candidate A was the 'civil service chap', Candidate B the one who was so 'political', and Jamie was the 'quiet, hardworking one'.

Thus it was that, aged twenty-seven, Jamie found himself Assistant Secretary of the Sturrock Foundation, earning a salary five times what he had been earning at Fairlawn – sufficient to fund a mortgage to buy a pleasant flat in Belsize Park, the middle section of what had once been a Regency house – and doing what he soon found out was fascinatingly various work, though comfortably at arm's length from most kinds of emotional involvement. Sir Ronald, the secretary, had quickly delegated to Jamie all the educational side of the Foundation, leaving himself more time to concentrate on the other side of the work of the Foundation, which was to provide support for the arts generally.

Ten years later, the Board of the Foundation had finally chucked Sir Ronald upstairs, to be deputy chairman to the duke, whose attendance at meetings was becoming desultory, though he was as sharp as ever at everything except names. After an acerbic falling out over the choice of a successor as secretary – did they want an accountant to manage the money, or did they want someone more generalist to hand it out sensibly? – Jamie had been asked to be acting secretary while the Board sorted themselves out. When they didn't, he had found himself, aged not quite forty, secretary of a Foundation responsible for handing out some fourteen million pounds a year: only in the British Isles, only for worthy causes (and worthiness explicitly excluded anything which might be regarded as too political) and preferably leaning in the direction of education, health, the arts and religion. He was constantly busy and, even with his instinct to be orderly to the point of the obsessive, sometimes under huge pressure: everybody always wanted everything yesterday, especially the members of the Board. 'But, you know, Hamish,' he told his uncle at the latter's retirement party, 'actually managing a Board isn't much different from running a class of very bright and lively prep school boys; one just has to teach them to put up hands before they ask questions.'

He had almost entirely lost his South African accent by now; occasionally, someone would wonder aloud to him if he had spent time in one of the former colonies, Australia perhaps, but – even within his own circles – Jamie Cathcart was known to be a very private person, and one tended not to ask him personal things. Outside the Foundation, and outside the organisations the Foundation helped with money, he was hardly known, and that too suited him very well. He had fenced off his life, and especially that part of his life that had belonged to Jenny Dicey and, in time, the hedges behind the fences grew so high that hardly anyone outside the family knew why the fences had been put there in the first place.

Now, in Cape Town, waiting for his brother, he had more time on his hands than he had had for years. He tried to keep the evenings free for Peter, but Peter was working hard again, despite the amputation, and was often weary when he got home. Sharon was there too, of course, as protective as ever of Peter, not in the slightest inclined to urge him to go out anywhere, and another reason for Peter to be quite keen on an early night.

Occasionally, Jamie felt a little excluded from his brother's presence by Sharon's constant solicitude: it wasn't anything as strong as jealousy he felt, just a desire that he might have his brother to himself for an hour or two. Yet his brother's passion for Sharon was clearly not diminishing with acquaintance; this was pleasure that did not cloy. Anyway, even if Jamie was not at all sure he should stay on in Cape Town, from what he heard, the Sturrock Foundation was still managing very well without him; after all, Sir Ronald knew his way around the office perfectly well, if not always very efficiently.

Sometimes, he felt almost guilty that he was having such a long holiday. There were terrible things happening in South Africa, some of them in the townships not ten miles away; but in a ghastly sense apartheid had worked: the black townships were thoroughly separated from the white suburbs and towns and, though the black workers poured in every morning, starting long before most white people were awake, they poured out again every evening – and, when there was trouble, it was often in the black townships themselves. There was infinitely more black-on-black violence than one would have expected from the picture of South Africa drawn in the Western press. Black-on-white violence was relatively rare – and certainly more rare than white-on-black violence. Many white visitors from abroad found it difficult to believe that the rich, spacious, beautiful and well-tended country they saw – all they were allowed to see – was the same country they read about: the poor getting poorer, living in overcrowded slums, filthy, diseased, chaotic – and, gradually, making themselves more and more ungovernable. On the surface, all was repression; underneath, the contradictions were becoming so violent that, unbeknown to all but a few particularly well-informed, very powerful and far-sighted people, there was actually a reformation being brewed. For most people, there was merely a sense that things couldn't go on like this much longer; there was underlying everything a sense of impending frenzy, a frantic and restless uncertainty that pervaded all parts of life, even in the apparently peaceful Cape Peninsula.

Jamie had always been a walker. Jenny hadn't been as keen as he was but she was as extraordinarily fit as all dancers had to be, without even realising it, and she could if necessary out-walk him. So often their weekend entertainment had been a walk up Table Mountain and back down by another route, or a walk up Silvermine, or a walk in the Tokai Forests. To get Jamie out of the Pimlico flat, Jenny had forced him to explore London on foot and, after her death, his main activity over a weekend was to walk: he walked the London parks, then Hampstead Heath, then the Thames embankments, then caught underground trains to the perimeter of London and walked back again, and then began to walk the coastal paths. He learned that, if one waited for the weather to be suitable, one never did anything in England; so he bought himself proper waterproofs, expensive walking shoes, a set of walking maps, a compass and a haversack from an army surplus store so like the one he had given to Fred Carelse that sometimes he forgot it wasn't his father's old haversack which he hoisted on to his back most Saturday and Sunday mornings.

Now, with time on his hands in Cape Town, he began to walk again; he bought (given the exchange rate, for what translated into very little English money) a good strong pair of lightweight boots in a factory outlet out near Noordhoek; he borrowed a small haversack from Peter; he had a waterproof jacket with him, though someone used to English weather seldom needed anything in Cape Town other than a sun hat. On those days when he wasn't lunching with an old acquaintance or visiting a Franschhoek farmhouse, he would set off on a long walk: up Table Mountain and back; over the mountain to Hout Bay; along the coast to Simon's Town; up and over the Silvermine route; and every step seemed to make Jenny come alive for him again. He knew how envious he was of Peter's love affair with Sharon. He quite often found himself having to avoid deliberately staring at Sharon as she wandered around the Wynberg house after she had got back from work with Peter and had had her shower. And he knew Peter knew why he got up suddenly from his armchair to look out of the window, rather than at the temptation of Sharon with her dark hair still wet and dressed in a white silk dressing gown and apparently nothing else as she laid the supper table.

It was a Wednesday, late afternoon, two days after his visa had once again been extended, this time for six weeks, and he was on the path just above the fast road, the so-called Blue Route. He was walking hard because he had slightly miscalculated the time it would take him to get down from the contour road which led from the cable car station back towards the Rhodes Memorial, and he didn't want to be back too late at the Wynberg house, when he saw, walking ahead of him, twenty yards ahead, someone who seemed from the back so familiar that, for a moment or two, he thought it must be her. He could hardly believe it wasn't, though he knew it couldn't be. She seemed to be limping a little; she was dressed just as if she had been to a ballet class and hadn't had time to change, except that she was wearing running shoes, not points: her socks were rolled down over the ankles and she was wearing pink tights, a pair of shorts, and a skimpy top. The dark hair fell as straight as it had always done, then curled in over her shoulders. He walked faster, still not believing what he saw, and then he ran a few steps so he could catch up. 'Hullo,' he said. Without stopping, she turned to look at him, pushing away the heavy dark hair from her forehead so she could see who it was.

'Hullo,' she said, very matter of factly. 'Oh, I know you. Hullo again.'

It wasn't her – it wasn't really like her at all. It had just seemed like that from the back, he supposed. Or perhaps … No, it wasn't. He didn't know her at all, though she didn't seem afraid. When he hesitated about what to say next, she smiled at him, then said, 'I came to your lecture. You were very good.'

'I didn't see you.'

She smiled again and, for a moment, his heart went out from him again, lurching. 'You weren't looking for me,' she said. 'Where are you walking to?'

'Back to my brother's house – he bought a house in Wynberg. May I ask why you're limping?'

'I've hurt my bloody knee. I thought it was better, but when I tried to run it went into spasm again. So I'm just walking for a bit.'

'Do you know you walk like a dancer – a ballet dancer, I mean?'

'I gave up dancing years ago; I like being out in the open. Damn and blast this sore knee.' Her accent was very strongly South African. He could hardly bear to look at her though he kept sneaking glances at her, striding along next to him, trying to match his paces. 'You walk nearly as fast as I run,' she said.

'Dancers don't usually run,' he said.

'You're funny,' she said. 'I'm not a dancer; I was never any good.'

'You still walk like one. Am I allowed to ask your name?'

'Yes,' she said, 'yes, I'm called Alexandra. Well, that's the formal name. Most people call me Allie or sometimes Alex – and my mother calls me Sasha. At school I was Sally-Ally. No one calls me Alexandra.'

'So many names ...'

'That's because I'm a chameleon, really.'

'Can I call you Allie?'

'Of course. And you're Jamie, aren't you? That's what the chairman called you at the lecture: Jamie, not James.'

'Jamie – please.'

They had stopped walking now, and she had turned to look up at him, her dark wide-set eyes a little puzzled now. 'I think I'd better turn back,' she said. 'The knee isn't easing up.'

'But you can't do that,' he burst out, suddenly desperate. 'Why don't you walk home with me? '

'My, my, Jamie Cathcart, but you are a fast worker. Of course I can't come home with you. For starters, I'm even sweatier than you are.'

'Sorry. Am I very smelly?'

'No,' she smiled again. 'I like men who smell of clean sweat.'

'You could shower at home.'

'Honestly, I'm not coming home with you.'

'I don't mean it like you think,' he said. 'I'm not going to attack you or hurt you.'

'I know that already, or I wouldn't be talking to you.' They were standing in the middle of the path, oblivious

226

that other walkers and runners were having to swerve to get past them. She was staring up at him, puzzled but unafraid.

'Can I see you again?'

'Well, you could invite me out. I like being taken out to supper.'

'When?' he demanded. 'Tonight?'

'Well,' she laughed now at his urgency. 'I am free to-night – and I'll be hungry. All right: I'll come out to supper with you tonight. I said "supper", mind.'

'I'll fetch you at seven. All right? Shall I walk back with you? I'd like that.'

'No,' she said. 'No, I'm going to try to run back. That may ease the knee.' She turned and, very gingerly, began to run back up the tarmac path while he stood to watch her, still only half able to believe what had happened. Suddenly she stopped and turned back to him. 'How do you know where to fetch me from?' she called.

'I don't. Sorry – I'm being a bit silly. Are you at the university?'

'At the women's res. I'm a sub-warden there.'

'I know where that is.'

She smiled back at him. 'You do know a lot about me now, don't you?'

By the time he was back at the house, it was close to six-thirty. 'Can I borrow the car?' he shouted to his brother as he changed to shower. 'And, Sharon, dear, don't cook for me; I'm going out.'

His brother appeared at the doorway on his crutches. In the daytime, going to the office, he had been trying out an artificial leg, strapped across his lower body and (Peter said) 'abominably and abdominably uncomfortable', so the moment he got home he tended to go back on to crutches. 'Do you think you'll be able to manage the hand throttle?'

'I expect so. This is quite important.'

'A date? I thought you were a misogynist.' His brother

was grinning at him, though – as Jamie looked up – he was conscious that Peter didn't look well; his face was thin and shadows accentuated his pallor.

'Are you all right?' he asked. 'Do you mind if I go out?'

'Of course not. We'll probably go to bed soon. I'm feeling a bit washed out: too much rushing about on the new leg. Who's the woman?' Jamie did not answer and Peter knew not to push: it was an article of faith, inherited from their father, that the Cathcarts were private people.

Be that as it may have been, it was Jamie who did most of the talking that evening, talking more than he had done for half his lifetime, filling in what he thought of as the missing years: Fairlawn, the school flat, the Foundation, the flat in Belsize Park, the walking, Hamish and Sarah and the cousins. His Jenny had always, he remembered, been brilliant at getting people to talk about themselves, while she smiled and listened, every now and then brushing the long dark hair back from her forehead, and Allie was the same. It was only near the end of their meal at a Cape-Dutch restaurant that she had directed him towards ('I've only been once,' she had said, 'because it's expensive, I warn you – though with English pounds it won't seem so'), out on the edge of the beach at the Strand, that he said suddenly, 'You've been asking me things all evening, and you've hardly said anything.'

'You've done much more interesting things than I have. South Africa's pretty dead in some ways.'

'Poor Allie,' he leaned across the table, and she let him take her hand in his. 'Is this strange for you, my barging in like this?'

She shook her head at him. 'It's not barging. I suggested supper, remember?'

'I haven't asked you if there's … if you have a lover, or someone.'

'I was engaged, a couple of years ago, to a young doctor, but he ditched me because his family wanted him to marry someone else – an arranged marriage. He's Indian, you see – I hadn't realised how Indian.'

'Were you hurt?'

'Yes, badly at first; I wouldn't accept it. I made scenes and I attacked him outside the medical school once. I'm very fierce; I have claws.' She made as if to scratch the back of his hand.

'I know about claws.'

'You can't – not mine.' she said. 'At any rate, not yet. It probably wouldn't have worked anyway; I'm told he's very happy now – there are two children already.'

'No one else?'

'Not really. I've been very careful since then.' She looked down at her hand in his, then looked up again. 'I'll tell you something else, though. A true confession, really: when that time-server, Huston Stillman, introduced you, and you stood up to lecture, tall and quiet, careful but very sure of what you thought and said, I said to myself: that's the sort of man I need.'

'Even though I'm so old? Look – grey hair,' and he turned his head so she could see.

'When you stopped me this afternoon, you looked about eighteen. You were so funny.'

'Why?'

'I think you're a bit out of practice at picking up women, aren't you?'

'I'm catching up. I think I've caught up,' he said, staring at her, suddenly distracted. 'Do you always wear earrings?'

She smiled as she put her other hand up to fiddle with them. They were very African, each with three patterned strands of small coloured beads, weighted down with a half-moon of silver. 'Someone told me that men look at your neck if you wear earrings. I put these on for you.'

'I like your neck,' Jamie said. 'It's almost Egyptian.'

'Do you know what it means if a girl takes her earrings off?' Jamie shook his head as Allie pushed the heavy dark

229

hair back from her face. 'Do you remember you said to me this afternoon, would I come home with you? And I told you off?'

'I didn't think you were telling me off.'

'Well, I was really. I thought you were being … is the right word "forward"? Is that what English people say?' She smiled at him; her dark eyes were bright and the colour rose in her cheeks. 'Will you think I'm terrible if I say now that I'll come home with you, if that's what you still want? It's me being forward now.'

'That's what I want.' He had not, in fact, got as far as thinking about that; it was sufficient joy to be sitting with her, talking, listening, looking, and – though he had been talking about the past – all time had become present tense: now, now, now. What next hadn't really entered his head.

'That's what it means when a girl takes her earrings off,' Allie said and carefully she unclipped each, turning his hand over so she could place them carefully in his palm, and then closing his hand on them. 'Shall we go now?' She took her cardigan from the chair behind her – there was still some chill in the night air – and, wordlessly, he got to his feet and followed her to the door. She stopped him. 'I think you'd better pay, hadn't you?' she said, *sotto voce*. 'We'll get arrested otherwise.'

The waiter was hovering, clearly anxious that something had gone wrong which took these customers away so suddenly, though they had seemed to be enjoying their meal as well as each other's company. Jamie said to him, 'Sorry; we've got to go. The meal was delicious.' He scarcely looked at the bill the waiter presented, merely took out his wallet; the size of the tip left the waiter in no apprehension that there had been a problem.

In the car, Allie said to him, 'Will your brother mind? Your bringing me home? It's tricky taking people into my flat.'

'Of course not. He'll be in bed anyway, with Sharon.'

'Who's Sharon?'

'His girlfriend; she's living there.'

'The Cathcart brothers seem to get around.' She was being rather shy with him, leaning against the door of Peter's Volkswagen, looking ahead at the road rather than at him. 'Won't we disturb them?'

He'd forgotten that she didn't know the house. 'No,' he said. 'It's quite spacious, really. I think you'll feel at home there.'

'I'm feeling a bit shy, really,' she said.

'Please don't be,' he said. 'I've been waiting for you, you see. I realise now.'

* * *

And it was as it had always been: passionately, even desperately urgent, and then – later – a slow play of their senses – touching, looking, tasting, feeling, whispering. She said to him, 'It's a long time since I came first that way and then the other,' and so he made her come again, very slowly. In the early morning, she woke him to wonder if she shouldn't get back to her flat in the women's residence – he had discovered the night before that she was a research student, writing a thesis on part of the history of South African trade unions as well as earning a pittance by acting as sub-warden in the women's residence – but as she leaned naked over him, he began to kiss her breasts, and she didn't leave after all. When Jamie heard Peter and Sharon leave for the office, he got up to make coffee and they drank it in bed before dozing off again in each other's arms. By the time they left the flat, it was nearly eleven.

'I've simply got to do some work today, Jamie,' Allie said. 'And I'll need to sneak into the flat to change out of my dress into something else.'

'Can I take you out to lunch?' he said. They were walking into Wynberg to find a taxi to take her up the hill to the university.

231

'If I say yes, I know what you'll want to do this after-noon,' she laughed at him. 'So, no. But you can take me out tonight again, if you want – unless you have something else on.'

Of course he had nothing else to do and so, for the rest of the week, that became the pattern of their lives together. Jamie would collect her in Peter's car at seven from outside the women's residence, and they would go somewhere different each night to eat (Hout Bay, Kalk Bay, the refurbished docks). 'It's funny,' Jamie said, 'having enough money to eat out every night. Do you remember how poor I used to be?'

'No,' she said. 'You keep forgetting. You're muddling me up again.'

'I'm sorry. I know I do. You have sort of … somehow … you're not; but I muddle you up. Does that worry you?'

'No,' she said, staring at him. 'It should, I suppose, but it doesn't. For one thing, it makes me feel less bad about going to bed with you the first night I met you.'

'But I love you. Doesn't that make it different?'

'Dangerous,' she said. 'Not different. I'm not used to someone being in love with me so suddenly.'

'This isn't sudden.'

'It feels very sudden to me.'

'I worry I may seem very old to you.'

'I've forgotten that too,' she smiled at him. 'You'd better remind me.'

At ten or ten-thirty, they would quietly let themselves into the Wynberg house and go to bed together. Peter and Sharon seemed to be going to bed earlier and earlier each night. Next morning, after Peter and Sharon had left for work, they would have breakfast, and then walk down into Wynberg for Jamie to put Allie in a taxi to take her to the university. He would walk slowly and rather forlornly back to the house, then put on his walking boots and go off somewhere for the rest of the day, getting back in time to have a shower, then a drink with Peter and Sharon before going off to meet her again.

On the Saturday morning, having forgotten that Peter didn't work then, Jamie was momentarily surprised to find Sharon in the kitchen; she was wearing an apron and seemed to be cleaning the whole place. 'Oh, hello, Sharon,' he said. 'May I introduce you? This is Alexandra – Allie.' The girls shook hands, very formally. Rapidly, he took Allie into the garden to where Peter was sitting on a bench in the sun, crutches beside him, and a pile of books next to him.

Peter didn't try to stand, but held out a hand and, when Allie made as if to shake it, pulled her down and closer so that he could kiss her on both cheeks. He looked quizzically at her.

'We've met before, haven't we?'

'Have we?' Allie smiled.

Peter frowned. 'I'm sure we have. Some sort of political meeting – downtown, perhaps. A UDF meeting?'

'I'm quite involved,' she said. 'Are you?'

'Hardly at all,' said Peter, 'and even less now I'm down to one leg.'

'That's a good excuse,' she said matter-of-factly. 'How are you coping?'

'I've been feeling a bit dodgy this week,' he said quietly.

'Should you go back to Dr Immerman on Monday?' asked Jamie, suddenly aware that he had been so absorbed in his own renewed joy that he hadn't thought of his brother's illness all week.

Peter grimaced. 'I expect she'd want to readmit me and start doing biopsies, and then pump me full of stuff.' He grinned wickedly. 'I don't suppose even Groote Schuur does private rooms with double beds, eh, Jamie?'

Sharon, who had come outside with a tray of coffee, orange juice and croissants, said, 'Now, Peter, don't you start on that. Jamie, can you and Allie pull that table over here?'

'I can move,' Peter said, starting to reach for his crutches.

'No, you won't,' said Allie and Jamie simultaneously

and between them they shifted the old wooden table and three chairs nearer Peter's bench so that Sharon could put down the tray and distribute mugs of coffee, croissants and glasses of orange juice.

'One forgets the luxury of late breakfasts in the sun,' Allie said contentedly, her mouth full of croissant. 'Do you ever get this in England, Jamie?'

'Not in England, but sometimes in Tuscany in August.'

'Tuscany?' said Sharon. 'Is that in Italy? I've always wanted to go to Italy. My grandfather was there in the war.'

'So was Peter's and my father,' Jamie said lazily.

'I expect my grandfather was your father's batman,' Sharon said; there was an edge in her voice that made the others look at her sharply.

'Sorry,' said Jamie. 'Was I being tactless?' He didn't think that he had been, and didn't see how what he had said could be taken as personally directed; but this was South Africa, and sensitivities abounded, especially when one got anywhere near race. Had something that seemed to him so mundane as carrying a tray outside scratched the delicate surface of her self-esteem? Allie clearly thought so because when Peter asked if he might have a second cup of coffee she was on her feet before Sharon had stirred. 'It's my turn,' she said.

'I'll help you,' Jamie said, standing up to help with the tray.

'All right,' Allie smiled at him. 'I've not really seen much of you being domestic.'

When they were in the part of the big room that served as kitchen, Jamie said quietly, 'Oh dear, I seem to have offended Sharon.'

'Oh, no,' Allie answered. 'I doubt that. She's just not sure of her place here, so perhaps I seem even more like an interloper. She watches, doesn't she? Constant scrutiny.'

'She's very good to Peter.'

'He watches her too. She's very pretty – much prettier than me.'

'You're beautiful, not pretty.'

'You're very kind, Jamie Cathcart, but I'm not sure I know the difference.'

'Beauty goes on; one grows out of prettiness, doesn't one?'

'Perhaps; I've not thought. Your brother is in love with Sharon, isn't he? It's not just a fling?'

'This may sound contradictory, but I don't think he's got the time for "just a fling", if you understand me.'

'Yes,' Allie said, reaching up to kiss him. 'Yes, darling Jamie, I think I understand. We'd better go back out now. Will you carry the tray?'

* * *

Later, Allie asked Jamie if he would like to go to a party with her that evening. 'It's quite political,' she said. 'Some of the people in the UDF. We don't often get together socially, but there's been some tension recently, and we thought something like this might help.'

'Just how involved are you, Allie?'

'Quite a bit,' she said. 'But, these days, you don't have to do very much to be counted as involved. It's enough for the security police that you are seen talking to people.'

'Have you been arrested?'

'A couple of times at demonstrations, but I've not been in detention, not like you.'

'That was a long time ago,' Jamie said firmly.

'I bet they still hate you all the same.'

'Are their memories that long? I wonder. I think it's just civil-servant efficiency with files.'

'Do you think your brother and Sharon will want to come too?'

'Would it be all right with Sharon?' Jamie meant, would it be all right for a Coloured woman to come to the party with a white man? In many ways, his mind was still fixed in the South Africa of 1966, when a mixed-race couple could be arrested merely for walking together.

235

'Oh, there'll be lots of mixed couples there – all genders too, I guess.'

Despite this, Peter said that if Sharon didn't mind, he wouldn't go: he simply didn't feel up to big parties and standing around for a couple of hours. He really needed to sit. 'Dr Immerman on Monday,' Jamie said firmly, but Peter merely shook his head.

'Do go without me, Sharon, if you like. Jamie and Allie will drive you.'

'Of course not,' said Sharon. 'If I can't go to Tuscany, I'd rather be here and, anyway, I want to go to Tuscany with you, not without you. Same for the party. If you want me to go to the party, I'll go. If you don't, I won't.'

'I'll take you to Tuscany, I promise, Sharon love, as soon as I've learned how to walk properly on that damned tin leg,' said Peter, and reached across to make her come to sit close to him on the bench in the sun.

* * *

Two months later, after Peter's death, that moment of longing, summed up in the forlorn notion of his taking Sharon away on holiday, seemed to be the last glimmer of hope that Peter had had of a future without illness – but perhaps (Jamie thought) he had known already what young Dr Immerman had to tell him less than a week later: that the cancer cells had outrun the surgeon's knife and were already lodged further up inside him, and in particular in his liver. She would do, she said, as she had promised, and make sure there was no pain, but there was nothing else she could do, and nothing else she would do. Anything else would just be pretending. She was very, very sorry; but the amputation had always been a last chance, really.

'It's odd, isn't it?' Peter said, as Jamie wheeled him back towards the car. (Without even discussing the matter, they had left the tin leg behind in the consulting room, knowing that, later, they would be telephoned to come to collect it, and would forget yet again.) 'That Dr Immerman. She's been lovely, and I know she'll look after me, and I'm not scared of the pain, really, though I wish I didn't feel so bloody washed up all the time. She'll go on looking after me, but I have a sort of feeling she's already looking beyond me at the next patient. I'm not looking forward to telling Sharon.'

'Do you want me to tell her?' Jamie said. He suspected that Peter's insistence that she go to work that morning, as usual, preferring that Jamie and not Sharon should take him to the hospital – on the grounds that Jamie had nothing else to do but go for some enormously long walk somewhere – was because Peter had known perfectly well what the doctor was going to tell him.

'No, no, I must. But can I ask you one thing, brother mine? I'd quite like to leave the house as well as some money to Sharon – but, really, half the house is yours.'

'No, of course, you must leave her the house. I've got the flat in London and it's more than big enough. I've paid off the mortgage now and I really hardly spend half what I earn. I'll tell you what: I always thought that I'd be leaving my money to your children ...'

'And I thought I'd be leaving my money to yours. It's odd neither of us has had children.'

'I suspect it isn't, really.'

'Oh, I'm not sure about that: think about Sharon – think about Jenny; and Allie too, now.'

'Do you want to marry Sharon? Before ... before you know what I mean.'

'Before I die? No, not really. I think it's going to be a big enough burden anyway, coping with the business of my dying. I wouldn't want her to have to cope with widowhood too.' He was silent as he steered the car carefully through the midday traffic down the main road to drop Jamie in Wynberg. 'Shit, Jamie, I'm scared of dying.'

'I know, brother, I know. I wish I could ...' He couldn't bring himself to finish the sentence he had begun.

'You wish you could die for me, do you? So do I,' he laughed briefly. 'No, I don't. I reckon it's something I'm going to have to do on my own. Do you know any priests?'

'Not in Cape Town, not socially; a few in England. The Foundation is meant to be Christian.'

'Do you go to church?'

'Hardly ever; sometimes when I stay with Hamish and Sarah. It seems less hypocritical then. Oh, and there's a big annual service-cum-celebration of the Sturrock Foundation at St Paul's every year. The lord mayor and the aldermen turn out in fancy dress, and I read the lesson, and so on.'

'I wouldn't mind being a Christian again. It seemed to make a difference to Mum, those last months.'

'I'm sure we can find someone for you to talk to if that's what you want. There'll be someone at the cathedral, no doubt. I'll telephone or I'll go in this afternoon.'

'I don't want a bigwig; just somebody ordinary, who believes in more than we can actually see. Do you know what I mean?'

'Yes, I do.'

'Are you going to marry Allie?'

'Good Lord. You know, I haven't even thought about it. I guess it's part of my wanting ... my muddling her up with Jenny. Do you think I should ask her? I don't want to scare her away.'

'If I were you, brother, I'd ask. You don't want the same thing to happen again like last time.' He laughed, suddenly and mirthlessly. 'I'll tell you what. Find me a priest, find yourself a priest. Marry the girl, quickly, before I die, and I'll come to your wedding on my crutches. I'll even be your best man if you can't think of someone else.'

'Are you joking, Peter?'

'No, not really. Having a laugh before the old bastard,

Mephistopheles, gets us all. What's the name of the dog with all those heads?'

'Cerberus.'

'Oh, yes, for the salt. And the boatman's name? Had you thought of that?'

* * *

The party had been, as far as Jamie could tell, a great success. There had been very little of the careful cliquishness which seemed to dominate exile politics in Europe and America and, as far as he knew, everywhere else too. Here, in the home country, where there was real danger in almost everything that was done – and danger even to those who happened to be standing nearby, sometimes without any intention of involvement – there was also a magnanimity about those who were working alongside, and about disparate opinions. This organisation was what it claimed to be: a conglomerate gathering of all sorts of democratic and anti-apartheid folk – middle-aged women in the Black Sash, ardent advocates of the Congress movement, trade unionists, student activists, Christian socialists, even some old-fashioned liberals of the kind most of those in black politics affected to despise, though they nearly always made personal exceptions of those who did real work or took risks and did not merely mouth platitudes.

In this gathering, it was immediately clear that Allie was – for all her claims of being merely a go-between – a significant person. All and sundry greeted her and, soon after their arrival, she said, 'Listen, darling, I've got some shop to talk, some people to see about things; this is a party, but it's also politics. I'll abandon you for a while and then I'll find you. You'll be all right, won't you? You'll find you know some people here, I think.'

And so it had been: seeing Dr Liebermann in a corner, he made his way over to join the circle gathered round him. 'Hullo, Jamie Cathcart,' the old man said. 'You've not gone back to England then?'

'Not yet, Professor. Not yet.'

'Well, you could stay here. A few more like you would be welcome. Too many have gone; I get more letters from Australia than I get from Johannesburg nowadays.'

'A new diaspora?' Jamie suggested.

For ten minutes, Dr Lieberman explained why the flight of whites from South Africa should not be described as a diaspora; diasporas had enriched most cultures but the desertion from difficulties at home had merely weakened the chances of a decent multiracial settlement. 'And, yes, I mean "multiracial", not that fashionable nonsense about "non-racial" because this is going to go on being a culture of disparate races for many years yet, even when apartheid falls apart, as it is bound to do shortly. No one is going to be able to close the gaps by waving a wand, or by passing laws, or by tossing pennies in a wishing well. Getting rid of bad laws won't get rid of oppression; oppression is also a state of mind; in part, it depends on acquiescence. In a new South Africa, whatever the optimists say, you'll still get parties like this in what will still be largely white suburbs – lots of whites and a few blacks. All that will happen is, over a generation or two, there will be more blacks and, in due course, more Coloured people – not Cape Coloureds, but black-white mixtures. That will be our strength – and I shall not be here to see it.' He referred to his own mortality with complete equanimity.

The point about Liebermann isn't, Jamie thought, that he doesn't listen to other people. He does; he loves it when people interrupt him with a disagreement or a question, and he accepts interruption happily. Is it because, during all those years when he was silenced – by being in detention, or under house arrest, or simply banned – he thought through all the questions on his own and came up with original answers? He has obviously come to terms with

240

himself in every sense: with his age, with his limitations, with his frailties.

After a while, Allie came to find him. 'Hullo, Prof,' she said, and then said to Jamie, 'There's someone I want you to meet in a minute or two, Jamie; he used to know you in the old days. He's busy now, but I'll come back for you in ten minutes. Are you all right?'

Jamie nodded. The rest of those who had been listening to Liebermann had taken the opportunity of Allie's coming up to them to drift away to join other conversations, leaving Jamie on his own. When Allie had gone, Liebermann took him by the arm. 'Jamie,' he said, 'allow me the privilege of an old man. Having put my foot horribly in your affairs in relation to Jenny Dicey – I should have known she had been killed; perhaps I did and had forgotten (I do forget more and more, especially what is unwelcome) – I think I am about to do the same again. Are you with this girl now, this Alexandra?' Jamie nodded. Liebermann gripped his arm surprisingly hard for a man who must have been well into his seventies, possibly even eighties. 'My boy, you will be careful, won't you? Very, very careful?'

Jamie said quietly, 'I am a careful man by nature, Professor.'

'I think you are a man who trusts and in politics that is very dangerous.'

'But this isn't politics.'

'Everything in this country is politics. This Allie: she is a real activist, I am told. She moves between many camps and she carries messages: to be a messenger is very dangerous in hard times – I think that is something out of Homer.'

'Not my period.' Jamie tried to make a joke of the warning, though he knew he should take it seriously. Others might think this was an old man well past real wisdom; Jamie saw him otherwise and suspected he knew much more than he ever let on. Though he was profligate with

241

theories, ideas, strategies and policies, he was immensely discreet with names and details.

'I think you know I am being serious, Jamie Cathcart. You must tread very carefully with that young woman though you are right: she is another beauty. Those Slavic cheekbones, those dark eyes … not what South Africans call pretty, but what a Central Europeans know to be a beauty. Still, my boy, be careful.'

'I will,' Jamie promised and made a mental note that he really must find out from Allie a little more about what she actually did. There was clearly much that he didn't know.

The person she wanted him to meet was Phakamile Mtirara – one of those from Barney's 'discussion group' of more than twenty years before, and one on the list of names which Maasdorp had asked him to give his assent to. Jamie had used then as his excuse an incapacity to remember African names, though he had known Phakamile precisely because it was, in 1966, quite uncommon for a black person not to have a Europeanised name, and Phakamile was fiercely Africanist in attitude when Africanism had still been regarded as racist.

The spirit was still there, though the body had aged savagely. Phakamile was clearly delighted to see him again, all the same, giving Jamie a prolonged comrades' handshake – a normal handshake with an added ritual which involved grasping each other's thumb in the middle of the handshake – and pulling him down to sit on the sofa next to him. Before Jamie had a chance to ask questions himself, Phakamile questioned him: what had he done since detention, where was he living now, what work did he do, was he still playing his violin, why was he back, how did he know Allie, did he ever see Barney? He knew that Barney was very big stuff now, a VIP travelling the world for the ANC in a dark suit and shaking hands with prime ministers and presidents; he had all the usual stay-at-homer's ironic suspicion of the exiles and their sybaritic lives, though clearly he knew much more than ever appeared in South African newspapers. Did he know that Fred Carelse was now a millionaire in Canada, heading up a family firm that had diversified from building into DIY superstores? Jamie had known about Barney, but was astonished to hear about Fred. 'Fred? Fred Carelse? Are you sure?'

'I'm sure, all right,' Phakamile laughed breathlessly, hawking and spluttering at the end of his laughter. Fred had come back a year before and had put up in – of all places – the Mount Nelson Hotel, like a foreign ambassador; and he had had discussions with a cabinet minister about starting up a superstore outside Cape Town.

'What a turn-up for the books, eh? I never thought Fred would be that kind.'

Phakamile seemed at ease with the knowledge.

'Did Fred try to see you when he was back?'

'No, I don't think he made any links at all; his family are all in Canada now, and he didn't have time for his old comrades. It's the way things happen.' He seemed without bitterness, though he spoke barely above a whisper; there was clearly something very wrong with his lungs, for even speaking seemed to make him breathless.

'What happened to you, Phakamile?'

'Oh, not much in terms of events. I was detained when you were in 1966. They kept me for longer, and then they got me on conspiracy to promote a banned organisation, and I did altogether fifteen years on Robben Island. No remission for political prisoners, see; they only let me out because they thought I was going to die there, and they wanted no martyrs. As you see, I am not very well. A quarry is not a good place for a man with asthma.'

'I'm surprised they didn't ban you, or house-arrest you, when they let you out.'

Phakamile smiled. 'Oh, they banned me. I told them they could stuff the banning orders up their trouser legs.

243

Listen, the worst they can do is to put me back inside again, and I will die very quickly then. Or they can put a bomb under my bed. I have stopped being afraid of them. It is amazing how much more simple things seem when you get rid of the fear.'

Jamie asked about the others in the group. Phakamile didn't know about all of them, he said. Poor old Ahmed Singhal had died in solitary confinement, the police said of a heart attack induced by a hunger strike, but everyone was sure he had been tortured to death. Khotso had been murdered by the police; they said he had been trying to escape, but when his sister – a nurse at Groote Schuur – had identified the body, she had noted that the bullets had hit him not from behind but in front. When she made a fuss and talked to the newspapers, the police had locked her up in solitary for a month. Of the others, some had gone quiet, one or two had sold out, and some had disappeared from view totally. It was the way things panned out, Phakamile said: you simply had to accept what happened to people. No, they had never found out who the informer had been; they didn't even know for sure there was one. There had been a rumour, but nothing more. One day, perhaps ...

Later, in Peter's car on the way back to Allie's flat at the women's residence because, rather than going back to Peter's house, she said that she would sneak him in there for once, through the back door ('I know they'll fire me as sub-warden if they find you there, out of hours, and you'll have to leave at dawn, but I want you to be in my flat, for once,' she said), after he had told her what Phakamile had said, he asked Allie what precisely it was she did.

'I try to make people talk to each other,' she said. 'I don't actually do anything; it's just talking to this one, and then to that one, and then trying to get this one and that one to talk directly to each other.'

'And you carry messages?'

244

'Who told you that? All right, I carry messages and sometimes the messenger gets blamed when it's the message that's wrong.'

'What sort of messages?'

'Well, I can't really tell you that: that X wants to talk to Y about Z. As simple as that, really.'

'I don't understand.'

'Jamie, for instance: I'm trying to get Congress people to talk to ... well, to other people. And we try to connect to the comrades in the townships though that's very difficult because they trust no one, not even each other.'

'You don't talk to the police, do you?'

'I try not to but, Jamie, you know, we are going to go on needing policemen even after liberation. Someone will have to talk to them.'

'Not the security branch, I hope.'

'No, no one trusts them. But take someone else unpopular – for instance, the people in the big banks. Even they know that there's going to have to be change, sooner rather than later, and they want to talk to the people who are beginning to take over. You know, there's really another kind of government in the townships now. The police go in to kill and to burn, but they hardly govern any more. And we can't go on like that. You can't have everybody killing everybody else.'

'Well, in some countries they seem to go on for quite a time: Ireland, for instance, or Israel and Palestine.'

'We've got to do better than that.'

'Does being a woman help?'

Allie smiled. 'Maybe we aren't so aggressive; maybe we're better peace-makers than men are.'

'You make it sound very simple.'

'Well, it is really. Except of course some people want things to stay as they are. They don't want change – they make money out of what exists, or they think they'll lose their place in the queue. That's the dangerous bit because you are never quite sure who is who.'

'I hope you're careful. Professor Liebermann told me to be careful of you.'

'Oh, the prof,' she laughed. 'He's a bit old-style now, really: an ideologue, isn't he? Things may change only on preordained lines?' She was quite scornful.

'I think he's more interesting than that.'

'You're a generous man, Jamie.' They were at the back of the women's residence. 'You can park here, and then you are going to have to be very quiet, even when you are making love to me.'

* * *

Peter got on with the business of dying swiftly and (for someone who had claimed to be 'shit-scared') calmly. There were practical arrangements to be made, and a lawyer came to the house to sit with him and Jamie to sort out practical details: the house was to be Sharon's, and there was a substantial sum in cash and shares for her, though she would probably go on working. The rest of the money was to go to Jamie, to be used as he thought fit, though if he ever had children Peter said he hoped the money would be given to them. 'Perhaps you can use it for the occasional holiday in Cape Town, brother,' he said. 'It's probably not enough to buy you a nice house here, but you could get something further up the coast if you wanted. I used to think I might, one day – you know, at Plettenberg Bay or in the Wilderness area.' His partnership in the business would lapse when he died, anyway; that was already in the papers signed when it was set up. Things would have been different if he had gone on to retirement, but when they set up the partnership they'd planned on staying alive.

Jamie went into the diocesan offices behind the cathedral in the centre of Cape Town in the hope of finding a clergyman who might be prepared to minister to his dying brother. A stony-faced woman in an office called 'Reception and Enquiries' established that neither he nor his brother was a regular churchgoer nor had a parish either would regard as his own. And that was clearly that: this was not a church for them; this was a church for its members. Jamie didn't argue. 'Thank you very much for your help,' he said, and walked out.

There was a little Anglican church he had noted in Wynberg when he was walking Jenny down to a taxi each morning. On his way back to the house – he had caught the train into town – he noticed the west door was ajar, and he wandered in. A caretaker with a broom in hand directed him towards the vestry where he found a tall, spectacularly thin priest in a white cassock sitting at a desk.

'Can you help me?' he said without preamble, half-expecting another rebuff.

'Of course,' said the priest, standing up. 'How?'

'My brother is dying of cancer. He wants to talk to a priest. He doesn't go to church – and he's living in sin with a girl. I'm not really a Christian myself any more.'

The priest got to his feet. 'Would your brother mind seeing me now?'

'Don't we have to make an appointment or something?'

'It doesn't sound as if there's much time for appointments. Are you in a car?'

'I'm walking.'

'I think I've seen you walking around and about. I too prefer walking – you see so much more, and people will talk to you on your feet. May I walk with you now?' His accent was more German than South African.

'Please.'

As they walked towards the house, the priest talked; it was almost at once apparent that, despite his white cassock, his Christianity was of an uncomplicated kind. As far as Jamie could tell, he was an almost entirely literal evangelical in whose head no paradox had ever lodged, and into whose heart no metaphor had ever crept. If you

247

prayed, God heard you. If you were ill, God would cure you if He could, unless He had some bigger purpose in your suffering, in which case you had the joy of knowing that your suffering had a purpose, just as Jesus Christ's own suffering had had. When you died, you went before the judgement throne and your sins would be forgiven, provided only that you had repented in time. He spent much time with people who were dying and he could help, he thought.

If it were me he was seeing, Jamie thought, I'd have him out of the door in five minutes. He's clearly a good, kind man, possibly even saintly – judging by his skinniness, he certainly doesn't eat very much – but I can't be doing with such simple-mindedness. The only way I can cope with things like the resurrection from the dead or the virgin birth or the ascension is by thinking they are metaphors, and the importance of religious services is merely that they are part of ancient ritual, and a way we have of keeping the past alive. I fear (Jamie thought) Peter will have him out of his bedroom before the man has got to the third clause of the *Lord's Prayer*.

Jamie was wrong. When the priest hadn't emerged from the bedroom after nearly an hour, he thought he had better intervene. He took in a tray of tea and some biscuits, the biscuits for the priest rather than his brother because Peter had seemed to have lost all appetite already. They were still deep in conversation, scarcely noticing the mugs of tea he handed to them. He put the biscuits within reach of the priest and left them alone.

When at last the priest came out, Peter was fast asleep, propped up on the pillows like an old man. 'I shall come back tomorrow,' the priest said. 'Peter has asked me to come at a time when I shall be able to talk to Sharon too. Do you want to talk to me too?' He smiled.

'No, no,' said Jamie hurriedly. 'It's good of you to give up your time like this.'

'This is my work.'

248

'I don't even know your name.'

'I am Father Andrew. You will find it easier to call me that than my complicated surname.'

'Which is?' Jamie persisted.

'Von Dorenberg – yes, my family was German, from Namibia, but I am South African now. I find it simpler to be called Father Andrew. I shall see you tomorrow at six o'clock. Your brother will sleep for some hours now. I hope he will be more peaceful when he wakes.'

From then on, until Peter was moved to a hospice five weeks later, Father Andrew spent an hour with him almost every day, except on Sundays. Sometimes he would come in the evening when Sharon was home from the office, and he would sit with them both, Sharon sitting on the bed holding Peter's hand and the priest in a chair under the window. Often, as far as Jamie could tell, the three of them merely chatted. Sometimes, Father Andrew appeared to be praying over Peter – as far as Jamie could tell, with Peter's assent. Occasionally, he read aloud from the small Bible that he habitually carried in his cassock pocket. Once, when Jamie went in with a tray of tea and biscuits as he used to do whenever Father Andrew had been there for any length of time, both Sharon and the priest were sound asleep, Sharon with her head on Peter's shoulder, the priest in the armchair. With his right hand – his left was supporting Sharon – Peter put a finger on his lips, smiling, then whispered, 'They are both exhausted – isn't it hilarious? I'm dying and awake, and they are asleep.' Father Andrew stirred in the armchair but did not wake, and Peter gestured Jamie silently out of the room.

He was on a constant supply of morphine now, with a charger strapped to his chest so that he could top up the drug if the pain began to overwhelm him; but he said he was seldom in much pain. He just felt pretty sick most of the time. He was eating almost nothing, and got thinner and thinner as each day passed. He said to Jamie, 'I sort of feel I should make an effort and get out of bed, but I'm overcome with lassitude at even the thought of walking down the hall. Is it the drugs or is it the liver? I am having the most extraordinary dreams – I guess it's like being a heroin addict. It's much more exciting than alcohol, I can promise you. I'm glad I won't have to get off it.'

At Sharon's request, Jamie had moved a mattress from the storeroom at the back of the house on to the floor of Peter's room so that she could move there from their double bed. Yet as often as not, when he took a tray of tea in to Peter in the morning – because almost all he could keep down was weak tea, heavy with sugar – he would find Sharon in bed with Peter and, judging by the way she pulled the covers up to her neck when he knocked to come in, she was naked. Once, after Sharon had gone to the office – she was going in by train now, later than when Peter had driven her – Peter said he would like to sit out in the garden. As Jamie helped him into a dressing gown and slippers, Peter said to him, as roguish as a schoolboy, 'I'll tell you something funny, brother: even blokes who are dying can still make love, given the right girl and a bit of encouragement. She doesn't even mind the one-legged bit.'

Jamie wasn't about to ask for details of the form the 'encouragement' took. Perhaps, thought Jamie, it's possible the 'one-legged bit', even the impending death itself, actually helps, not in a physical sense – though he guessed that one-leggedness might have its peculiar advantages – but because Sharon is given some kind of special authority by Peter's being so dependent on her. She is empowered by his helplessness and her sexiness is in some way enhanced by his dying. He knew that sometimes, in a very different context, he felt the same: when he made love to Allie, he wasn't creating life, he was fending off death.

Some nights, Allie slept at the Wynberg house and some nights he slept in her sub-warden's flat at the university.

However, in the daytime, Jamie hardly left the Wynberg house now; the one thing Peter seemed to be concerned about was not being left on his own. One day, Jamie left him for only an hour and a half to go to shop at a supermarket for food and found him distraught and almost incoherent with anxiety on his return. 'I don't know why,' Peter said, 'but please, brother, don't leave me on my own like that. I didn't know what was happening.'

'I told you I was just nipping down to the shops,' Jamie said, as he helped Peter back to his bed, but he resolved then that there would always be someone there for him. He had by now arranged with the Sturrock Foundation that his holiday would become long leave. 'You had better shift me on to half-pay, hadn't you, Ronald?' he had told the chairman on the telephone. 'I've been away longer than I planned already.'

'No question of it, Jamie,' said Sir Ronald. 'The Foundation can hardly go around organising conferences for employers on good industrial relations and then treat its own chief executive inhumanely. No, you look after your brother. I'll keep the office warm for you.' Jamie hoped he wouldn't keep it too warm, and he was a little concerned about this 'conference for employers'. Sir Ronald had once been an enthusiastic convert of the Oxford Group – in its post-Victorian guise – and was a little inclined to a view of industrial relations that wouldn't disgrace the scientologists. There had been a proposal for a conference from some board members which Jamie had managed to shift from a list of firm commitments to a list which privately he summed up as falling into the category of 'Wouldn't it be nice if we had the money? I shall make sure we don't.' In his absence, it seemed that the conference had moved category again; but if he wasn't there he could hardly complain.

Peter began to struggle for breath sometimes, almost as if he were having an asthma attack. Jamie telephoned Dr Immerman and she called in to see him that evening.

Afterwards, she said to Jamie, 'I think he's probably got a tumour on one of the lungs – perhaps on both. I'll arrange for an oxygen cylinder to be sent and a mask; then he'll be able to breathe more easily. I can take him back into hospital if you can't manage and there's a new hospice in Constantia that seems very helpful and kind.'

'He wants to be here,' Jamie answered. 'There's no point in your trying to do something about the lungs?'

'There isn't, I'm afraid. We could x-ray him, but we know what we would find. You'll have to face this, Mr Cathcart: your brother is riddled with cancer now – all we can do is to try to make him comfortable. He's not in pain, is he?'

'No, no – at least I don't think so. Having the charger seems to work. How long now, do you think?'

'No one can say. Not long, probably. He's very thin – there's not much resistance.'

'Should we try to make him eat?'

'I don't think you should make him do anything he doesn't want to do, and I think anything he wants you should give him.'

'I tried to tempt him with champagne last night, but he wouldn't; he did say he loved watching the rest of us drinking it – he said it made us all rosy.'

'He's a brave man, your brother. He's been brave since before he came to see me. I wish I could do more.'

'No, Doctor, you've done everything you could have done. We are very grateful; we really are.'

Towards the end, when Peter began to need proper and constant nursing, and when his sleepy lassitude turned to spells of unconsciousness, Sharon and he took the decision to move him to a hospice in Constantia. They weren't sure that he even knew that he had been moved but, after five days of his drifting in and out of a coma, he whispered to Jamie that he would like, if they didn't mind, to go home. There was a drip up at this stage, and the staff at the hospice tried to prevent a move back but, when

Sharon took Jamie's side, they capitulated, and an ambulance moved Peter back into his own room in the house in Wynberg that evening. As far as they could tell, he was aware that he was back, though he seemed unable to talk. Then, because his breathing was so irregular and shallow, they put the oxygen mask on again, and Sharon lay down on the bed in her clothes, stretched out next to him, while Jamie sat in the armchair under the window. When Jamie woke at first light, as the muezzin chanted, he thought simply that there had been another change in Peter's breathing. When he tried for a pulse, he could find none. So he woke Sharon and telephoned Dr Immerman.

Peter had asked that his body be cremated. 'Please: no fuss,' he had said. 'Just get the mortal remains out of the way swiftly.' Father Andrew came with them (Jamie, Allie and Sharon) to the crematorium, said some prayers, comforted Sharon, and said he would collect a little casket of ashes from the undertaker later.

The next day, there was a short memorial service in the church in Wynberg. Jamie had expected just Sharon, himself, Allie and Father Andrew but, in the event, Sharon's family turned up in force: father, mother, grandmother, three sisters, a brother, and a couple of what he supposed were cousins but may simply have been friends. They were all in their Sunday best, sharp suits or club blazers, black ties or black scarves, black shoes and black handbags, all a little shorter than Sharon, none even remotely as good-looking. Clearly, they had turned out to support the star of the family.

Most of Peter's office turned up too, including Jessica Barnard, in a linen coat and skirt that clearly hadn't been bought anywhere except in London or New York, and a man he guessed was her husband. He wasn't sure whether he was expected to know Jessica, but she greeted him warmly and sympathetically, kissing him on both cheeks as she hugged him. Had it been tact that had kept her away from Peter while he was dying, he wondered?

Although the congregation was much bigger than he had expected, Father Andrew kept the service as unfussy as Peter would have wanted: three traditional prayers, a reading from the New Testament, one hymn (*Abide with me ...*) and a brief address by Father Andrew, in which he said he hadn't know Peter long, but that he was a brave man who had faced dying with real grace and courage, particularly as he hadn't himself had much faith in Jesus Christ's promises of eternal life for believers. Despite that, since Christians believed that God's mercy was infinite, and since Christ hadn't died for good people only but also for sinners, he himself believed that Peter would be judged mercifully, and was now peacefully in God's arms. To his surprise, because he had been holding his own emotions in very firm check, Jamie found that these simple words reduced him suddenly to paroxysms of uncontrollable grief, and he had hardly been able to stand for the last part of the service. Then they stood in the sun outside while Father Andrew buried Peter's ashes in a garden of remembrance at the back of the church. Most of those present joined in scattering some earth on top of the casket before Father Andrew replaced the little square of turf he had dug.

Sharon's family and a few of the office staff came back to the house for tea, sandwiches and cakes, though Jamie found a bottle of brandy in one of Peter's cupboards and offered drinks to those he thought looked as if they would welcome them. Standing in the garden later, when most people other than Sharon's family had left, he said quietly to Allie, 'I know that the will hasn't been proved yet, but I have a sort of feeling that Sharon's people think this is her house already. I know she has been wonderful – so brave, so resourceful – but the family are very much at home already.'

'Come on, Jamie, darling, isn't that a bit unfair? There's a different tradition about death and funerals in Coloured families; they are more inclined to make these things a party. You're very English now, you know.'

Jamie looked at her affectionately. She had comforted him in church as if he had been a child. 'You do realise, don't you, Allie, that I'm going to have to go back to England in the next few days?' She nodded, looking hard into his face, brushing back the heavy dark hair from her forehead. 'I don't want to, but I have to.'

'Can I come with you?' she asked quietly. He stared at her in astonished silence. 'I won't if you don't want me to,' she said, but she was smiling as she said it because she knew.

'What about ... what about your research, and the sub-warden's job, and everything?'

'There's a queue of people wanting to be sub-warden. I can finish my research in England – it might be better to have a degree from London than from Cape Town, given the way we are seen now, or I can still submit it here – but there are other reasons. I want to show you something, Jamie.' She pulled him to his feet to lead him past Sharon's family talking quietly in the sitting-room area, and then on to the verandah. She pointed down the street to a car parked some twenty yards away. There were two men sitting in the front of the car. 'That's a police car, Jamie; we know the number – and those are two security policemen in the front. They've been watching this house for five weeks now, noting every coming and going. Father Andrew noticed them first, and told me.'

'Shouldn't we go inside? They'll see us and know that we've seen them.'

'Oh, they want us to see them. They are probably trying to panic me.'

'My God, they must have got bored.'

'Don't you start to feel sorry for them, Jamie Cathcart. Those men will do anything they are ordered to, without compunction.'

'Are they watching you or me?'

'I think they are watching you because they want me – they are waiting for me to trip on the edge of the pavement.

255

They've had a car outside my flat at the women's res too, and they went to see the warden about me. They are trying to put the wind up me.'

'Allie, are you in trouble?'

'I don't know. I may be. You never know here; sometimes even simple things upset them.' She laughed briefly. 'Do you remember saying that you were surprised, last time you went for a visa extension, how quickly they gave it to you? You said something like, 'I thought they almost wanted me to stay'. Maybe they did. Once they realised we were together ...'

'How would they know that?' They were back in the garden again, sitting at the wooden table.

'Oh, I think they've been following us. A couple of times in town I thought there was someone on our tail. It's one of the reasons I'm always so pleased you walk so fast. Sometimes I run just to make the buggers sweat.'

'Do you want me to run you over a border? I could take you in Peter's car tonight. I know how. I've done it before.'

She shook her head. 'You can't do now what you did twenty years ago; the border is wired or it's mined now – every inch. Remember: they have to stop armed people getting in now. In the old days – when you were around – they didn't much mind people skipping out. Now they do. No, I've got a better way.' She grinned. 'Let me show you. I went to collect this from a friend this morning; she stores it for me.' She fished about in her handbag and, to Jamie's surprise, produced a standard South African passport.

'If the Special Branch are after you, would you be able to get out on that?'

'Open it,' she said.

The photograph was of a pretty girl in glasses and make-up with blonde hair drawn back from her forehead into a ponytail. 'Good heavens,' Jamie said, 'it's you, isn't it? You as a blonde intellectual. Good God, I didn't know the colouring made so much difference.'

'I cheat, too,' Allie laughed. 'I wear falsies that push me up and out – and a lot of men are staring so hard at my boobs that they don't look at my face. You haven't looked at the name.'

'Alexandra Durer,' he read. 'Did you apply under a false name?'

'No, of course not. You need a birth certificate and signatures to say you are you and all that. No, it turned out that my birth certificate is in my mother's name – she must have had me before she was properly married to my father. Jolly useful mistake, really. That's a proper passport. I've tested it, and it worked. I went to the USA on it last year, with a visa and everything. I had no problems getting out or getting back.' She was grinning at him, enjoying his astonishment at her cheek and her bravery. 'When are you going?' she said. 'Can I come with you?'

'Hadn't you better come on a different plane? If they are watching you?'

'But they won't be watching me; they'll be so busy watching you they won't see a blonde bombshell four or five behind you in the queue or, if they see me at all, they'll be watching my boobs and my bum. I wear an incredibly tight skirt that shows almost everything I have. But you won't be able to look at me – not one single glance, even if you want to. Eyes front the whole way – at least until we are over Angola. Then I'll come to sit next to you.' This was a game, this was entirely exciting, there was no room for fear or doubt. Why then was his heart gripped with such foreboding? He had lost her once; he couldn't bear to lose her again.

'Are you really in such trouble you've got to do this, Allie? Can you tell me?' He was suddenly conscious of how little he really knew her: her history, her habits, her ideas, her past.

'I don't know.' She was serious again. 'I've never been watched like this – as openly as this. They want me to know that they are following me. They want me to know that they are watching you too. They are being so blatant it has to be deliberate. They are trying to frighten me, I think. They used to be quite crafty about listening to the telephone and opening the mail, but they are almost breathing down the 'phone now, and sticking the envelopes together again with sticky tape. I may have upset both sides, you see: I've been pushing quite hard – and now they're pushing me. Someone had to do something; we couldn't go on with everything getting harder and crueller forever. I think I've upset some of the UDF people ... I didn't want to, but the UDF is riddled with informers too. You have no idea how much jockeying goes on. And, for the first time, I'm getting scared – because I may have made mistakes, and I don't even know what they are. That's why I think I must leave. I'll be able to come back one day – with you, I hope.' She took his hands in her own. 'It's also you, my own Jamie, you see. I don't want you to go, but I know you've got to go – so maybe I'd better come with you.' She leaned forward to kiss him, and then whispered something throatily in his ear that he couldn't quite hear.

* * *

Thus it was, four days later, on a Thursday evening, at Cape Town International Airport – in those days still named after an Afrikaner prime minister – Jamie Cathcart found himself in the queue to leave the country. Somewhere behind him in the queue there was a blonde girl with hair drawn so sharply back it changed the shape of her face, wearing those large horn-rimmed glasses favoured by intellectuals and the seriously short-sighted, but which contrasted with the cupid's bow of her much made-up mouth, the tight T-shirt and the even tighter skirt, who carried a passport with an Afrikaans- or Spanish-sounding name – Alexandra Durer.

258

He had not seen Allie in her disguise, indeed, had not seen her since she had let it be known that she would be away for several days, attending a conference in East London with a friend. Then there had come a visitor at the front door of the Wynberg house, a large, ugly woman in a shapeless dress who didn't give her name, but who told him she had a message that a friend of his had managed to get a place on the British Airways flight out of Cape Town on the Thursday evening, and hoped he might be on it too. The car had still been there, he noticed, parked twenty or thirty yards down the road, with two men watching from the front seat. He had taken himself and his open airline ticket into Cape Town by train and, after producing his passport, had booked himself on the direct flight from Cape Town to Heathrow. He had to pay a bit extra because his ticket was from Johannesburg to Heathrow, and there wasn't any way in which the return part of his ticket from Cape Town to Johannesburg could be made use of, the woman in the booking office had said, politely but firmly. All she could suggest was that he might take his ticket into the main airline office to see if a refund on the used part was possible; she was sorry but that was the way things were. Fortunately, there were still several empty seats in the business section, she said, and hoped he had had a very good holiday in the Cape. Hadn't the weather been perfect the last few weeks?

He had his passport in his hand again, with his boarding pass and his ticket, just in case. The queue ahead was moving quite smartly through the barrier and past the desk where the immigration officials examined each, then the screens in front of each, then referred to another list before they took out the form with the visa and stamped the passport. He guessed they wouldn't be quite as quick with him as they had been when he last arrived, but he couldn't see that any trouble could be made. Each of the extensions of his visa had been carefully recorded, and the latest extension still had more than a month to run. Allie had promised that she would arrive early at the airport; she would hang about the departures lounge until she saw him, she had said, and then she would wait a moment or two before going through herself. She didn't want to be too close behind him, but she did know that he'd be nervous. It was essential that he shouldn't look for her. As far as anybody in Cape Town knew, she was away at a meeting in East London. As he arrived at the airport – he was leaving with more luggage than he had arrived with because Sharon had urged him to take some of the family things from the Wynberg house as mementos of his brother, and so he had needed a taxi – he thought he spotted her in the distance, but he had deliberately and quickly looked away. 'Even on the plane,' she had told him in their last whispered conversation in the car outside her flat at the women's residence at the university, 'you're going to have to keep your eyes off women – especially any blonde bombshell who waggles her tail at you. I suppose you can look at the air hostesses, just to keep in practice, but not otherwise.' They had both been trying to make as much light of their anxieties as they could, though both had known that what had worked once mightn't work again – and, anyway, though Jamie didn't say this to Allie, you never knew with the Special Branch: they might have let you out once and back again, just to fool you into thinking you were safe. They played tricks the whole time; that was their nature.

He was at the desk now. As casually as he could, he laid his passport down, then the boarding pass. The official wouldn't, he thought, want to see the ticket and he had put it into his briefcase. The official looked at the name, the face in the passport, the boarding pass, then pushed his stool back, stood up and signalled to another official, standing some way off. The second official came into the booth, there was murmuring, the passport was checked again, and the official took it and the boarding pass before coming out of the booth to say to Jamie, 'Mr Cathcart, if you please, will you step this way?'

Something's wrong, Jamie thought to himself. Something has gone wrong. Something is going wrong. He hesitated and then, without even thinking, looked back at the queue behind him. She had promised she wouldn't be too far behind. She should be there. She should be able to see that something was going wrong, and she might be able to slip away. She could pretend she had left a bag behind at the booking-in counter, and she could slip safely away from the airport.

She wasn't there. There were two queues now, one for each of the desks, but she wasn't in either. There must have been thirty or forty people waiting and she wasn't there.

The official had grabbed his arm now. Perhaps he thinks I'm going to make a run for it, Jamie thought. Stupid bastard, he's got my passport and my boarding pass in his hand. He can't seriously think I'm going to scarper. She wasn't there. Where had she gone? Why wasn't she there? She had promised.

'If you please, Mr Cathcart,' the official insisted.

'Why?' he demanded. Several people were looking now, obviously wondering why the tall Englishman in a checked shirt, rather distinguished-looking with his tie and his greying hair, clearly very lean and fit for someone his age, was in trouble with the immigration authorities.

'Please come to the interview room, Mr Cathcart.'

There was nothing for it but to comply, Jamie realised. He risked another glance at the queues, but she still wasn't there. Something had gone wrong, and there was nothing he could do about it.

For a moment he didn't recognise the man at the desk in the interview room. Then he saw who it was. 'Twenty years, Jamie, twenty years. What a long time it has been.' He held out a hand and, instinctively, Jamie shook it, though he let go as soon as he could.

'Captain Maasdorp,' he said in acknowledgement. He was still very smart in his expensive blazer with silver buttons and no badge, and dark blue trousers that nearly but didn't quite match the blazer – still overweight too, Jamie noted.

'Colonel Maasdorp, now. I have been promoted, just like you. I suppose I should call you 'Mr Cathcart' now, shouldn't I? I am told you are a significant figure in your United Kingdom. Quietly significant – very English at that. The most important people there don't have names, do they? Those who wield the real power.'

'What do you want, Colonel Maasdorp?'

'I merely wanted to renew acquaintance after all these years, Jamie. Do you mind if I call you "Jamie"? Please feel free to call me "Peter" – unless you want to be formal, like a proper Englishman.'

'If you propose to hold me here, Colonel, I think I am entitled to ask to see someone from the embassy.'

'We have no intention of holding you, Jamie. You are here quite voluntarily.'

'Then I wish to go. I have a plane to catch.'

'There is plenty of time for that. I shall send one of my officers with you to make quite sure you find the right gate. Please sit.'

'I'd rather stand.'

'Suit yourself, Jamie, suit yourself. I shall sit. Today was my day off. I had planned to go fishing.' He laughed, apparently genuinely. 'You have a real skill in disrupting my days off, Jamie. I have a very long memory. I still enjoy fishing; if anything, I enjoy it even more now. As I grow older, the fish seem to get wilier.'

Jamie nodded. Perhaps Allie hadn't come to the airport at all. Perhaps she had had a warning. Perhaps she was trying another route.

Maasdorp rocked back on his chair and smiled up at Jamie. Sitting down to talk to someone standing is meant to put one at a disadvantage, Jamie thought; but it doesn't feel like that. Shall I sit? Perhaps not.

'Tell me, Jamie,' said Maasdorp. 'Where is your beautiful young girlfriend?'

Perhaps they haven't got her, Jamie thought wildly. Perhaps she's got through without their noticing. Maybe she decided to go in front of me for some reason. She might be waiting for the announcement for people to begin to board the flight to Heathrow. There was still a chance she was safe. 'I don't know what you are talking about,' he said as flatly as he could. 'I would like to catch my plane now.'

'In a minute, Jamie, in a minute.' All pretence at bonhomie was gone now. 'Why did you lie to us?'

'What do you mean? Lie? I haven't talked to you for twenty years.'

'You lied about your reason for coming back to South Africa: you said it was because your brother was dying. That's why we were compassionate; that's why we let you in. I said to the Minister, "In this case, compassion will be mistaken." But he overruled me.'

'Even you, Colonel, have to know that my brother died a week ago. You've had people watching the house.' Even as he said it, he knew that he had gone a step further than he needed to.

'I know your brother is dead, but you came back for other purposes, didn't you?'

'I came back to see my brother before he died. He's dead now, and I am leaving.'

'What about your beautiful young girlfriend, Jamie? Very young for you, isn't she? You always had a weakness for beauty, didn't you?'

Jamie closed his eyes to help him swallow his rage. 'I've nothing to say to you on that or any other subject, Colonel Maasdorp.'

'Your other girlfriend was beautiful too, was she not? The one called Jenny? She died in London, didn't she? The car …?' Maasdorp gestured, his hand sweeping across the desk as if he were clearing something away. 'No one

263

should mess with us, Jamie Cathcart: no one.' There was no pretence at anything but menace now, in eyes or voice. Jamie stared across the desk, knowing for sure now what had happened, but unable to speak.

'Your brother, on the other hand ...' Maasdorp continued, silkily.

'Leave my brother out of this ...'

'You think I speak ill of the dead, Jamie, do you? We didn't like your brother's habits, you know. Black girls ...' He gave a small grimace of distaste.

'Sharon's not black.'

'She's black enough. I know the law has changed – and more's the pity, as far as we think. But we can see what happens to a country when it goes mongrel, Jamie – like your new country has done. As your brother would have done if he hadn't died.'

'My brother loved Sharon, and it was mutual.'

'Was it, Jamie, was it? She's done very well out of it, hasn't she? A nice house in a white neighbourhood? Lots of cash, too, for her family to share? Even a whore doesn't get that much usually.'

Keep your mouth shut, Jamie tried to tell himself. Keep your mouth shut, keep your temper bottled up, keep anger at bay. The man is playing with you. Silence is your only option. You have no other power – and Jamie knew that he wasn't used to being without any power at all. 'Where's Alexandra, Jamie? Where is the beautiful Allie? Alexandra Morten? That's her name, isn't it?' He pretended to look for it in the papers in front of him on the desk.

Say nothing, Jamie told himself. Keep silent. It's the only course of action.

To his surprise, Maasdorp stood up. 'You've decided to keep silent, I see,' he said. Is he bringing the interview to a close? Jamie wondered. Why? 'Friends of the beautiful Allie say she has gone to a meeting in East London. So they say. And you will tell me too that she has gone to a meeting in East London? Yes?' Jamie kept his head still. 'No? You're not saying? Very well. You may leave now. I think you will find your flight is being boarded at the moment. One of my officers will take you to the right gate. I shall call you Mr Cathcart now, I think. You may leave and, if I were you, Mr Cathcart, I would not return. Next time ...' And he shook his head, almost as if he were sad.

At the door, Jamie turned to look at Maasdorp. You are a monster, he thought to himself; you are a monster. I think you know what was done to Jenny and, if anything has happened to Allie, if it takes me the rest of my life, if it takes my death, I shall come back to seek you out and I will destroy you with as little compunction as you have when you kill a fish or a baboon. Jenny is dead, my brother is dead and I do not know where Allie has gone. I had thought that, at least, she would be with me soon. I had thought that those twenty blank years of agendas, lunches, visits, inspections, accountants' reports and auditors' recommendations, dinners, board meetings, letters of congratulation, minutes of actions undertaken, decisions delayed – all of them merely a desert – might at last turn into a garden again.

* * *

The bakkie has been parked in the veld, about half a kilometre down a dirt track leading away from a side-road, for nearly two hours before the other car, a grey saloon, arrives. The three white men in the saloon car sit talking for a moment before getting out. One – who gives the orders – walks over to the bakkie where two men, one white and one black, are waiting. They, like the three men from the car, are wearing automatic pistols in holsters, but none is in uniform. In the meantime, the other two men open the boot of the saloon, then stand back, waiting. The man in charge walks with the two men from the bakkie about twenty yards into the veld to look at a trench which the black man had been digging before the second car arrived. Apparently satisfied, he calls out something to the men waiting by the boot of the car.

The story varies here. In one version, the person taken out of the boot is still alive, though almost certainly unconscious; in that version, her hands and feet are tied, and the cord from her feet is also tied around her throat, so that if she tries to straighten her legs she strangles herself. There is then another variation: in that version, one of the men cuts the cords binding her feet together so that he can remove her jeans and pants. He then invites the other men to make use of what is visible to all of them. Whether it is only one who does so, or more than one, is disputed. In another version, she is already dead when she is taken out of the boot and the men merely cut the cords by which she has strangled herself and strip the clothes off. There is no rape in that version. In a fourth version, she is already dead when she is put in the boot of the car, and the cords are merely there to constrict the body into a smaller shape.

All versions agree that the girl's body is then carried over to the trench and thrown in, together with the cords and her clothes. One of the men fetches from the back of the bakkie a large plastic container of petrol, which he pours over the body and around it in the trench. He uses the last few drops in the container to dampen the girl's blouse, then carefully lights the blouse and throws it into the trench, leaping backwards to avoid the whoosh of the exploding petrol. All five men wait until the flames have died down a little before they return to the grey car where they are all – including the black man – offered cigarettes by the man in charge. After a few more minutes, the black man returns to the trench and begins to fill it in with the earth and stones he had dug out earlier. When the trench is nearly full, three of the other men return, leaving the man in charge sitting in the car. While the black man completes his digging, two of the other men tear off branches from a bush nearby and use them to sweep away all footprints and, in due course, all evidence of the grave. The bakkie is then driven off and the man in charge returns on his own from the grey saloon, keeping carefully to the stony ground. Satisfied that all is in order, he rejoins his companions, and the grey saloon is driven off too.

PART THREE

Chapter 9

The Foreign Office official had left his large desk – admirably devoid of paperwork, Jamie noted – and was standing at the window, looking down, presumably at the people in the street; it was a busy Tuesday morning in London and, despite double-glazing and fourteen floors, there was still a constant growling, grating and grumbling of traffic from the streets below. 'The dreadful thing about this business of disappearance,' he said, 'is precisely the not knowing. A little bit of hope is in some ways worse than certainty, isn't it?'

I don't hope any more, thought Jamie. I suppose, all those years ago, I had a small fraction of hope left in me for about twenty minutes. First, I somehow persuaded one of the air hostesses to show me the passenger list, and then – just to make trebly sure – I waited until the seat-belt signs were switched off and I walked around the plane, looking at all the passengers; but I knew already – I knew from the moment I turned round to check the queues behind me. Proper hope died then; that bastard Maasdorp with his smile and his sneering merely confirmed what I already knew. But Mr Pinstripe Suit (CMG already and going further) is right: I would still like to know what happened.

The official was back behind the desk. 'After the war – in 1945 and '6 – when the newsreels of the concentration camps were being shown in cinemas, my mother told me ... she had a friend, a German Jew, who had got out in the early '30s, but most of her family hadn't ... This friend used to make my mother go with her to the cinema to see these newsreels, just on the off-chance she might recognise one of the family. All those millions ...' He was quiet. 'My mother said this friend of hers – Trudi, I think she was called, very conventional – couldn't bear to sit and watch; she used to stand at the back of the cinema, with the usherettes I suppose. I suppose it was a kind of penance, too, for being alive at all.'

And I suppose, Jamie thought, that's what you think I am doing here: penance. Well, that's perhaps part of it. There's something more besides; but we shall come to that in due course.

The official pulled open his top drawer and took out a file; he was clearly going to get down to business, Jamie thought to himself, after that oh-so-discreet warning. 'Now, about this young friend of yours: Alexandra Morten, also known as Alexandra Durer. I take it you've made your own enquiries over the years?'

Jamie had done what he could though there had been little enough he could do. Almost everybody he thought he might be able to ask had been swept up in the arrests that had happened in the weeks after he had left. Even old Dr Liebermann, in his eighties, had been re-detained; Phakamile Mtirara had died inside prison, ostensibly of an asthma attack; Father Andrew had been blinded in an attack with hand grenades on his church; Huston Stillman had emigrated to Australia. Jamie wrote to Sharon Danialls at the Wynberg house, only to receive a letter back from a new owner informing him that he had bought the house from Mrs Danialls the month before, but didn't know where she had moved to, and couldn't look it up for him because her name had changed when she had remarried – her reason for selling the house to him.

Jamie then went to a detective agency in London that claimed to have an international network. Yes, they had a connection with a South African firm and would gladly get that firm to make enquiries about Miss Alexandra Morten who had some years before been a research student at the University of Cape Town and a sub-warden in a women's residence there, all this without revealing Mr

Cathcart's name. After nearly three months, he had an embarrassed letter from the London firm returning his cheque; their South African partner, having made some preliminary enquiries, had declined to take the investigation any further. 'In the circumstances ...' and so on. A subsequent telephone call to the London firm elicited the information that, like most detective agencies in South Africa and elsewhere, their connection had been staffed by ex-policemen. At Hamish's suggestion, he wrote to the most liberal of the Members of Parliament in South Africa, internationally famous for having stood up to the Afrikaner Nationalist government and its state-apparatus when most other whites kept their mouths shut in fear and trembling. She wrote back to say she had seldom come across a higher or thicker wall of silence than that which surrounded Allie Morten's apparent disappearance, and had therefore to assume something very unpleasant and unhappy had happened. Officially, Allie Morten had left the country on a South African passport, but there was something odd about the wording of even that explanation. She wished she could help more, but ...

Jamie replied gratefully. Would there be any chance of her interceding with the authorities so that he – who had after all been born in the country – might be granted a visa to come back to try to find out for himself? He had been refused a visa again recently. Her reply was swift: what she had discovered made her sure that he would not get a visa until there was a change of regime and, even if he got a visa, she had to advise him to keep away until then. 'For reasons that I have to say I don't completely understand,' she wrote, 'you appear to have made some enemies in very high places. Sad though I am to have to say this, my advice must be that you keep away from South Africa for the time being. A return would be dangerous – for you, and for anyone you associated with.' Since the British press had recently carried several stories about the probable existence of a group in South Africa specialising in the assassination of political activists, and almost certainly attached to the police, the advice was pointed.

He asked the Chairman of the Trustees of the Sturrock Foundation if he would be prepared to use his old Foreign Office connections to find out anything at all. 'Why, of course, Jamie, my dear boy. What a dreadful story. I realised something bad had happened to you, but I thought it must merely be – no, I don't mean 'merely' – just the death of your brother so young. I'll get someone to find out.'

Every few months, Sir Ronald would say to him, 'I've chivvied the Foreign Office again and they say things are being looked into. Nothing happens very fast. There are all sorts of stirrings in South Africa, you know.'

The official closed his file. He had clearly decided not to read aloud from it. He looked across the desk at Jamie, then said, 'Our people in Pretoria say that there was a rumour, a few years ago, that the security police had disposed of a woman's body in the ... what do South Africans call it? In the bush.'

'In the veld, probably,' Jamie said.

'Yes, yes,' said Mr Pinstripe Suit. 'That's the word. Common enough word. Anyway, there are various versions, but the body seems to have been that of a young woman, almost certainly a white woman. There are details I won't burden you with; these people appear to have been totally brutal.'

'Please: details,' Jamie said quietly.

'If you insist. There are different versions, too. It's likely the girl was dead already; the body had been transported in the boot of a car. This body was put in a grave and I'm afraid it seems it was burned before the burial was ... was completed.'

Jamie sat silently, looking down at his hands on his knees. After a long time, he heard himself say, 'Is that all?'

'I'm afraid it is, Mr Cathcart. I'm sorry.'

He did not, Jamie could hear, mean merely he was sorry

there were no more details. He looked up. 'You – and your people – have been very helpful – beyond the call of duty. I am glad to know. You are pretty sure, are you?'

'I've no idea, I'm afraid. This is what we've been told. It's all that I have to tell you, all that I can tell you.'

As he shook hands with Jamie at the entrance to the lift, the official said, 'Is it any consolation to know that, from everything we hear, there are big changes coming in South Africa soon? Enormous changes – and, at last, changes for the better.'

There were too, almost miraculously confounding Jamie's pessimism, which had assumed that there would have to be more and more bloodshed, more and more civil disturbance, more and more armed intervention, more and more international strictures, more misery, more murder, more disappearances. Nelson Mandela was released from gaol, apparently without conditions; there was a government of national unity; the Archbishop said this was a rainbow nation; and the first proper elections the country had ever known swept the African National Congress to power, though not (for the time being at least) to absolute power. Jamie Cathcart applied again for a visa. Months later, a letter came – surface mail – from Pretoria to say that he (like all other British citizens) now no longer required a visa to enter the country. The restrictions no longer applied. He was free to come and go as he wished.

He did not hurry. There was no need to hurry now. If there had been any modicum of hope left, it was that Allie would have resurfaced when the changes happened. No one came back.

The Truth and Reconciliation Commission began its work, travelling around the country to hear the stories. Witness after witness came forward with stories of almost unbelievable cruelty, pathos, revenge, mayhem, conspiracy, accident, murder, torture, detention. Men wept when they told how they had seen their fathers murdered on suspicion that they were informers; police assassins confessed that they had put car bombs in place that had killed, not the people for whom they were intended, but family members and friends; mothers told of their struggle to find out where and when their sons had been killed and where their bodies lay; sisters told how they had realised their brothers had been shot out of hand by the police; mothers told of false accusation, of babies taken away and placed in foster homes, of actual and apparent torture, and on and on. The lists of the people the witnesses wanted to talk about, and the briefest of details of their suffering, were alone enough to cause terror and compassion: Harry Mabija – death in detention; Phineas Adonis – shot with birdshot; Christopher Mosebi – died of head injuries inflicted by police at school premises; Alakie Koopman – died as a result of house being tear gassed; Sylvia Vuizwa Moleleki – shot with birdshot; Father Michael Lapsley – severely injured by a letter bomb; Nzimeni Patrick Bosman – tortured by police and unlawfully arrested; Ellen Moshweu – shot by police; Tommy Kgatiwane – shot; Izakiel Mokone – killed by hand grenade during march; Khotso Flatela – died in exile; David Mabeka – tortured/detained under state of emergency; Lathli Mabilo – shot and killed; Reuben Gallant – shot at close range in left eye with tear gas; William Rabuku – disappeared in exile; Thabo Moorosi – severely tortured and detained … and on and on. But never Allie Morten, never Allie Durer. There were lies too, lies and half-truths. Some witnesses lied, even when the chairman wept as he begged them to rid themselves of the burden of their own guilt. Some policemen told enough to earn themselves amnesty; others appeared but told nothing at all; others merely hinted at passive involvement on the orders of the more senior.

Jamie went back to the London detective agency. He had another name, he said; all he wanted now was an address. This came back quite promptly, though with a warning attached from the Johannesburg firm. 'Don't

274

mess with this one,' the warning said, explicitly. Jamie took some of the leave due to him – much had again accumulated – and went to South Africa for a short holiday – bird-watching, he said, which was why he needed the field-glasses. He hired a land cruiser, and drove a long way to check that the address he had been given was the right one. There were fishing rods in the bakkie parked in the drive of the modest bungalow and when the owner next went fishing he did not notice a land cruiser following a long way behind.

Jamie had already taken careful advice from a famous gunsmith in London. He had, he said, been invited by a friend to go hunting with him in a remote area of Zimbabwe: quite serious hunting, possibly even a lion. He hadn't shot for years, he said, but he had once been a reasonable enough shot, and now he wanted a good hunting rifle. Could they advise him? They certainly could and would happily help him get a licence and the necessary permission to get the rifle shipped out to Zimbabwe for the expedition; a good hunting rifle was the 7x57 Rigby. That should serve his purposes well, they said. He examined the gun and its accoutrements, made careful notes, and later telephoned to say that he was sorry he had put them to so much trouble, but the expedition had been cancelled because of the troubles on the border.

Now, on his bird-watching holiday, he went to a gunsmith in Cape Town. He wanted to buy himself a 7x57 Rigby, he said. Could they help him? The problem was that he lived in England, but wanted to hunt baboons with an old friend of his in the Karoo whose mealie lands were being devastated by a huge gang of really vicious baboons. He knew he had to go to the police for a licence application, and he knew that the police were pretty slow about granting licences these days, though God knows people in South Africa had cause enough to want to defend themselves; but his problem was he didn't have an address in South Africa. Could he give the shop's address?

The manager was only too pleased to oblige; he'd shot baboons himself, he said: when they got out of hand on a farm they were a menace. If necessary, Mr Cathcart could use the manager's home address; he'd be very happy to oblige a customer in this way. When the licence came through, he'd personally telephone Mr Cathcart in England. Oh, and I'll need a state-of-the-art telescopic sight, Jamie said. He thought it might be sensible if he paid a deposit. If by any chance a licence were refused, they could let him have the deposit back – but at least they'd have an assurance that he was a serious customer. They knew that already, said the manager, but a deposit would of course be acceptable. He looked forward to seeing Mr Cathcart again in six or seven months' time. The baboons had better watch out, eh? They had some trouble coming their way.

* * *

He left the jeep parked out of sight of the road behind the blue-gum trees, but then moved quite openly and quickly, working his way through the thorn bushes towards the river. Only when he had gone about a mile did he begin to move more cautiously, checking his direction against a rough map he had drawn the day before, and looking back to double-check that he had not been observed. Once, because he thought he heard a noise somewhere to the side, he stopped completely, sheltering behind a thorn bush, and watching carefully to make sure no one was following. Satisfied that he had heard nothing of significance, he shouldered the rifle again and moved on. Twice, he took a compass from the breast pocket of his hunting jacket and checked the direction in which he was moving, though the lie of the land seemed obvious. He dropped down to the bed of a stream that would serve as a tributary to the river if it ever rained, and for the first time hesitated there, looking at the sand; it was so dry that his boots left no detectable prints and, anyway, there were so many other prints – cattle, goats, sheep, buck perhaps, humans probably. Still, to be safe, he left the cover of the stream and climbed up the other side to work his way carefully down through the thorn bush on the edge of the stream towards the dam across the river.

About two hundred yards before the dam, he turned sharp left and, keeping well below the skyline, worked his way upwards to a point behind the brow of the hill. It was hot in the sun, particularly as he climbed the rocky out-crop near the top, but a slight breeze from the dam cooled the sweat on his face. A few yards short of the top of the hill, he took the rifle from his shoulder and, holding it carefully in the crook of his elbows, dropped to his hands and knees to crawl upwards to a gap between the rocks and a thorn bush, from which he could look down at the dam.

The bakkie was parked in the dried grass at the side of the dam wall. The man fishing in the dam hadn't even bothered to close the driver's door and stood now, fifty yards further up the dam, on the edge of the water, his khaki haversack nearby. For several minutes, the man with the rifle on the hillside watched to make sure that the fisherman was alone; then he felt in the pocket of his jacket, to take out a telescopic sight which he clipped to the rifle. Carefully he adjusted his elbows on the ground until he was balanced, then brought the rifle to his shoul-der and the barrel up slowly, using the bakkie as target until he had the sights clearly focused: a bare hundred yards to the haversack, he reckoned, and some fifty yards further to the bakkie. He shifted his position slightly, then checked the sights again, switched the safety catch off, took a breath, held it, and squeezed the trigger once, then again.

The fisherman looked up suddenly as the shots rever-berated from the rocks above him, and swore, but made no effort to move away from where he was fishing; he seemed not to have noticed that a back tyre of the bakkie had collapsed. The man on the hillside fired again, the same pattern of two shots, one after the other, and this time the fisherman realised his bakkie was the target. He dropped his fishing rod and began to run towards the bakkie, shouting furiously, first in Afrikaans and then in English. The next shot shattered the windscreen, and now the fisherman stopped, realising that there was someone on the hillside above him. He stared upwards to where he thought the man with the rifle must be, and shouted again; this time he could be heard. 'For fuck's sake, are you fucking mad, man, shooting like that? What the fuck do you want?' Then he began to run again, this time towards his haversack. He probably has a weapon in there, thought the man on the hillside; he had guessed he might have a rifle or a shotgun in the bakkie; he might have a pistol or revolver in his haversack instead. He waited until the man was ten yards away from the haversack, then fired twice into it, making it jerk and leap in the dust. The fisherman stopped, then moved a pace nearer the haversack. He looked at a different point of the hillside, trying to see where the hidden rifleman was, and shouted again: 'What do you want, you fucking lunatic? When I catch you, I'll fucking kill you.'

Once again, the rifle on the hillside answered, and the haversack jerked as the bullets tore into it. The man turned sideways now, and began to run for some thorn bushes on the edge of the dam that might provide cover. The man on the hillside let him run for twenty yards, then carefully fired, just once, into the ground ahead of the running figure. The man stopped; he was clearly winded even by that short run. He faced the hillside again, panting and then shouting, now more or less incoherent in rage and terror, though he seemed to have at last spotted the vantage point from which the rifle-fire came.

The man on the hillside waited for the cursing and shouting to subside into silence, then got to his feet slowly, with the rifle still against his shoulder. The man at the dam could see now who held the rifle and swore just once more, then was silent again. There was nowhere to run now, nothing more to be said. The rifleman planted his feet wide for balance. Slowly the rifle came up until the cross hairs of the sights were on the man's sweating fore-head, and then the sights moved down to the larger target. The baboon has his fist wrapped so hard around the pips he cannot get it free, and he doesn't know enough to open his fist and let go of the pips. Then the old instruction came back to him: *breathe in; hold steady; then ...*

Hold steady. Shift the sights sideways two yards, three yards, until they are focused (through a haze of tears) and are once again fixed on the haversack. Squeeze now, and again and again, so that the haversack is leaping about almost as if it were alive, until the magazine is suddenly empty. *Well done, thou good and faithful servant.* Well done, brother. That's right, my Jamie.

The man realises then, and turns to run. He looks back as he runs and he stumbles, then runs again and falls; but he is on his feet again, more than half expecting the shoot-ing to start again, and running for whatever remains of his life. He is at the bakkie now, and he scrambles in and, despite the shredded tyres, drives off across the dried mud, the bakkie tilting so much it almost topples over, then along the top of the wall of the dam, and – leaving a trail of dust and small stones – down the track towards the road.